Dirty Thoughts

Also by Megan Erickson

Make It Last
Make It Right
Make It Count

Coming Soon
Dirty Talk

Dirty Thoughts

A MECHANICS OF LOVE NOVEL

MEGAN ERICKSON

AVONIMPULSE
An Imprint of HarperCollinsPublishers

Excerpt from *Dirty Talk* copyright © 2015 by Megan Erickson.
Excerpt from *Heart's Desire* copyright © 2015 by Tina Klinesmith.
Excerpt from *Desire Me Now* copyright © 2015 by Tiffany Clare.
Excerpt from *The Wedding Gift* copyright © 2015 by Lisa Connelly.
Excerpt from *When Love Happens* copyright © 2015 by Darcy Burke.

EPub Edition JUNE 2015 ISBN: 9780062407733

Print Edition ISBN: 9780062407740

AM 10 9 8 7 6 5 4 3 2

To all who like their men a little dirty…

Acknowledgments

So I HAVE to confess that I never intended to write this book. Or this series. But then readers began to ask questions about the Payton brothers after reading *Make It Right*. They wanted to see why Cal was so gruff, and they wanted someone to knock that smirk off of Brent's face.

And so I started thinking. And thinking some more, and Cal began to shout his story in my head, and I thought, what the heck? Why not?

And thank God for my editor, Amanda Bergeron, because she loved this idea as much as I did. Her enthusiasm for it has been such a motivation to me to do these characters justice. Her edits throughout this process were amazing and thoughtful and made this book so much better. I learned so much during the editing of this book, and I'm really grateful.

As always, my agent, Marisa Corvisiero, was right by my side, as excited about this book as I was and championing it for me.

My critique partners were awesome as I was drafting, letting me share passages where Cal was swoon-y and where Brent was a loveable jerk. Thank you to Natalie Blitt, AJ Pine, and Lia Riley for being there for me. I love you guys. Lia—I owe you for this series title, because Mechanics of Love is genius, and that's all you, baby!

I adore the team at Avon Impulse, I have to say. I love the authors. I love the editors and the publicists and the design team. You make Avon a wonderful place to be. You make it a family. And I'm proud to be a part of it.

Thank you to my husband and children who dealt with my crappy holiday cheer because I was in my head, writing this book in December but all the time wishing it was summer. Confession: this book takes place in the summer mainly because I was really hating on winter, and I was tired of being cold. Oh, and I wanted to write a sweaty, oil-streaked, shirtless Cal.

Thank you to the writing community, to Meg's Mob for wanting this book (especially Jullie Anne) and, as always, Andi—you'll never be one of the "little people."

Chapter One

CAL PAYTON SIGHED and braced himself as the opening guitar riff of "Welcome to the Jungle" reverberated off the walls of the garage. Sure enough, several bars later, his brother, Brent, began his off-key rendition, which didn't sound much different from his drunken karaoke version.

Which, yes, Cal had heard. More times than he wanted to.

He growled under his breath. Brent kept screeching Axl Rose, and if Cal wasn't stuck on his back under this damn Subaru, he'd be flinging a wrench at Brent's head. "Hey!" Cal yelled.

There was a blissful moment of silence. "What?" Brent's voice came from somewhere behind him, probably in the bay next to him at the garage.

"Who sings this song?"

"Are you kidding me?" Brent's voice was closer now. "It's Guns N' Roses. The legendary Axl Rose."

"Yeah? Then how 'bout you let him sing it?"

There was a pause. "Fuck you." His brother's footsteps stomped away. Then the radio was turned up, and Brent started singing even louder.

Cal blew out a breath and tapped the socket wrench on his forehead, doing his best to tune out Brent's increasingly loud voice. Cal vowed to buy earbuds and an iPod before he murdered his brother with a tire iron.

He turned his attention back to the exhaust shield he was fixing. The customer had complained of a loud rattle when his car idled. Sure enough, one of the heat shields covering the exhaust system under the car was loose. It was an easy fix. Cal used a gear clamp to wrap around the pipe of the exhaust system to prevent the shield from making noise.

It didn't necessarily have to be done, but the Graingers were long-time customers at Payton and Sons Automotive. And they always sent those flavored popcorn buckets at Christmas. He and Brent fought over the caramel while their dad got the butter all to himself.

He finished tightening the hose clamp onto the pipe and then banged around the exhaust system with the side of his fist. No rattle.

He slid out from under the Subaru and patted it on the side. He squinted at the clock, seeing it was almost quitting time. Their dad, who owned half of the shop—Cal and Brent split ownership of the other 50 percent—had already gone home for the day.

Cal put away the tools he'd used, purposefully ignoring Brent as he launched into a Pearl Jam song. Cal rubbed his temple, wiping away the bead of sweat he could feel rolling down his face. The back room had a small table and a refrigerator, so Cal made his way there to get a water.

In the summer, they kept the large doors of the garage open, but the air was thick and humid today. The American flag outside hung like a limp rag in the still air.

Cal wore coveralls at work and usually kept them on to protect his skin from hot exhaust pipes and any number of sharp tools lying around. But as he walked back to the lunchroom, he stripped his upper body out of the coveralls so the torso and arms of the clothing hung loose around his legs. Underneath, he wore a tight white T-shirt that still managed to be marked with grease and black smudges from the work day.

In the back room, he grabbed a bottle of water from the refrigerator and leaned back against the wall. After unscrewing the cap, he tilted it back at his lips and chugged half the bottle.

After the Graingers came to pick up their Subaru, he was free to head home to his house. Alone. That was a new luxury. He used to live with Brent in an apartment, and it was fine until he realized he was almost thirty years old and still living with his younger brother. He was tight with his money, which Brent teased him about, but it'd been a good thing when he had enough to make the deposit on his small home. It had a garage, so he could store his bike and work on it when he had free time. Which wasn't a lot, but he'd take what he could get. If his father would quit dicking him around and let him work on motorcycles for customers here, that'd be even better. But Jack Payton didn't "want no bikers" around, ignoring the fact that his son rode a Harley-Davidson Softail.

Cal's phone vibrated in the leg pocket of his coveralls. He pulled it out and glanced at the caller ID. It was Max, their youngest brother. Cal sighed and answered the call. "Yeah?"

"Cal!" Max shouted.

"You called me."

"What's going on?"

"Workin'."

"You're always working." Max huffed.

Cal took another sip of water. "That's what people do."

"Hey, I work."

"You play dodgeball with a bunch of teenagers." Cal knew Max did a hell of a lot more than that at his physical education teaching job at a high school in eastern Pennsylvania, but it was fun as hell to get him worked up. Cal smiled. One of the first times that day.

"Hey, I had to hand out deodorant and condoms to those teenagers this year, so don't give me that shit," Max said.

"Condoms?"

"Yeah, they're kinda liberal here," Max muttered.

"Huh," Cal said, scratching his head. They sure never handed out condoms in school when he was a teenager.

"Anyway," Max said.

"Yeah, anyway, what'dya need?"

"How do you know I need something?"

"Why else do you call?"

"I want to hear your pleasant voice?"

Cal grunted.

"I just wanted to know if you had any plans for your birth—ouch!" There was rustling on the other line, some mutters, and a higher-pitched voice in the background. Then Max spoke again. "Okay, so Lea punched me because she said I'm doing this wrong."

Cal smiled. Lea was Max's fiancée, and she was a firecracker.

"We wanted to come visit you and take you out for your birthday. All of us." Max cleared his throat. "And you can bring a date too. If you want."

A date. When was the last time he'd introduced a woman to his family? Hell, when was the last time he'd had a date? "The five of us should be fine."

"So that's okay? To celebrate? I mean, you're turning thirty, old man."

Cal let the *old man* comment roll off his back. "Yeah, sounds good." He paused. "Thanks."

Max seemed pleased, chattering on about his neighborhood and how he was enjoying being off work for the summer. Cal drank his water and listened to his brother ramble. Max hadn't always been a happy kid. Cal had tried his best after their mom left the family shortly after Max was born. Their dad was pissed and bitter and immersed himself in working at the garage. So as the oldest brother, Cal scrambled to hold the reins of his wild brothers.

He hadn't done such a great job, he didn't think. His brothers survived in spite of him, not because of him, he was sure. Brent was still a little crazy, and it had taken Lea to straighten Max out in college. Cal tried not to dwell on his failure and instead appreciated that at least they were all alive and healthy.

It was why he valued his own space so much now. His alone time. Because he'd been a surrogate father at age six, and he was fucking over it.

Although, by the time he hung up the phone with Max and slipped his phone back into his pocket, he had a warm feeling in his gut that hadn't been there before his brother had called.

He was flipping the cap of the water in his fingers and finishing the last of the bottle when Brent poked his head in the back room. "Hey."

Cal raised his eyebrows.

"Someone's asking for you."

Cal tossed the empty bottle in the trash. "The Graingers?"

"Nope, they just came and got the Subaru and left. This is a new customer."

Cal threw the empty bottle in the recycling bin, turned off the light to the back room, and followed his brother out to the garage. "We're closing soon. Is it an emergency? Are they regulars?" He pulled a rag out of his pocket and began to wipe his dirty hands. He thought about washing them first in case this customer wanted to shake hands.

Brent didn't answer him, didn't even look at him over his shoulder.

And that was when a small sliver of apprehension trickled down his spine. "Brent—"

His brother whirled around and held his arm out as they walked past a Bronco their dad had been working on. "I think it's better if you take this one."

Cal squinted into the sun and when his eyes adjusted to the light, her legs were the first thing he saw. And he knew—he fucking knew—because how many times had he sat in class in high school staring at those legs in a little skirt, dreaming about when he could get back between them? It'd been a lot.

His eyes traveled up those bare legs to a tiny pair of denim shorts, up a tight tank top that showed a copious amount of cleavage, and then to that face that he'd never, ever forget as long as he lived.

He never thought he'd see Jenna MacMillan again. And now, there she was, standing in front of his garage next to a Dodge Charger, her brunette hair in a wavy mass around her shoulders.

Fuck.

OKAY, SO ADMITTEDLY Jenna had known this was a stupid idea. She'd tried to talk herself out of it the whole way, muttering to herself as she sat at a stop light. The elderly man in the car in the lane beside her had been staring at her like she was nuts.

And she was. Totally nuts.

It'd been almost a decade since she'd seen Cal Payton, and yet one look at those silvery blue eyes and she was shoved right back to the head-over-heels *in love* eighteen-year-old girl she'd been.

Cal had been hot in high school, but damn, had time been good to him. He'd always been a solid guy, never really hitting that awkward skinny stage some teenage boys went through after a growth spurt.

And now...well...Cal looked downright sinful standing there in the garage. He'd rolled down the top of his coveralls, revealing a white T-shirt that looked painted on, for God's sake. She could see the ridges of his abs, the outline of his pecs. A large smudge on the sleeve drew her attention to his bulging biceps and muscular, veined forearms. Did he lift these damn cars all day? Thank God it was hot as Hades outside already so she could get by with flushed cheeks.

And he was staring at her with those eyes that hadn't changed one bit. Cal never cared much for social mores. He looked people in the eye, and he held it long past comfort. Cal had always needed that, to be able to measure up who he was dealing with before he ever uttered a word.

She wondered how she measured up. It'd been a long time since he'd laid eyes on her, and the last time he had, he'd been furious.

Well, she was the one who'd come here. She was the one who needed something. She might as well speak up, even though what she needed right now was a drink. A stiff one. "Hi, Cal." She went with a smile that surely looked a little strained.

He stood with his booted feet shoulder width apart, and at the sound of her voice, he started a bit. He finally stopped doing that staring thing as his gaze shifted to the car by her side and then back to her. "Jenna."

His voice. Well, crap, how could she have forgotten about his voice? It was low and silky with a spicy edge, like Mexican chocolate. It warmed her belly and raised goose bumps on her skin.

She cleared her throat as he began walking toward her, his gaze teetering between her and the car. Brent was off to the side, watching them, with his arms crossed over his chest. He winked at her. She hid her grin with pursed lips and rolled her eyes. He was a good-looking bastard but irritating as hell. Nice to see *some* things never changed. "Hey, Brent."

"Hey there, Jenna. Looking good."

Cal whipped his head toward his brother. "Get back to work."

Brent gave him a sloppy salute and then shot her another knowing smirk before turning around and retreating into the garage bay.

When she faced Cal again, she jolted, because he was close now, almost in her personal space. His eyes bored into her. "What're ya doing here, Jenna?"

His question wasn't accusatory. It was conversational, but the intent was in his tone, lying latent until she gave him reason to really put the screws to her. She didn't know if he meant, what was she doing here at his garage, or what was she doing in town? But she went for the easy question first.

She gestured to the car. "I, uh, I think the bearings need to be replaced. I know that I could take it anywhere, but…" She didn't want to tell him it was Dylan's car, and he was the one who had let it go so long that she swore the front tires were going to fall off. As much as her brother loved his car, he was an idiot. An idiot who despised Cal, and she was pretty sure the feeling was mutual. "I wanted to make sure the job was done right, and everyone knows you do the best job here." That part was true. The Paytons had a great reputation in Tory.

But Cal never let anything go. He narrowed his eyes and propped his hands on his hips, drawing attention to the muscles in his arms. "How do you know we still do the best job here if you haven't been back in ten years?"

Well, then. Couldn't he just nod and take her keys? She held them in her hand, gripping them so tightly that the edge was digging into her palm. She loosened her grip. "Because when I did live here, your father was the best, and I know *you* don't do anything unless you do it the best." Her voice faded. Even though the last time she'd seen Cal, his eyes had been snapping in anger, at least they'd showed some sort of emotion. This steady blank gaze was killing her. Not when she knew how his eyes looked when he smiled, as the skin at the corners crinkled and the silver of his irises flashed.

She thought now that this had been a mistake. She'd offered to get the car fixed for her brother while he was out of town. And while she knew Cal worked with his dad now, she'd still expected to run into Jack. And even though Jack was a total jerk-face, she would have rather dealt with him than endure this uncomfortable situation with Cal right now. "You know, it's fine. Don't worry about it. I'll just—"

He snatched the keys out of her hand. Right. Out. Of. Her. Hand.

"Hey!" She propped a hand on her hip, but he wasn't even looking at her, instead fingering the key ring. "Do you always steal keys from your customers?"

He cocked his head and raised an eyebrow at her. There was the smallest hint of a smile, just a tug at the corner of his lips. "I don't make that a habit, no."

"So I'm special, then?" She was flirting. Was this flirting? Oh God, it was. She was flirting with her high school boyfriend, the guy who'd taken her virginity, and the guy whose heart she'd broken when she had to make one of the most difficult decisions of her life.

She'd broken her own heart in the process.

His gaze dropped, just for a second, and then snapped back to her face. "Yeah, you're special."

He turned around, checking out the car, while she stood gaping at his back. He'd…he'd flirted back, right? Cal wasn't really a flirting kind of guy. He said what he wanted and followed through. But flirting, Cal?

She shook her head. It'd been over ten years. Surely he'd lived a lot of life during that time she'd been away, going to college, then grad school, then working in New York. She didn't want to think about what that flirting might mean, now that she was back in Tory for good. Except he didn't know that.

"So, you think the bearings need to be replaced?" Cal ran his hand over the hood. From this angle, all she saw was hard muscle covering broad shoulders, shifting beneath his T-shirt.

She shook herself and spoke up. "Yeah, it's making that noise—you know, that growl."

He nodded.

The only reason she knew was because she'd spent a lot of weekends and lazy summer afternoons as a teenager, lying in the grass, getting a tan in her bikini while Cal worked on his car, an old black Camaro, in his driveway. She'd learned a lot about cars and hadn't forgotten all of it. She wondered if he still had that Camaro.

"Want me to inspect it too?" Cal was at the passenger's side door now, easing it open.

"What?"

He pointed to the sticker on the windshield. "I can do it now, if you'd like. You have to get it done by end of next month."

She opened her mouth to tell him sure, but then she'd have to give him the registration and insurance card, and then he'd know it was Dylan's car. "No, no, that's all right."

He frowned. "Why not?"

"I just…"

He opened up the passenger's side door and bent inside.

"What are you doing?" She walked around the car, just as he pulled some papers out of the glove box. She stopped and fidgeted with her fingers, because he'd know in three…two…

He bent and tossed the papers back in the glove box. "I'll have it for you by end of the day tomorrow." He started walking toward the office of the garage.

He had to have seen the name, right? He had to have seen it. She walked behind him. "Cal, I—"

He stopped and turned. "Do you need a ride?"

"What?"

"Do you need a ride...home, or wherever you're going?"

She shook her head. "I'm going to walk across the street to Delilah's store. She'll take me home."

His gaze flitted to the shop across the street and then back to Jenna. He nodded. "All right, then."

She tried again. "Cal—"

"You picking it up or your brother?"

The muscle shift in his jaw was the only indication that he was bothered by this. "I'm sorry, I should have told you..."

He shook his head. "You don't owe it to me to tell me anything. You asked me to fix a car—"

"Yeah, but you and Dylan don't like each other—"

That muscle in his jaw ticked again. "Sure, we don't like each other, but what? You think I'm going to lose my temper and bash his car in?"

Uh-oh. "No, I—"

He shook his head, and when he spoke again, his voice was softer. "You didn't have to keep it a secret it was his car. I'm not eighteen anymore. I got more control than I used to."

She felt like a heel. And a jerk. She wasn't the same person she was at eighteen, so she shouldn't have treated Cal like he was the hothead he'd been then. "Cal, I'm so sorry. I—"

He waved a hand. "Don't worry about it, Sunshine."

That name—it sent a spark right through her like a live wire. She hadn't heard that nickname in so long, she'd almost forgotten about it, but her body sure hadn't. It hadn't forgotten the way Cal could use that one word to turn her into putty.

He seemed as surprised as she did. His eyes widened a fraction before he shut down. "Anyway"—his voice was lower now—"we close tomorrow at six. Appreciate it if you'd pick it up before that." He jingled the keys and shot her one more measuring look, and then he disappeared into the garage office, leaving her standing outside the door, her mind broiling in confusion.

She should have known Cal Payton could still knock her off her feet.

Chapter Two

DELILAH'S DRAWERS SAT across the street from Payton and Sons in a small strip mall that held a Subway, a Dollar Store, and a popular Mexican restaurant.

Jenna's friend Delilah had opened up Delilah's Drawers, a clothing consignment shop, shortly after they'd graduated from high school. Delilah had liked alliteration and thought it was a cute play on words—as if people were looking into her dresser drawers for used clothing. She'd already signed paperwork and made promotional material with the name before someone told her they thought the name referred to Delilah's underwear.

But Delilah, being Delilah, held her chin up and kept the name. No one even mentioned it anymore, since she'd been in business for close to ten years. It wasn't like Tory got many visitors.

Delilah had a steady stream of clientele. There was another consignment shop in the area that had been there since Jenna was a kid that carried children's clothing. So Delilah cornered the market on higher-end women's clothing, shoes, and accessories.

The bell over the door rang as Jenna stepped into the shop.

"Be there in a minute!" a voice called from the back room.

"Take your time!" Jenna called back and walked to the front counter to gawk at her favorite part of Delilah's shop—the jewelry. Jenna had a weakness for large earrings, and after that whole situation with Cal at the shop, she could use some retail therapy.

She'd been naive to think that seeing Cal again would be no big deal. It'd been so long since they'd been together, so long since they'd even seen each other. It was a shock to her system that he could still cause a wave of arousal to crash over her body. All those old feelings weren't dead and buried. They'd just been lying dormant. And now she'd gone and offended him because she'd wanted to avoid an awkward situation. *Good call there, Jenna.* That *situation hadn't been awkward at all.*

She sighed and fingered a set of gold chandelier earrings with fake jade accents. They'd go perfectly with that cream-colored top she'd just ordered…

"Hey, you."

Jenna smiled at her friend. Delilah was a five-foot-nothing beauty, whose parents had adopted her from China when she was a baby. Jenna wasn't tall by any means, but Delilah made her feel like a linebacker. Today, Delilah wore a sleeveless navy jersey dress with gladiator sandals and a long necklace made of coral beads.

"Hey, you," Jenna said, hugging Delilah tightly. "I've missed you."

Delilah squeezed her and then pulled back. "Missed you too. Glad we're going to get some girl time in, now that you're back."

Back. What a weird word. She'd never planned to return to Tory. She'd gone to school in New York and worked there for years. Her plan had been to stay there, but as time went on, it became apparent she wasn't happy. As much as she loved the city, she was tired of the pressure, of the people, of the cost of living. She hadn't been willing to give it up, though, because a little bit of it felt like admitting defeat. But when her father offered her a job back home as the publicity director for his financial firm, she took it. After an employee discrimination lawsuit—that her father ultimately won—the firm's public image was in the crapper. Her father had called on the old "family must help family" adage, and so here she was.

Being back in Tory had rekindled some old dreams she used to have—a nice house with a yard in the suburbs. A husband and kids. Growing up, she'd never been close to her family. They'd lived in a big house, which only gave them the excuse not to interact with each other. Unlike Cal's family. Despite Jack's absence in the Payton sons' upbringing, the brothers had been close. She'd admired that. Craved it, even. Back in high school, Cal had dreamed about starting a family, hoping to do a better job than either of their parents did.

But that had been the dream then, and slowly, she'd let it fade. It was still there, though, if she squinted hard enough. And seeing Cal again had already wiped away some of the cobwebs that had covered that dream.

She'd been back in town for a week, having rented a little two-bedroom colonial in a decent neighborhood until she figured out where she wanted to be long term. She started work on Monday and planned to dive in headfirst to improve how the area viewed MacMillan Investments. Not that she was a huge fan of the firm, but it was family, and at the end of the day, her last name was on the letterhead.

But that was next week. For now, she was going to spend time with her oldest, truest friend. Jenna gestured around Delilah's shop. "It looks great in here. Business okay?"

Delilah fixed a gauzy tunic on the rack next to her. "Yeah, it hasn't been bad. Tory is getting better. More businesses are opening, which means more people and people with money." She winked. "But they still like to buy cheap."

"And you have great stuff."

"I have excellent stuff." Delilah snapped her fingers and stepped to another rack. She shuffled through the hangers quickly. "Actually, a dress just came in, and all I could think was, this would look fabulous on Jenna."

"Oh, Delilah—"

She snapped her fingers again. "What was I thinking? I put it aside so no one would buy it." She walked around her counter and bent down behind the register. Smiling, she held up a sleeveless, green- and cream-colored chevron dress. "See? Isn't it gorgeous? And there's a little green matching belt."

Jenna fingered the material, which was lightweight. The fabric flowed beautifully. "I could wear this to work with my—"

Delilah shook her head. "No, how about you wear this out for dinner and drinks with me tomorrow?"

Tomorrow was Thursday. It wasn't like Jenna had to get up for work until Monday. She raised her eyebrows. "Are you asking me or telling me?"

Delilah didn't even blink. "I'm telling you."

Jenna smirked. "Of course you are."

"Come on." Delilah shimmied the dress. "I know you're used to high-class New York drinks, and all we have here is Tory, Maryland, drinks, but I think you can lower your standards a little bit."

Jenna laughed. "Oh, stop. As much as I loved New York, I certainly was never as close to anyone as I am to you." And maybe that was why it'd been so easy to leave. And so easy to come back home.

Delilah pretended to wipe away a tear. "You really know how to talk to a girl."

Waggling her fingers, Jenna said, "All right, so tell me how much the dress is, and I'll take it off your hands."

"Well, you can just take it—"

Jenna shook her head and dug her wallet out of her purse. "Stop. Don't you dare give this to me for free, Delilah Jenkins. Don't you dare."

Her friend pressed her lips together. "Fine."

"Fine. And throw in those gold chandelier earrings too."

As Jenna signed the credit card slip, Delilah leaned on the counter and placed her chin in her hands. "So. Cal Payton."

"Cal Payton," Jenna repeated, her lips comfortable forming the name, like they'd never forgotten.

"How'd he react when you dropped off the Dill Pickle's car?"

Jenna pushed the slip to Delilah, who placed it in the register drawer. "Do not call him Dill Pickle."

"It's either that or Dylan the Dick."

Jenna held back a laugh. "Okay, fine. Dill Pickle it is."

Delilah beamed, surely pleased she won that argument.

Jenna leaned a hip on the counter, crossed her arms, and told Delilah what had happened at the garage, including how she'd offended Cal.

Delilah's eyes widened. "Huh."

"What's 'huh' mean?"

"Wow."

"What's 'wow' mean?"

Delilah furrowed her brows.

Jenna threw up her hands. "Will you talk?"

Delilah shrugged and held her hands out, palms up. "I don't know what you want me to say! That's weird. It's weird Cal showed emotion, and it's weird that it bothered him that much. And it's super-weird he was honest with you."

Jenna chewed the inside of her cheek. "Weird bad or weird good?"

Delilah was silent for a minute. "I...I would actually say good. I've been worried..." Her voice trailed off, and her gaze drifted. "I've been worried about Cal for a while. Not that I talk to him much or see him much, for that matter, but when I have, it's seemed like he was turning more and more into...well..." Delilah winced. "Jack."

Jenna clamped down on the inside of her cheek so hard that she gasped. Jack Payton, Cal's father, was a bitter, scowling man. At least, that's the way he'd been back when she and Cal had been together. "I take it that Jack..."

Delilah shook her head. "He's not any worse, but he's not better."

Jenna sighed and picked at a sales sticker on the counter. "I never wanted that for Cal."

"I know, sweetie."

Jenna looked up. "Cal was never going to leave Tory, though. He was always going to stay here. I mean, I made the right decision. I didn't want to ruin his life. Or mine."

Delilah laid her hand on top of Jenna's. "It's not even worth it to look back. You know that. It's not like you can change anything."

Jenna swallowed, dreading the next question but asking it anyway. "Does he...have a girlfriend?" She didn't recall seeing a wedding ring.

"I don't know. I don't think so. To be honest, I don't see him around a lot. It's a small town, but most rumors are about Brent, not Cal. Although they are the most eligible bachelors in Tory."

She didn't know which relationship status for Cal she preferred more. Even though the thought of Cal in a serious relationship with someone else hurt, it also hurt to know he was alone. "I kind of hate this, Delilah. I had no idea this would still be all…fresh." She looked into her friend's deep brown eyes. "I thought time healed everything."

Delilah's face softened. "I don't—"

Jenna's phone rang, cutting into the moment. She pulled her cell out of her purse and rolled her eyes. "This is Dylan. I'm sorry. I have to take it."

Delilah waved her on. "Don't even worry about it. I have to close out the register anyway before we leave. Say hi to Dill Pickle for me."

Jenna huffed a laugh and then answered the call. "Hello?"

"Hey, did you get my car fixed?"

Jenna clenched her phone hard so she didn't say something nasty to her brother. He wasn't a bad guy. But he had a serious lack of interpersonal skills. "I dropped it off. It'll be ready tomorrow night. I'll pick it up for you."

A pause. "Where'd you take it?"

"Um…"

"You took it to *him*, didn't you?"

Jenna's hackles rose. "Yes, I did, actually. Because we all know that's the best garage in town, and I wasn't driving an hour to the dealership."

"He's probably going to put a condom in my gas tank—"

"Oh, grow up, Dylan." Jenna was over this. Her brother was thirty-four years old, and he needed to act like it. "Cal is a professional, and he'll treat you like any other customer. If you *do* find a condom in the gas tank, it will be *me* who put it there!" She ended the call and huffed out a breath.

A strangled sound came from in front of her, and she lifted her gaze to Delilah's wide eyes. "Did you just tell off your brother?"

Jenna winced, immediately regretting letting her anger get the best of her. "Crap. I should call and apologize, shouldn't I?" She hovered her finger over the phone button.

Delilah reached across the counter and snatched the phone from Jenna's hand. "Don't you dare, Jenna Mac-Millan. I'm proud of you for yelling at Dill Pickle. Damn, that was the best thing I've heard in a while."

Jenna ran her hand through her hair. "I lived and dealt with his dickishness for eighteen years. I'm over it. He can't talk to me like that."

Delilah raised her eyebrows. "Talk to you like that or talk about Cal like that?"

Jenna opened her mouth, then shut it, then opened it again. "Tomato, tomahto."

Delilah smiled knowingly. "Whatever. Let me get this register closed out, and I'll take you home."

"Can we stop for some wine on the way home?"

"Of course, sweetie."

Jenna didn't have wine glasses yet. But on second thought, maybe she'd just drink straight from the bottle.

CAL HAD JUST sat down in his recliner with a newly opened beer when there was a bang on his front door. He stared at the baseball game on TV and waited. The knock was louder this time. He waited longer and cocked his head. Three more knocks and a muffled, "Let me in, asshole!"

"There it is," Call muttered to himself. He set his beer on the coffee table with a sigh and walked to his door. He turned the deadbolt, unlocked the knob, and opened the door. He turned around immediately, walking back to his recliner. The door shut behind him, and then two thuds sounded as Brent toed off his boots.

Cal picked up his beer and sat down. He heard Brent pad into the kitchen and grab a beer from his fridge. Cabinets opened and closed, and Cal rolled his eyes because he knew Brent was hunting for food.

His brother still lived in the apartment they had shared. It was a decent place, and now Brent had a spare bedroom. But Cal...well, he wanted his own place. He wanted a garage and a yard and a deck where he could set up a grill.

Cal had found this two-story home on an acre of land, and even though it was old, he could manage a lot of the repairs himself. He had no neighbors nearby. *None.* He could walk around in his backyard naked if he wanted to. Not that he did, but he *could*.

He had a small basement, and the first floor had a family room, a half-bath, and a nice kitchen with an island, with a door out to his small deck. On the second floor were two bedrooms, plus a full bathroom with a big shower. He loved that damn shower.

It was worth the mortgage, even if he thought sometimes he should have kept the address from his brother.

Brent sauntered into the living room while chugging his beer. He lowered the bottle and wiped his mouth with the back of his hand. "Hey."

Cal narrowed his eyes. "I moved out for a reason, you know. I like quiet."

"I'll be quiet."

"First, you can't be quiet. And second, by quiet, I mean *alone*."

Brent dropped onto the couch. "Come on, you don't mean that."

"I really do mean that."

Brent ignored that. "I'm bored."

"Get a puppy."

Brent had selective hearing. That was not news. "So how about we talk about Jenna MacMillan." Brent waggled his eyebrows.

Although Cal knew his brother was doing it to get a rise out of him, he couldn't help wanting to wipe the leer off of his brother's face. "That's the last thing I want to talk about."

"Okay, so she was hot in high school; I'll give you that. The legs and the hair. But she got, like, way hot now."

Cal growled into his beer.

"We're just talking."

"No, *you're* just talking. I'm trying to watch the game."

Brent's gaze flicked to the TV. "Um, you don't like either of these teams."

"I dunno; thinking I like them a whole hell of a lot right now."

"Anyway, you plan to do anything about it?"

"About what?"

"Quit playing dumb."

Cal sighed. "It didn't work back then; it wouldn't work now. Just let it go." He wondered who he was saying that to—Brent or himself.

He'd done everything he could to separate himself from that dumb, angry, impulsive eighteen-year-old kid who'd fucked up his future. The kid who'd lost the best thing that had ever happened to him.

For ten years, he'd been sure that kid was gone. Done. Buried with a tombstone. Covered over with a neat, orderly, simple life where Cal kept a lid on his emotions.

But he hadn't anticipated the one wild card in his life to come back and dig up old wounds and feelings. Jenna still saw him as that same angry, hot-tempered teenager, not trusting him with the knowledge that the Charger belonged to Dylan.

And the worst part was, that bothered him. It dug under his skin like a splinter, painful enough to feel the need to set her straight.

Why couldn't he have kept his mouth shut? He was good at that—the not-talking thing.

Except around Jenna. Around her, he'd always lost control. Spilled his guts. She'd been everything to him once, in a way no one had been before or after. Other than his family, no one could get extreme emotions out of him. He liked it that way. It was safe and comfortable.

He'd been in Jenna's presence for ten whole fucking minutes, and the body of their past was already dredged up to the surface. He'd felt exposed, like he'd rolled over and shown her his tender belly. That wasn't safe. That was the exact opposite of safe.

He squeezed his eyes shut and gulped down his beer. When he looked over at Brent, his brother grimaced.

"So maybe I shouldn't have said anything," Brent muttered.

"Ya think?"

"I didn't know that there was still—"

"There's nothing!" Cal raised his voice, and Brent flinched. Cal took a deep breath and steadied his voice. "There's nothing *still*. Okay? I don't know why Jenna's in town, but I'm sure she'll be going back to wherever she came from after I fix her brother's car. It was nice to see her and all of that, but that's about it."

Brent swallowed. "What if she's in town…for a while?"

"She's not." She couldn't be. He was sure of it. This wasn't meant to be anymore, her here in Tory. Single.

Not with him.

Jenna had always wanted a family. A husband and kids and cats and all things that he didn't want. At least, not anymore.

Back when he'd been with Jenna, he'd thought about having those things with her, and he might have done it, if she hadn't ended things.

Cal's dad had pretty much checked out after his mom left, so Cal had been responsible for his brothers for a long time. He wasn't eager to fill that dad role again. Been there, done that, got the T-shirt. Now he wanted to come home from work in silence and drink his beer and eat crappy food and not have to answer to anyone.

So he'd made his decision, and he was nothing if not stubborn. He had his inner circle of family, and it was a firm boundary. He didn't want the same things he'd wanted at eighteen. In fact, he wanted just about the opposite of what that impulsive kid had wanted. He'd committed to bachelorhood now, and it would take an act of God to shove him off course.

Although, Jenna MacMillan had always been an act of God in his life. Just the sight of her had brought back a lot of those feelings of a bright, family-filled future. And he wasn't eager to pay those feelings any attention.

Cal sighed. "Can we drink and watch the game now, please?"

Brent pursed his lips. "Okay."

The silence lasted five minutes before Brent started talking about the girl he'd taken out last week, and Cal decided he was definitely getting his brother a puppy for Christmas.

Chapter Three

FAMILY. IT WAS always fucking family that made him grit his teeth and clench his fists and feel that white-hot bolt of anger deep in his chest. At least he'd learned how not to let it manifest physically. "You know I have the certifications. I don't understand why you're so against this."

His father didn't even bother turning around from the tool drawer he was rooting through. "Already explained it."

"Yeah?" Cal said. "Well, explain again, please."

His dad turned around and stared at him. Sometimes, after Cal showered in the mornings, he wiped away the condensation from the mirror and stared at his eyes, wondering if they looked like his dad's. He'd inherited the slate-gray irises from him, but Cal wondered if he'd also been passed down the chill they caused.

"I told ya. I've had this garage for almost forty years, and I ain't fucking with it. And if you fuck it up after I die, I'll come back and haunt your ass."

"Like you have a soul," Cal muttered.

His dad's lips twitched. "Heard that."

"Didn't whisper it."

"I don't want to deal with motorcycles. I don't want them taking up room here—"

"Told you we could add on a special bay—"

"And we can't spare your time. I need you for the cars—"

"We can hire someone else—"

"And I don't want the clients, and I just don't want to deal with it."

Cal ran his tongue over his teeth. "I own part of this garage too."

"Well, I own more." His dad gave Cal his back and turned his attention to the drawer.

That was how his dad ended conversations. There was no politely wrapping up discussions in the Payton family. Nope. Why waste the words? Showing your back was much easier.

Cal walked away, tired of arguing anyway. Plus, Brent was singing again, and it was giving Cal a headache.

He stepped out back and lit up a cigarette. Payton and Sons was on the main drag of Tory, surrounded by strip malls, a couple of gas stations, a bed-and-breakfast, and a grocery store. Their garage had four bays, plus a small office and back room. Cal was proud as hell of the garage and, if he wanted to really be honest with himself, proud of his dad. Their mom, Jill, had devastated Jack when she left. She'd devastated everyone, really, leaving her family behind.

Other than Jack, her leaving had been hardest on Cal. He'd been six, so he'd remembered her more than Brent or Max did. He'd remembered what it'd been like when she was there. How she bought him and Brent matching pajamas every Christmas Eve. How she loved to laugh. So when she left and subsequently remarried out in California, he'd had something to miss.

Jack was a hard man to live with, but when she left him, she'd abandoned her sons too. And the only correspondence Cal got from her were cards signed, *Love, Jill*, on major holidays and his birthday. Which was more salt in the wound than anything.

Cal inhaled sharply. The cigarette helped to calm his nerves a little over the situation with his dad.

He'd finished his work for the day and gotten a call from a friend of a friend who was inquiring about motorcycle repair. Again, Cal was reminded that he wasn't doing what he most wanted to do, which was repair bikes. Not that he didn't like working on cars. He enjoyed that. But bikes were where his main interests lay. His dad couldn't be persuaded to list the shop as a Harley-Davidson certified repair site.

They'd been having this argument for the last couple of years. It was *déjà vu*. And it had only gotten worse since Cal went out and got the certifications himself.

After he finished his cigarette, Cal spent the next hour completing paperwork in the office. He hated it and usually left it up to Brent, but he didn't want to be in the garage with his dad, so he'd volunteered to do it. Childish, but whatever.

And he didn't want them to know that he was nervous. He'd been anxious all day about whether he'd see Jenna. He'd had Brent call her to tell her the repairs and the price, to which she'd given the go-ahead.

If Dylan came to pick up his car, Cal would say as few words as possible to him and then ignore him as Dylan looked down his nose at Cal.

But if Jenna showed up—which was what Cal thought was going to happen—that was another story.

He'd thought about her all night, despite telling himself he wouldn't. And in that odd conscious state between sleep and wakefulness, that was all his brain wanted to dwell on. *Jenna*. She's been his first girlfriend. His first everything. He hadn't thought about her in a long time, preferring to relegate all the MacMillans to a far recess of his brain.

They'd stayed there, right where he put them. Out of sight, out of mind. So much that he'd forgotten about them, and he'd taken it for granted. Because now Jenna was back and refusing to be locked back into that box. He'd have to work extra hard to get her there again when she left.

By closing time, she still hadn't showed up at the garage. Jack left, and Brent asked Cal if he wanted him to stay. Cal waved him on home. He'd wait another half hour or so, and then he'd call Jenna.

He didn't have to wait much longer. A MINI Cooper screeched into the parking lot, loud music blaring. Only one person in Tory drove a MINI Cooper, and that was Delilah Jenkins, so he figured Jenna had arrived.

She had. He saw her heel first as she stepped out of the car, a light beige color that made her legs look even more tan. She shut the car door, and the short skirt of her green and white dress in some sort of striped pattern swirled around her long legs. She was dressed up, and her hair was done in waves around her shoulders. She gestured toward Cal, so she must have spotted him through the glass walls of the office. She patted the roof of the MINI Cooper, and then Delilah backed up, peeling out of the lot.

Cal didn't even bother pretending to look away. He didn't pretend much of anything, and she'd know he'd been waiting for her.

Her heels clicked on the tile floor as she stepped into the shop.

The sight of her constricted his chest. She had more makeup on today, and it made her eyes look bigger, her red lips fuller.

She looked ready to go to some fancy high-class wedding or something. When he was a teenager, he'd been self-conscious sometimes about how he looked—all rough around the edges, where she was soft, smooth curves. His wrong-side-of-the-tracks to her right-side. But she'd seemed to like that about him, so he hadn't fought it. He hadn't tried to be something he wasn't. He knew back then, though, if she'd asked him to, he would have changed for her. He would have done anything for her.

And now, as she stood all clean and beautiful and soft in his dirty shop, he wondered if she'd grown out of that bad-boy phase. Because he was too old to change now.

She was staring at him, lips slightly parted, eyes wide, and a definite flush down her neck, which disappeared beneath the low neckline of her dress. He'd seen that look before, but it'd been a long time ago. He shook his head, telling himself he wasn't up for memories.

He stood up and walked out from behind the counter. His jeans were a little grubby today, and his gray T-shirt showed the typical smudges of dirt and grease. He jingled the keys to the car. "Wonderin' if you were gonna come."

Her hands lifted hesitantly to her hair. "I know. I'm so sorry. I was busy…" Her fingers fluttered. "I lost track of time."

"It happens."

She took a step forward. "You stayed late for me?"

He shrugged. He didn't make it a habit, but she didn't need to know that. He gestured toward her dress. "You're going out with friends since you're visiting?"

"Visiting?"

He frowned. "Yeah, visiting. Tory."

She swallowed. He watched her pale skin flush redder. "Oh, I'm not visiting. I…uh…live here now."

He blinked at her. "Come again?"

"Yeah, I accepted a job with my father's firm as their publicity director."

He was going to guess that had to do with the recent lawsuit that had been splashed all over the papers. Dylan MacMillan and MacMillan Investments had been sued by a former employee who claimed they fired her when they found out she was pregnant. They won the case, but Dylan's reputation—along with the company's—had taken a hit in the community. Brent had thoroughly enjoyed reading letters to the editor, railing against the company. He used fake voices when he read, which even Cal had to admit was pretty funny.

When Cal just stared at her, she kept talking. "I was in New York, working for publicity at a women's magazine but…I don't mind being back." She laughed nervously. "I'd rather raise a family here."

It was taking him a while to catch up. "You're living in Tory now." He had to make sure he had his facts straight.

She bit her lip and nodded.

So this wasn't temporary. He wasn't going to give her back her brother's car and be able to tell himself this was the last time he'd see her. He'd know she was here now, in town, where he could run into her at the grocery store or while getting gas or—*fuck*—on a date with some suit from her father's firm.

Fuck.

He turned around and took a step toward the counter, needing to get her out of here, needing time to process this, get it straight in his head, so then he could fasten all his armor in place. This was okay; he'd be okay. She was just a girl from high school—

"Is that okay?" Her voice shook a little from behind him.

He stopped and gripped her car keys so tightly, he knew the imprint would be in his palm.

He faced her. "Why wouldn't it be okay?"

"I don't know. I…"

"I don't own this town, Jenna."

She pursed her lips. "I know that. Never mind. Forget I asked that."

"Why would you think it wouldn't be okay?"

She held his gaze. "Because no matter how much time has gone by, we still have a past. I thought we had closure, but the way you look at me, I'm not so sure of that. And I'm thinking I look at you the same way."

Eighteen-year-old Jenna had been bold but unsure what to do with it, like she couldn't harness her confidence.

Close-to-thirty-year-old Jenna, apparently, had grown into her boldness.

It was a major fucking turn-on.

He stepped closer, careful not to touch any of her fancy clothes but close enough that he could if he wanted to. The heat rolled off her body, and for a moment he wanted to melt into her. "How do I look at you, Sunshine?" he asked softly. He'd given her the nickname back in high school because everything about her was bright, from her clothes to her smile to her personality. Everything was better when she was around, like she was his own personal vitamin-D provider.

She rolled her lips between her teeth and let them out. He wanted to cup her face, rub some grease on her cheek, and swipe his thumb across those lipstick-coated lips. A trade.

"Like we're still at River's Edge." She spoke hesitantly, haltingly, like each word was an effort. "Sometimes, I close my eyes, and I hear the leaves rustle above us. I can see the glow of the moon on the water, and I can smell the cigarette smoke from your clothes. You still smoke?"

She'd only said a couple of sentences, but he was right back at River's Edge, holding her warm body in his arms, rubbing his stubbled chin in her hair while she drank a can of Bud Light he'd stolen from his father's fridge.

Those nights were some of the best of his life. Until he fucked it up. And she'd let him go. "I still smoke sometimes."

Her arm moved, like she was going to touch him, but then she flinched back. "They'll kill you."

"Why do you think I keep buying my dad cigarettes?"

She barked out a harsh laugh and then clapped her hand over her mouth. "That was so mean, Cal Payton," she said around her fingers.

He smirked, glad the moment was broken. He didn't want to see her hazel eyes wistful. Going down memory lane was not on his life agenda.

He took a step back. Her body swayed, like she wanted to follow, but she kept her feet planted. He held out the keys, and she took them. "Car's out front. Brent got your payment over the phone and e-mailed you the receipt, right?"

"Yes."

"Then you're good to go." He did turn around now and retreated behind the counter. He didn't need to stand there within arm's reach of her when he had no intention of touching her. He didn't need to smell her hair or whatever perfume she had on.

He didn't need it. He had his life. His good, solitary life without being responsible for other people. Jenna was just reminiscing. She could do that all she wanted, but she could leave him out of it.

She jingled the keys. "Okay, well, thank you so much for working on it. I know you guys are the best."

There was the flattery again. "No problem. You have fun, uh, doing whatever you're doing tonight."

She smiled. "Delilah and I are going out. She said there's a new place over in Hattery that serves great martinis."

He wouldn't know. Hattery was a little salty for his taste. "Drive safe, then."

"Thanks again."

"Any time."

She turned around and walked out the door, her heels clicking on the floor.

When her car pulled away, he dropped his forehead onto the counter. This was going to take some time. He'd have to get used to possibly running into Jenna in town. When he did go out, he tended to head south to Brookridge. So if he hooked up with a woman, there wasn't much risk of running into Jenna. He'd tried the relationship thing a couple of times after Jenna left. And he didn't know if it was that he missed her or missed what they had. The women after her had complained about his lack of communication and *emotions*. He didn't know how to do that anymore. With Jenna, it had all been so easy.

His brothers received his emotions now, when he had them to give, and that was it. Everything else, he kept to himself. And he'd been fine with that, until Jenna's eyes had met his again and brought up all those memories.

He sighed. *Fuck.*

Chapter Four

JENNA FORGOT THAT she hated martinis.

Okay, so maybe she didn't hate them, but she'd rather have a nice glass of merlot or something.

Martinis were pretty to look at, all suave in their delicate glasses with the olive-laden toothpicks. She felt sophisticated holding them too.

But then she remembered that it felt fake, like she was playing pretend, just like she'd done for so many years in New York. That wasn't who she was. She was Jenna MacMillan from small Tory, Maryland, and dammit, she wanted a glass of wine. Boxed would do. Honestly, she'd drink it out of a sippy cup. She wasn't picky.

She took a sip of her pomegranate martini and grimaced.

"I'm starting to get a complex, because you look like you're in pain, sitting here with me." Delilah raised her thin-mint martini to her lips. Jenna thought the concept sounded delicious, but the smell was not enticing, kind of like toothpaste.

"I'm sorry." She placed a hand over her friend's. "It's not you; it's this drink."

"You don't like it?"

Jenna shook her head and pushed her drink into Delilah's grasping hand. Jenna was driving, so she'd limited herself to one drink. And since she'd only had about three sips, she was confident in her sober status. Delilah was driving too, but despite her small stature, the girl had a high tolerance.

After Jenna had picked up Dylan's car, she'd driven to her place. She dropped off her brother's car and got into the used car she'd bought a week earlier. She hadn't needed a vehicle in New York, and even though Dylan said she could drive his, she wanted something for herself. It wasn't anything fancy, just a late-model Honda Civic.

Then she drove to Hattery to meet Delilah, chastising herself the whole way for getting all weird with Cal. Why, *why on earth,* of all things, had she brought up River's Edge? She'd dwelled on those memories of the back of Cal's truck for years. She'd daydreamed about being seventeen again, no care in the world, no responsibilities. All that had mattered when she'd been in his truck was *him*. His whispered words in her ear that were only for her, his questing fingers, his strong lips. She'd built it up so big in her head that it had almost become a fantasy. They were larger than life now, those memories. They were private. So she had no idea what had possessed her to spew them at Cal's feet.

Delilah was sipping happily, glancing around the bar, named Olive Tree. It was cute, one of those places that was only lit by a couple of strategically placed wall sconces and candles on the high-top tables. The walls were decorated, appropriately, in an olive tree motif. Other than martinis, the bar served tapas. They'd ordered *chopitos*, which was fried baby squid. Jenna ignored what it was, because it was, in fact, delicious. Which worked, because she could really go with eating some of her feelings right now. She'd already decided the artisanal cheese plate was next, because it came with some dark chocolate.

"So," Jenna said, "you seeing anyone?"

Delilah licked a drop off the side of her martini. "I went out with a guy from your dad's firm last week, actually."

"Yeah?" Jenna perked up, eager to hear about someone else's love life. "How did it go?"

"Oh, it went terrible," Delilah said cheerfully, munching on her *chopitos*.

Jenna stared at her. "You sound really broken up about it."

Delilah laughed. "I'm not really looking for anything right now. The store keeps me busy. I go out with friends, and now you're back. I only said yes because he said he'd take me to that new Peruvian place in Brookridge. Which was excellent, by the way. I recommend the stuffed poblanos."

"And you didn't even have to put out?" Jenna smirked.

Delilah winked. "Oh, *he* put out. By the way, he had a gorgeous cock, but he didn't know what to do with it. Such wasted talent."

Jenna waved her hand. "Please don't tell me who this is, because I have to work with him."

Delilah zipped her lips.

"Thank you."

"My pleasure. So speaking of big dicks—and not the good kind—did you get Dylan's car fixed?"

Jenna snorted a laugh. "Yep, thanks for dropping me off."

"And?"

"And what?"

"Did Cal bend you over the counter?"

"Delilah, I swear to God, I can't take you anywhere."

Her friend erupted into giggles.

The thing was, Jenna had been content to casually date for years. Like Delilah, she'd been busy in New York. She had her friends and her job, and a serious relationship wasn't something she wanted.

But being back in Tory was affecting her attitude. Back in high school, all she'd wanted was to go to college and then come back with a fancy to degree to her hometown...and to Cal. But that was before they broke up, and then it was no longer a future she saw happening. But now she had those visions again of lazy afternoons lounging on her front porch, while Cal worked on his car. Maybe with a couple of kids running around. And a dog. It'd been so long since she'd wanted that.

It was a shock to think that Cal still had this effect on her. She'd given up on that teenage notion of soul mates long ago.

"I just don't know," Jenna said. "I'm surprised all these feelings about him are still there. Do I just miss the familiarity we had? Or am I grasping at straws or…?" She looked at her friend helplessly.

Delilah bit her lip. "You and Cal always had something special. Everyone knew it, that your relationship was so much bigger than high school. We were all surprised when you broke up—"

"You know why that happened." Jenna's voice surprised her when it came out as almost a growl.

Delilah didn't react. "I know that, sweetie. You didn't have a choice."

"I think he resented me for it, though. He wanted to pay the price without his rich girlfriend getting him off the hook."

"Maybe. Cal always had a lot of pride."

"It's why he got in that situation in the first place."

Delilah pressed her lips together and nodded.

"But what's done is done," Jenna said. "I need to let it go. I'm not going to see him around too much, right? Like maybe in passing while we're both picking up milk at the grocery store? I can handle a couple more awkward conversations." *Without sharing all your innermost thoughts*, she added to herself.

Delilah reached across the table. "It'll be fine. And anyway, I'll keep you busy. I'm so glad you're back. I have a good time with my girls, but you're my favorite."

Jenna laughed. "You've always been my favorite too."

Delilah jerked her head in the direction of the small dance floor, where Van Morrison played softly from two speakers. "Why don't we dance?"

Jenna hopped down off her stool. "Now you're talking." Thoughts about Cal could wait. Tonight was a best friend kind of night.

So AFTER A night of drinking, dancing and laughing with her best friend, Jenna was too tired to stop her mind from wandering on the drive home.

She gripped the steering wheel as her thoughts ultimately led to Cal. It was so easy to remember the good times with him—the school dances where they slipped into dark hallways to make out, the times he'd take her driving late at night to go deer spotting. It'd been a long time since she let her mind sink into all the ways their relationship hadn't been perfect.

Cal had a temper, which he kept repressed until it blew like a gasket. Brent covered everything with a joke, and little Max had been kind of a mix of the two. Cal, though, was a storm waiting to happen. As a teenager, it had been exhilarating. That bad-boy edge had been attractive. She'd been devoted to Cal, because she knew his soft side—his gentle smile and the way he touched her.

She'd told him she'd come back to Tory after her college graduation or suggested he could move to her. Looking back, she wondered if he actually believed her, or if some part of him decided to self-sabotage.

It'd all come to a head at her high school graduation party, when Dylan cornered Cal and…well…it didn't really matter now what he'd said. It was a lot of nasty things and mean words, and Cal got angry. Really angry.

He lashed out with a fist, broke her brother's nose, and doomed their future.

Dylan probably had set him up—no, she was sure of it—but Cal hadn't had to take the bait. After that, her father had forced her to make a choice—break up with Cal, or Dylan would press charges.

She hated Cal for putting her in the position of having to make that decision. She hated her brother and her dad for forcing it.

Cal had been contrite but angry. He'd refused to break up with her, saying he needed to be punished for the mistake he'd made in hitting Dylan. She hadn't wanted to ruin his life like that, though. So that was it—to save Cal an assault charge on his record, she'd cut ties. She was bitter that she was the one who'd had to do it, that it had fallen on her shoulders. That at eighteen, her brother and dad had enough sway over her life to force that choice.

Yeah, so she was bitter about the whole damn thing. Still.

The crack that rent the air was like a gunshot, and Jenna swerved to the right onto the shoulder of the road and slammed on her brakes. She threw the car in park and sat there, breathing heavy, as goose bumps rose along her skin. She didn't want to get out of the car, because what the hell had that been? She was on a rather secluded, forest-lined section of road between Hattery and Tory.

Once she felt okay enough to drive again, she put the car in gear and slowly pulled onto the road. And that's when she heard the steady *wap*.

She'd blown a tire.

She breathed out an exasperated sigh and pulled onto the side of the road again. She turned the car off and sat there, listening to the pinging of the engine. She knew how to change a tire. At least, she'd known once, but it'd been a decade, and she wasn't sure that was so much like riding a bike. Plus, it was dark, and she was wearing a dress with heels. Not the most ideal situation to be in. She opened up her car door and peered back. It was the driver's side rear tire, which meant she'd have to squat half in the road to change it.

"Shoot," she muttered and pulled out her AAA membership card her father had given her when she came back into town.

She called the number on the card and told the operator she needed a tow. The operator told her the nearest tow truck could be there in about forty-five minutes. She thanked her and settled in for a wait.

Luckily, she had an iPhone, complete with Candy Crush, so she settled in to beat the stupid, frustrating level 125 once and for all.

She was close, oh so close, when the headlights of an approaching truck shined into her windshield. She put down her phone and watched as the tow truck driver executed an impressive three-point turn in the road and then backed up to the front of her car. Booted feet attached to a pair of sturdy, jean-clad legs dropped down from the cabin of the truck, and then a man with a baseball cap walked toward her, a pair of work gloves in one hand. A lit cigarette dangled from his lips. She wished now she had a jacket or something to cover up her bare shoulders, because she was on a stretch of deserted road with a strange man.

She gripped her keys and stepped out of the car—then immediately sucked in a breath. The headlights from her car reflected off Cal's steely irises.

Chapter Five

"CAL?"

He stared at her from under the brim. The ends of his dark hair stuck out around the edges of his cap. He inhaled and then took his cigarette out, crushing the butt under his boot. He blew the smoke off to the side, away from her. "Long time, no see."

She stared at the tow truck and then at him. "You guys do towing?"

"We have a contract with AAA. We got a kid who does it usually, but Brent and I fill in on his nights off."

"A kid?"

A slight smile curved his lips. "Okay, a young man, then."

She blinked at him. She'd just vowed to stay away from Cal and avoid any situation where she could be alone with him and that stretch had lasted approximately four hours.

He raised his eyebrows. "So you got a flat?"

"Yeah, it just blew."

He glanced at her car. "Is this one actually yours or another one of Dylan's?"

"This is mine. I just picked it up for something temporary when I got into town. It's only been a week."

He nodded and walked past her. After he opened up the driver's side door, he flipped up the latch to pop the trunk. "Let's check out the condition of your spare."

She followed him around to the trunk, where he lifted up the flap in the fabric lining to discover…no spare.

"What the hell?" she muttered.

He blew out a breath. "Who'd you buy this from?"

"Five Star Motors, over on Fairview."

He snorted and closed the trunk. "Asshole."

She assumed he'd had an unpleasant experience with the owner of Five Star. "I called a tow because I wasn't too keen on hanging my ass out in the road in the dark while trying to change it. Glad I didn't bother now."

His eyes looked lighter in the stark reflections of the car lights. "You made the right decision. It isn't safe here."

He held her gaze a moment too long, and she looked down at her feet, heat rushing into her cheeks. "So I guess you can give me a ride?"

"Let me get the car hooked up. Then we'll get you home." He glanced at her bare arms. "You need a jacket or something?"

Why did he have to be so nice? "I'm okay, thanks."

He nodded and walked past her, pulling on his gloves.

About ten minutes later, he had her car hooked up to the tow and was motioning for her to hop into his truck. He even helped her inside, with a steady hand cupping her elbow.

The inside of the cabin was surprisingly clean for a tow truck. She stared at a picture that was hanging from the rearview mirror. It was a laminated photo of a naked woman. Even Jenna had to admit that if her boobs looked like that, she'd pose naked too.

When Cal sank into the driver's seat beside her and started up the truck, she pointed at the picture wordlessly.

He barked out a laugh. "That's all Gabe."

"The kid?"

"Yeah, the kid. He needs a girlfriend or something."

She hummed under her breath, and he shook his head with a grin as he pulled out onto the road.

It was after five minutes of silence that he spoke again. "You…uh…you look nice tonight," Cal said softly.

She squeezed her eyes shut as goose bumps broke out on her arms. She'd heard pick-up lines. She'd heard them all. And she'd heard from the best. But none of them— none of them at all—lit up her body like an honest, real statement from Cal Payton. He said what he meant, always had. He thought she looked nice. Such a simple thing to say, but it meant a lot.

She looked over at him. They'd begun to reach the small neighborhoods outside of Tory, so the lights from the houses lit up Cal's face. His jaw was stubbled, and a little bit of silver streaked the hair sticking out under the cap. He'd always had the thickest hair. She wondered if, as he'd aged, he'd grown chest hair. She wondered what his body looked like at thirty, compared to eighteen. Would he be thicker? Would he still catch his breath when she wrapped her fingers around…

She took her gaze away from him before he realized that she was staring. Because dirty thoughts about Cal while she was alone was one thing, but dirty thoughts about him while he was sitting within touching distance felt…well…dirty.

Jenna fingered the hem of her dress. "Thank you."

She told him where the house was that she was renting, and he said he knew the neighborhood and remembered seeing the FOR RENT sign outside the house.

"So, did you have fun with Delilah?" he asked.

"Yeah, we had a nice time."

"How was that drinks place? Martinis, you said?"

She laughed softly. "I always forget that I don't like martinis."

He glanced at her with a small smile. "You never did like the liquor."

She pressed her lips together. They'd gone to a party once in high school. She'd drunk shots and some type of schnapps right from the bottle and then spent the whole night puking. Cal had stayed with her, holding her hair and rubbing her back. "Yeah, I still don't."

"That's okay." He reached over and patted her thigh. She was sure it wasn't a conscious decision to touch her. But nothing was simple between them. It never had been. The calluses on his palm rasped along her bare skin, and she sucked in a breath.

He had to have heard it, because he jerked his hand back. "Uh, didn't mean to do that." He scratched the hair that was curling at the nape of his neck. "Sorry."

She turned a little to face him. They were entering her neighborhood now. They'd pull into her driveway in minutes. "You don't have to apologize."

He didn't look at her, and a muscle in his jaw ticked. "Yeah, but I shouldn't have touched you. I just…" His voice trailed off.

She stared at his profile as he pulled into her driveway and parked. He rubbed his hands on his jeans and squinted at the one-car garage attached to her house. "Nice place."

She ignored his attempt to change the subject. She reached and brushed his arm lightly with the back of her hand. "Is this difficult for you? Like it is for me?"

He stared at the emblem in the center of the steering wheel and ran his fingers over it. She waited, unsure if he'd ask her to elaborate.

"There are times," he said softly, "that I wish I was good at lyin'."

Her heart sped up until it pounded in her ears, and she swore he'd see it beat through the skin of her neck.

"This is one of those times." His voice was gravel and grit and regret. He took off his hat and scratched his head and threw his cap into the back of his cab. "It's hard as hell. And after all these years, I never thought it would be."

His gaze finally met hers. His pale eyes glowed, reflecting off the light above her garage door. A slash of light cut across the bottom of his face, highlighting the five-o'clock shadow on his jaw. She wondered how that stubble would feel on her face, the soft skin of her belly, between her thighs.

"Cal…" She didn't mean to reach out, to touch him. What right did she have? Those blue-gray eyes were boring into hers, but they were giving her nothing. And she wanted just one touch, one shot at a connection. He closed his eyes as her palm cupped his jaw and her fingers traced over the hollow of his cheek, the corner of his mouth, and that dimple in his chin.

His stubble was coarse, but the skin beneath was soft, which was how she'd always described Cal himself.

Reluctantly, she pulled her hand back, but Cal's eyes sprung open, and he grabbed her wrist. She curled her fingers into a fist, inches from his face.

Those steely irises were giving her something now, daring her, and his parted lips were the incentive.

"Jenna." His growl was a warning. But she didn't know if he was throwing the caution tape between them or if he was pissed that she'd started to retreat.

She tried to remember what he was like at eighteen. But it was hard to find that impulsive boy in this controlled man. All she knew was that she didn't want to retreat. She'd only started because she'd thought he wouldn't appreciate the advance. But what she'd learned in New York was to be clear and firm about what she wanted and, most of all, to go after it.

Jenna uncurled her fingers so the pads brushed his bottom lip. And she gave one decisive nod.

There was a pause, and it was like time stopped for a minute. Jenna didn't move, didn't breathe, and she swore her heartbeat slowed to a crawl as she waited for Cal to react to her nod, to her questing fingers on his lips.

And then he yanked on her arm, not enough to hurt but enough to pull her across the bench seat of the tow truck and into his arms.

She didn't care about her heels or her dress. She didn't give a shit about any of it, because she was in Cal's lap, straddling him, her knees on either side of his hips. And his palms were on her face, fingers curling into her scalp and finally...oh, *finally*, his lips were on hers.

Cal could kiss, always could. Just the right pressure with the right texture of those maddening ridges on his lips. But back then, he'd been a boy. He kissed with the intent to move on to the main show.

The Cal she was kissing now was all man. A man who knew what a kiss could do, how it affected a woman. How a kiss was its own skill. And boy, how she loved kissing this man.

She squeezed his shoulders, fingers pressing into the muscle through the thin layer of his T-shirt. He moaned against her lips, and she opened her mouth. He went for it, delving his tongue inside her mouth, licking into her, tasting her, inhaling her. And God, maybe they were different people than they had been but this...this was the same. This hunger for each other, the intensity with which their bodies reacted in each other's presence. It was the same, if not magnified.

As his hands lowered down her neck, she wondered what else Cal could do now that he was all man. Those strong arms, those thick legs. How would he fuck? She could think dirty thoughts about him now, because his hands were doing dirty things to her body.

Those palms were moving over the swell of her breasts, and a thumb flicked her left nipple through the thin material of her dress and bra. She whimpered and rolled her hips, feeling the hard heat of him encased in denim between her legs.

She could still turn Cal on. She could still make him hard. It was empowering.

He broke the kiss and leaned back, watching his hands as they skimmed her ribs, spanned her waist, and then gripped her hips.

She liked watching him look at her, his eyes full of mercury heat. His fingers dug into her, and he gently guided her, rubbing her onto himself. His jeans were rough on the skin of her thighs, and the seam was chafing the skin raw on the inside of her knees, but she didn't care. She dug her fingers into his chest further, using her nails, because if she was going to have marks from this, then he'd have them too.

He licked his lips, his eyes still on his lap. "Lift up your dress, Jenna."

Her breath left her lungs on a whoosh. His voice was low and firm and so confident. This was what he'd been lacking when they were teenagers and frankly, this was what every man after him had been lacking too.

Cal knew what he wanted and wasn't ashamed to ask for it. Her nipples hardened, and she was sure he could see them through her dress. She was wet, but even if she hadn't been astride him, she would have been wet just from those words.

She uncurled her nails from his chest and lowered her hands. She placed her palms on her knees and then slowly ran them up her legs. She had goose bumps, not because she was cold but because every single inch of her body was hypersensitive to Cal's gaze, his touch.

He was watching her hands and when they reached the edge of her dress, he sucked in a breath.

She paused and bit her lip.

His tilted his head to the side and lifted his gaze to her. "Show me."

She curled her fingers around the hem as she worried her lip between her teeth. He was fully clothed, and she was straddling him, about to lift up her dress. His command pulled at something inside of her to obey, and so she did, skimming that light fabric up her thighs. He dropped his hands to her knees and watched his lap as she pulled up, up until the lower half of her dress was balled up at her waist.

She was wearing a white lace thong. Anything else might have been visible through her dress. Without her dress covering it, the air hit the damp fabric, and she moaned.

Cal didn't move. He was staring at her, at the small scrap of lace that covered her. The muscles in his jaw bulged as he flexed them, and his thumbs dug into the soft skin of her inner thighs.

He swallowed and licked his lips, leaving them parted. His hands began to move, following the same path hers had moments before. He stopped when his thumbs dipped into the crease where her legs met her body.

She tried to keep her breathing steady, but not knowing what he'd do next was driving her crazy. Her chest was rising and falling with her heaving breaths, and she wanted to scream, until he lifted his right hand and ran the backs of his fingers between her legs.

She shuddered at the touch. She was wet and swollen and so sensitive, she didn't think it would take much to set her off.

He leaned his head back on the headrest and finally, his gaze met hers. Not breaking eye contact, he moved his thumb and pressed it right to the damp fabric. She sucked in a breath. He moved it, questing, reading the cues in her body, the shifts in her hips until he hit just. The. Right. Spot.

"I want to see you get off," he said. Every word, every touch was full of intent. With one hand firmly on her hip and the other doing crazy things to her clit, he urged her to ride his lap. She let her dress go, and it stayed bunched around her waist as she clutched his arms. He watched her, the cords in his neck straining, the muscles in his shoulders bulging.

"You still get this wet for me?" His voice came through clenched teeth.

"What does it feel like?" she gasped.

"Feels like my Sunshine."

She threw her head back, the ends of her hair tickling the top of her bare ass. She didn't care where she was; she didn't care what this meant. All she knew was that

Cal's hands were on her again, his voice in her ear, his scent in her nostrils. She wanted him, and she wanted this moment more than her next breath.

She came on a silent cry that turned into gasping moans. Her whole body shook in his arms, and his low voice whispered some words in her ear that she couldn't decipher. Her brain had gone offline, and all she managed to do after her orgasm ripped through her was to slump onto his chest, panting hot breaths on the skin of his neck.

A finger lifted her chin. "You still kiss like a fucking dream." His lips coasted over hers, and his broad hands skimmed down her back to palm her ass. He flexed his hips once. "And you still feel like one too."

"Cal." He was hard between her legs. It was difficult to reconcile this Cal with the one she'd known before, but it didn't matter. She wanted him. And he wanted her. She leaned back and cupped his stubbled jaw, looking into his silver eyes. "Do you want to come inside?"

Chapter Six

Do you want to come inside?

Those words slammed into him, bringing everything into focus, and it was like a bucket of ice water had been dumped onto Cal's head.

What the fuck was he doing? No really. What *the fuck* was he doing?

He was about ten seconds away from fucking her in the cab of the tow truck. Jenna MacMillan. The only girl he'd ever loved. He hadn't seen her in ten years, and he acted like this, like the same out-of-control eighteen-year-old who couldn't keep his hands to himself.

She'd felt right under his hands, her lips had been perfection, and that was the problem. Nothing had changed between them from back then to now. He was still Cal Payton, a blue-collar piece of shit, and she was Jenna MacMillan, daughter of the richest guy in town. She still saw him the same, didn't she? The rough guy with rough hands who'd take her in a truck?

The definition of insanity was doing the same thing and expecting different results. Cal was many things but crazy wasn't one of them.

Jenna's flushed cheeks faded, and her brow furrowed as she stared at his face, which surely showed his dawning anxiety over this situation. "C-Cal?" Her fingers curled into the hair at the nape of his neck.

He closed his eyes and let his head fall back on the headrest. He dropped his hands from her legs, hating the way his palms itched to go right back where they were, like her skin was magnetic.

He swallowed and prepared to hate himself. "No."

Her body tensed on top of his. "What?"

"No, I don't wanna come inside. And you gotta get off of me."

There was a pause, and she flexed her hips slightly onto his erection, which made him grit his teeth. "But—"

"I'm holding on to my willpower by a fine fucking thread. So if you don't get off me in five seconds, Jenna, swear to God, I will be inside you. Now *get. Off.*" He used crude words and language on purpose. That's what she expected of him, wasn't it?

He didn't open his eyes until she slid off him. Where once there had been a simmering heat of attraction firing in this cab, now there was nothing but a chill. And it went right down to his bones.

He heard her take a deep breath and then her purse straps jingled. He opened his eyes and gripped the steering wheel, staring straight ahead at the door of her garage. She'd rented a nice house. He figured she didn't plan to stay there, but even if she did, it would be a nice place to raise a family. He could picture a basketball hoop over the garage door. A nice little swing on the front porch. Jenna standing at the door, a toddler clinging to her leg as he pulled into the driveway after a long day of work.

He didn't want that. He told himself he didn't want that. It wasn't for him. Jenna wasn't for him.

And as much as it killed him to listen to her gather herself together over on the other side of the truck cab, he had to stay firm. Another couple of minutes of awkwardness and anger would save them each from a future of heartache. Because this would end again, probably even worse than the last time. Which was pretty fucking bad, considering the broken nose and possible assault charge.

He heard her take a sharp breath, and he wondered what kind of battle was coming. "Cal—"

"I'll take your car back to the shop and get a tire on it. Brent'll call you when it's ready." He turned the ignition, still avoiding her gaze.

"Excuse me?" Her voice shook.

He turned to look at her, careful to keep his face blank. "He'll call you when it's ready," he said slowly.

Her nostrils flared as she inhaled sharply. "Can you explain, please, why you're pretending like I wasn't on your lap five minutes ago with my skirt hiked up to my waist?"

Of course she wouldn't let him get away with this. "That shouldn't have happened."

"That shouldn't have *happened*?" Her voice was reaching screech octaves. He heard, and he knew she did too, because she shook her head and turned away from him.

She smoothed her dress, and it pained him to see how much this hurt her. But he told himself it was for the best, despite the sour feeling in his stomach.

"Well, thank you for fixing my tire. I'll look forward to your brother's call." She opened up the truck door, hopped down, and turned to peer back into the cab. There was a flash in her eyes he didn't like. "Maybe *he'll* be nicer to me than his asshole brother."

Cal couldn't stop the sneer from curling his lips. "Don't play that game with me, Jenna."

She smirked, and he knew she'd willingly poked the bear. "Then don't play games with me, *Calvin*." She slammed the door shut and stalked to the front door of her house. She opened her front door and stepped inside.

He sat in the driveway for five minutes, beating himself up until he felt steady enough to put the truck in gear and drive away.

THE SOUND OF his motorcycle's engine below him, the vibration between his thighs, was the only thing soothing him, keeping him from running back to Jenna's house and begging forgiveness.

Because plain and simple, he'd been an asshole. He knew it. She knew it. But what was done was done, and Cal was a decisive son of a bitch. It'd been heaven to feel her again, but that was the last chance he was going to get.

He'd come home after dropping off Jenna's car and immediately hopped on his bike for a late-night summer ride. These were his favorite times to be out on the road. There wasn't much traffic, and the air was hot yet not blistering. He could wear his leather jacket with a T-shirt underneath, a backwards ball cap on his head and just…ride.

He'd tried to be a big shot around Jenna at first, all proud of how he'd changed, but then he'd pulled that move on her like a teenager. He had his reasons why they'd never work in the long run, but how could Jenna understand that? She hadn't gotten it all those years ago. She thought it was no big deal how much her family despised him. But they had more power over her than she wanted to recognize, and they'd sure pulled that card at the first shot they had to get her away from him.

And at eighteen, he'd played right into it like a chump.

He turned a corner and opened up the gas on the long stretch of highway in front of him.

Jenna. God, she'd been beautiful with her swollen lips and flushed cheeks, with that mass of brown hair surrounding them.

He'd wanted her so bad. He'd wanted to open the fly of his jeans, rip that piece of fabric between her legs to the side, and bury himself inside of her. If she was any other girl, he wouldn't have hesitated. But she wasn't. She was Jenna.

He had…things with Jenna. A past. Fucking *feelings.* Goddamn *feelings.* And they fucked everything up, because then a fuck wasn't a simple fuck. It was complicated and messy because he wouldn't want one time with her. He'd want it again and again.

So he'd made the right decision. He was about two cats away from being a hermit anyway, so he didn't think he'd see her around town much. He'd make Brent deal with her cars, although he sighed when he thought about how much fun that conversation would be.

He pulled into his driveway and steered his bike into the garage. He kept his truck parked outside, because he cared a hell of a lot more about his bike than that old rusted thing on four wheels.

He'd ridden a couple of used bikes before saving up for his current ride—a 2013 Harley-Davidson Softail Deluxe. It had a retro look, with whitewall tires, a thick fork, and triple headlights. He ran his hands over the black seat and the red and silver body.

So yeah, this beauty got the garage. His truck could rust out in the driveway.

Inside the house, he threw his keys onto the kitchen counter and walked upstairs, disrobing as he went, eager to get a shower to wash this day off him.

When he finally stood naked under the hot spray, his erection, which had never really gone away, decided to make a reappearance.

He reached down and wrapped his fingers around his shaft, stroking once as he braced his other hand on the wall in front of him. He widened his legs, feeling that familiar pull in his gut, the need to come.

He thought about the last girl he'd dated but blurred faces rolled through his vision, like a lottery slot machine, until it finally stopped to focus on Jenna's hazel eyes.

He groaned, stroking his cock harder, hating himself because he knew it was going to be a while before he was able to get himself off with anything but the memory of her.

Her tans thighs, that tiny scrap of white lace. Why hadn't he tugged it aside when he had the chance? Then at least he'd have the image of her—all pretty, pink, and wet for him.

Instead, he felt her on his thumb. He'd driven home in that damn cab with the scent of her all around him. On him.

He should have known a shower wasn't going to do anything to get her out of his head.

His balls tightened, and he breathed hard, his wet chest rising and falling as the water beat on his back, over his ass, and down his legs. If he hadn't formed a conscience, he could be in the shower with her right now, with those long legs wrapped around his waist, her hands in his wet hair, her head thrown back, body quivering, as he plunged into her again and again and again until she made that sound he remembered and shuddered around him.

He came hard and afterward, with exhaustion seeping into his bones, he leaned forward, bracing himself now with his forearm on the wall. He let his head fall with a *thunk*. He was breathing hard, and his legs were shaking. The water was beginning to lose heat now, and he knew if he didn't get out soon, he was going to be suffering through a cold shower. Maybe he should have started with that.

He snorted to himself as he quickly soaped down his body. That wouldn't have mattered. He had to shower sometime, and Jenna was going to pop into his brain no matter how much he avoided it.

He rinsed off and stepped out of the shower, drying off and then throwing on a pair of cutoff sweatpants. He crawled into bed, glad he didn't have to work tomorrow, because he was fucking beat.

He didn't want to deal with people tomorrow. No fucking people. They were complicated.

Cal hated complicated.

THE SHRILL RING of his cell phone woke him up. Cal blinked and glanced at the clock. It was eight in the morning on a Sunday, so Cal knew perfectly well it was Brent. He didn't bother glancing at the caller ID. "What."

"Wakey, eggs and bakey!"

Cal almost hung up on him. Almost. He didn't bother responding.

"Hello?" Brent asked.

"What do you want?"

There was a crashing sound in the background. "Hey, Gabe!" Brent's voice wasn't even muffled. He didn't bother covering the receiver. "Watch where you're walking. There's tools and shit, and I don't want you dropping my doughnuts you're carrying." There was a shout, probably Gabe answering him. "That's precious cargo!" Brent yelled and then said, "Okay, I'm back."

Cal massaged his temple. "You shouted in my ear."

"Really? Sorry about that." Brent didn't sound sorry. "So what can you tell me here about a seven-year-old Honda Civic that needs a new tire and is registered to a Jenna MacMillan?"

"I left a note."

"Yeah, I see your note, but there isn't a section for questions and/or comments, and that's no good because I have a lot of both."

Sometimes Cal wondered how it was possible for one person to be so fucking irritating. "I'm not taking questions or comments."

"But—"

"Put a damn tire on the car, and call her to come get it, Brent. There's nothing to fucking discuss!" He hung up the phone. Like a grownup. And when his cell rang again, he continued on the mature path he'd set that morning and ignored it.

And then he rolled over, tempted to break his one rule of "no fucking smoking in the house." Because it wasn't even nine in the morning on what was supposed to be his day off, and his nerves were already shot.

Fucking brothers.

Fucking high school girlfriends.

Fucking *feelings*.

Chapter Seven

It'd been one week, and Jenna was only starting to scrape the surface of how much work she was going to have to do at MacMillan Investments.

For starters, the morale was down. Even though Dylan had been cleared of any discrimination, the seed had been planted, and the three-hundred-plus employees—MacMillan was the biggest employer within a good seventy-five miles—were wary.

And wary employees who weren't secure in their jobs were not good employees, in Jenna's opinion. Her father thought a little fear for their jobs was healthy, that it would spur them to work harder to keep their positions. And he could think that, but Jenna vehemently disagreed.

Step one was to make the employees happier. Step two was then to work on the firm's image. Her father, Christopher MacMillan III, had groused about her plan, but she'd reminded him that he had hired her. If he didn't like the way she did her job, he could find another publicity director.

She stepped out into the parking lot, rolling her neck on her shoulders. It was a Friday, and she was leaving work a little later than she wanted to. She still had to meet her brother, father, and mother for drinks at Bellini, an Italian restaurant that was the nicest dining establishment in Tory. She considered trying to get out of it, but then they'd just reschedule, and she wanted to get it over with.

The door to the building banged open behind her as she walked to her car in the almost empty parking lot. "Jenna!" said a male voice.

She turned on her heel. Pete Connelly, a friend of her brother's, walked toward her, a large smile cracking through his short ginger beard.

She'd only met Pete a couple of times over the years, since he and Dylan had become friends, but he was always friendly toward her. She wondered what the hell he and Dylan had in common. They'd met at the office after Pete was hired.

She smiled at him. "Hey there, Pete."

He stopped in front of her and gestured toward the office behind them. "You working late too?"

She blew out a breath. "Just trying to get caught up."

Pete nodded. He was one of the managers and worked closely with Dylan. "Yeah, me too. Anyway, I just wanted to say that I'm glad you're here helping to get things back on track."

She raised her eyebrows. "So what you're saying is that things are *off* track."

Pete laughed sadly. "You know they are, Jenna."

She sighed and said softly, "Can I ask you a question?"

Pete eyed her but nodded.

"Is the main source of this derailment my brother?"

The big man looked at his feet, kicking a stray piece of gravel. "You know he and I are friends."

"Yes."

"So you know that I'm not trying to bad-mouth him or get his job."

"I know that."

He looked up. "But he's…changed. I don't know what it is. He's controlling and, frankly, he doesn't play well with others."

Jenna rolled her lips between her teeth. It was amazing how two people could grow up in the same household and be so different. At least she hoped she was different from her brother. Jenna never reveled in the MacMillan name. She rebelled. At sixteen, Cal Payton had been one hell of a way to rebel. He was everything her family wasn't, and in her mind, that had been a good thing.

Cal had been a way to get back at her parents, but then she'd gone and fallen in love with him.

Dylan, however, fed into the whole MacMillan name, demanding respect because of who he was rather than what he did. He'd been a bully growing up, plain a simple. A bully who used words and money rather than fists.

"Do you…" Jenna hesitated. "Do you think he should have won that discrimination lawsuit?"

Pete looked sick. "Please don't make me answer that."

"Shit." Jenna felt as sick as Pete looked. That was all the answer she needed. She placed a hand on Pete's arm. "I'm going to try to get this company back on track, in the eyes of the employees and of the community."

Pete nodded. "Your father is…well, he's your father. But at the end of the day, he does good work, and this business supplies a lot of jobs. This place matters, but your brother…" His voice trailed off.

"It's so hard because it's family," she said softly.

"I know." He sighed. "I need to get home to the wife and kids, but if there's anything I can do, let me know, okay?"

Jenna nodded. "I appreciate your talking to me."

He smiled as he backed away. "Any time."

Jenna watched him as he turned around, back hunched as he dug in his pocket for his keys. She sighed and continued walking to her car.

Her relationship with Dylan had always been complicated. He was her brother, and the importance of family had been drilled into her every waking moment. Yet she had nothing in common with him except they'd been conceived by the same parents. And as time went on, Jenna even questioned that. She tried to find anything good in Dylan, but other than his work ethic and dedication to the family business; there wasn't much. So to hear that his attitude was threatening the foundation of what her father worked for made her angry.

This business mattered to a lot of people. It mattered to this town. And her brother wasn't going to mess it up.

She reached her car and slid into the front seat. She wanted to go home and not think about it until Monday, but unfortunately, she was going to have to sit across from her brother for an entire meal. Which would be hard, because right now, she wanted to stab him with a fork.

Their relationship had always been tainted with a competitiveness that she hadn't wanted to participate in. Dylan was always, always trying to one-up her, to make himself look better by making her look worse.

She'd always wanted a close sibling, someone to joke around with about family holidays, someone she'd be happy to have as the aunt or uncle to her children. It was one of the reasons she'd been so attracted to Cal. In his own way, he was fiercely loyal to his family and to his brothers. They had a camaraderie she'd only dreamed of as a kid. A camaraderie she'd dreamed of replicating with her own Payton brood. A dream that would never come to fruition, especially after that disastrous make-out session in Cal's tow truck.

Jenna turned the ignition in her Honda and listened as the engine rumbled to life. She put the car in drive and made her way out of the parking lot to head home. The car was all fixed up now. Brent had recommended she get two new tires, and she'd give him the approval. Of course, she hadn't heard a peep from Cal. *He* never called, and *he* hadn't been there when she picked up her car.

It'd been a week since that night Cal had dropped her off at her house, and she felt like she was going through the stages of grief. First, she'd been in denial. She pretended it never happened. That lasted for a whole couple of hours before her brain switched right into anger. That stage...well, actually she was still in that stage.

She was pissed.

Maybe this had been something Cal had to get out of his system. He had to show her he could still light up her body and scramble her brain. And then once he did that, he could wipe his hands clean of her and move on. One little last jab, like, *Hey, Jenna, this is what you left behind.*

As if she didn't know. As if she wasn't aware that every guy who'd touched her since then had been held up to Cal's standard and found lacking. Not just in bed but out of it too. She lived in a world of political correctness. It was her job to say the right words the right way. To get by without the whole truth or maybe a little embellishment. It was how she'd grown up and how she did her job.

That wasn't in Cal's blood. He never had time to beat around the bush or say anything but directly what he thought. It was refreshing not to have to play games with him.

Which is exactly why she'd thrown that statement about his brother in his face. She knew it'd piss him off.

Good. She hoped he was still pissed. She hoped he was furious and had tossed and turned at night just as much as she did.

She wanted to move to the next stage. Or skip right to acceptance. That would be great. She wanted to accept that what had happened wouldn't happen again and then move on. But her brain—or maybe it was her body, which had a frustratingly accurate memory of how good Cal's hands felt—wouldn't let her.

So stuck in anger she was, and there she would stay for the foreseeable future. Cal was lucky she hadn't run into him at the grocery store this week, or she likely would have chucked a can at his head.

She pulled into her driveway and took a deep breath. This was okay. She could do this. She parked her car, not bothering to pull it into the garage since she would be leaving again so soon.

She hadn't had much time to decorate the house. The belongings that had filled her tiny apartment in New York didn't go far in this house, even though it wasn't much bigger than about thirteen hundred square feet. She dropped her keys in a bowl she kept on a small table inside the door. She kicked off her heels and padded on her bare feet into the kitchen.

Opening up the fridge, she contemplated having a drink before facing the gauntlet of an evening with her parents. Instead, she grabbed a bottle of water and collapsed onto her couch with it.

She wanted to take a nap. Or veg out on the couch watching mindless reality TV, but unfortunately, she had to drag her carcass to a restaurant, where she'd be required to uphold the MacMillan image.

She made a gagging sound and hauled herself off the couch to take a shower and get ready. The only good thing was that maybe this dinner would keep her mind of Cal for one blessed evening.

JENNA WORE A simple navy blue tank dress in a jersey fabric. It wasn't fancy, but it was comfortable. However, her mother clearly disapproved, because her eyes were doing that roving, disapproving thing. She pursed her lips. "Is that new?" Her tone showed she thought it was anything but new or appropriate for Bellini.

Karen MacMillan had never been what Jenna would call a nurturer. She raised her children to be proper little MacMillan children who ate with the right silverware and drank the right wine and always, *always* said the right thing.

Her mother, of course, was wearing a nice pale-pink sweater, a cream-colored pencil skirt, and pearls. The cliché made Jenna's teeth ache.

Jenna took a sip of her wine. "No, it's not new."

Her mother hummed under her breath and clinked her wedding ring on her wine glass. Her eyes continued to roam Jenna's body, and Jenna wondered what her mom would pick on next—maybe her hair, which could use a deep conditioning, or her eyebrows, which could probably be waxed.

Jenna's father cleared this throat, drawing her mother's attention. Jenna relaxed and this time, she gulped her wine.

"So, Jenna, you mentioned something about an employee appreciation event?" her father asked.

Jenna put down her glass. "I think that the first step to getting the company back on track is improving employee morale. I'm sure what they want most of all is a raise across the board, which you said you'd consider. But I also think throwing some sort of event, something that helps the community or gives to charity and involves the employees is a great way to create goodwill."

He was watching her, tapping his chin lightly. Dylan and her mother were talking about the recent construction to the local high school while Jenna's father contemplated her idea. But Dylan was watching their conversation with one eye, she noticed, and a frown on his face.

"Dad, we don't have to talk about this now," she said. "I'm working up a proposal with ideas on what we can do."

He blinked and then nodded. "No, I wanted to get a feel for what you're working on. I do like this idea, and I think you're right. I want my employees to feel secure in their jobs and proud of their company."

Jenna nodded. "And I do think this will help."

An uproar of laughter came from a table in the back. Multiple restaurant patrons craned their necks toward the sound as the noise continued. Jenna appreciated the reprieve from her father's scrutiny and chugged more wine. Her mother was fingering her necklace, her face pinched. "Heavens, they are loud. In a place like this? Maybe I should say something to the manager."

Jenna hid her eye roll. "Mom, they're talking and laughing, not pole dancing."

Her mother gasped, and Dylan let out a bark of laughter.

Jenna felt the blush rise in her cheeks. Damn wine.

"Jenna Marie," her mother said. "Since when do you talk like that?"

Since forever? "Sorry, Mom."

Karen straightened her cardigan and murmured under her breath, probably contemplating where she'd gone wrong that her daughter mentioned pole dancing at a nice family meal.

Jenna wished her mom would say, *We can't take you anywhere*, and actually mean it and not make her suffer through these family meals.

Midway through their meal, the loud voices from the back of the restaurant drew closer. Jenna took another sip of wine and what she saw over the rim of her glass nearly made her spit out the liquid across the table.

Jack Payton, striding through the crowd, wearing a pair of old jeans and plaid button-down shirt rolled up to his elbows. Behind him was Cal, head down, fingers fiddling with a toothpick in his mouth. Then Brent, and a young man who looked like a grownup Max, arm linked with a small, dark-haired woman.

Jenna set down her glass gently. The restaurant grew a little quieter as the family passed, like the calm before the storm.

Jenna's mother looked up, making a small gasp. She'd never liked Cal. Not one bit. He didn't fit in with their family, according to her, never mind that Cal loved Jenna and treated her with respect. Dylan muttered something as the family passed, but it hadn't been quiet enough, because Brent jerked his head up, eyes widening a fraction, before settling into his smirk. "Hey, look who it is! The MacMillans. Man, just who I've been *waiting* to see."

Jenna watched Cal as he lifted his gaze and swept it over the table—and over her. He wore his boots and a pair of dark blue pants with a light-colored button-down shirt. His hair was actually combed back, so his eyes glowed in the dim light of the restaurant. He looked handsome, although if Jenna was hard-pressed, she might say she liked his garage-look better. Because that *was* Cal.

He lowered his head, clearly avoiding all contact. He nudged Brent with his elbow, but his brother didn't move.

"Hey, Jenna," Max said, stepping out from behind Brent, ignoring the tension surrounded the table.

She smiled at him. "Wow, look at you. I haven't seen you since you were twelve or thirteen."

He gestured to the girl on his arm. "This is my fiancée, Lea."

The girl beamed. "Hello."

"Nice to meet you," Jenna said.

"Hey, Dylan," Brent said, and Jenna braced herself when she saw the quirk of Brent's mouth. "Gotta little sauce, uh…" He gestured toward his own cheek and coughed. "You know."

Dylan lifted his napkin, dabbing at the corner of his mouth with stiff movements. And then his eyes narrowed, and Jenna stifled a groan, because she knew what that look meant. It was the same look he'd get when he tattled on her when she didn't clean her room. "Ah, that must be the pasta pescatore. It was delicious. Did you have it?"

"Nope," Brent drew out the word, popping the *p*.

Dylan's smile was hard. "Of course not. The menu said 'market price.' You would have wanted to be sure you could cover the bill."

Brent didn't even hesitate. "God, I know. It was awful. I could only afford butter with spaghetti, and I'm starving." And then he reached across the table, as non-chalant as could be, and picked a piece of asparagus off Dylan's plate. He stuck the tip in his mouth and crunched down, chewing happily. "Wow, thanks, man." He looked over their table with wide eyes. "So this is how the real people live." He turned to his father. "They look great in their natural habitat."

Jenna clapped her hand over her mouth. She wasn't sure which was funnier—Dylan's red face or Brent's crunching noises as he finished off the asparagus.

Max turned to Lea and said quietly, "This is like *Family Feud* but without the answer board." He gestured around the restaurant to the people gawking at them. "I mean, we even have a live studio audience."

"Max, stop," Lea whispered.

"I happen to think Ray Combs was the best host, don't you?" Max whispered back.

Lea's posture immediately softened. "I was so sad when I heard about he died."

"I know. Horrible, right?"

Jack Payton cuffed Brent on the back of his head. "Will you mind your fuckin' manners?"

Brent stared at him. "My manners? Are you kidding me? You spent the whole dinner with your napkin tucked into your shirt."

"Oh, for God's sake, Christopher, please do something," Jenna's mom whispered. "They're making a scene."

Jenna wanted to roll her eyes. A scene. Heaven forbid a scene! All her life had been one giant "let's not make a scene" tut from her mother.

Jenna's father cleared his throat, but Dylan had to get the last word in. "Now that you've sufficiently disturbed every diner in this restaurant, I think it's time to leave."

Brent turned back to Dylan, his ever-present smirk on his face. "Honestly, I'm just getting started."

Then Jenna's father was talking. And her mother was making obnoxious sighing sounds. And Jack was tugging on Brent's arm while Brent continued to prod Dylan, who answered back with insults of his own.

Max and his girlfriend were still debating *Family Feud* hosts, and it would have been completely, completely embarrassing if it hadn't been hilarious.

Christopher MacMillan had hired Jenna to fix the image of his company, and here he was, the CEO with his family, in a restaurant full of the Tory elite who were eager to gossip, throwing down with the Paytons.

Jenna knew she'd get blamed for this, for bringing the Paytons into this…circle of their lives. But right now, in the midst of chaos, she didn't really care. She took a gulp of her wine, looked up, and met Cal's piercing gaze.

She'd expected him to join the fray. Or glare, or hell, she expected him to have walked out of the restaurant already. That's what he would have done before. But nope, he was watching her quietly with those slate eyes. They were unreadable at first. She thought about flipping him off or haughtily turning up her nose. But Cal hated that kind of attitude. And she didn't want to do it anyway.

Especially not as those eyes began to change, darken, as they studied her. As they really *looked* at her. His gaze dropped to where she held the wine glass stem between her thumb and forefinger. Then his eyes lingered on the neckline of her low-cut dress, and then they coasted up, up until they locked on hers again. When an outstretched hand knocked over a water glass on their table, Cal's lips twitched. Almost imperceptibly. But she saw it. Along with that twinkle in his eye.

He thought this was funny too. Hilarious, even.

She stretched her lips into a closed-mouth smile, then shook her head.

He grinned back and blinked once, twice, and then he was moving toward her.

His silent saunter in her direction was like slow motion in the chaos of the scene around them. He didn't take his eyes off her as he walked around the table, that shirt stretched across his broad chest, the top button open so she got a glimpse of a sliver of skin. When he was behind her, she stayed facing forward, not really seeing anything, because every other sense was hyper-focused on him. Focused on how he had smiled as he walked toward her, that sexy smirk. Focused on how his heartbeat pounded as his chest now brushed the back of her head. Focused on how he leaned down, his breath coasting over the fine hairs at the back of her neck. She closed her eyes, relishing his heat at her back.

"Even in this fancy place"—his voice was a vibration she felt in every limb—"you outshine everyone."

And then his heat was gone.

The raised voices around her dulled to mutters. And when she opened her eyes to turn around, the Payton family was leaving the restaurant, Cal at the helm.

Her first thought was, *Take me with you.*

Instead, she turned around and faced her family, swallowing the rest of her wine along with an overdose of glares, heavy sighs, and guilt, courtesy of her family.

Chapter Eight

CAL IDLED HIS Harley at the stop sign. He stared down Jenna's street and chewed on the corner of his thumb until it bled. Then he started on the other hand.

He should turn around and go home. After that night in his tow truck, he'd vowed to stay away from Jenna. Despite his resolve, she consumed his thoughts to the point of distraction. He'd stuck to his guns, right up until he'd seen her at the damn restaurant tonight.

Among all those people there dressed to the nines, Jenna had stood out. The beautiful smile, that mass of hair. It'd been like the sun beamed down on her from a skylight above her head. Only her. Like usual, his Sunshine was the brightest in the room. She'd shined like a beacon through that shit-show.

She'd given him that smile, the one that made him feel like they were on their own private island, despite the chaos around them. The rest of the world went dark, and it was just her, and she had eyes only for him, making him feel like the most important thing on earth.

She'd always made him feel like that. That he was worth something. That he mattered.

The feeling was mutual.

He should go to his house. Alone. But the thought of going home and seeing that birthday card on his kitchen table—the one from *Jill*—made his heart clench. He should have thrown it away when he saw her name, like he usually did. How the hell did she get his new address anyway? He suspected Brent had something to do with it, the damn peacemaker.

With a growl and a flick of his wrist, he roared onto her road and then cut into her driveway. She wanted the out-of-control kid? The impulsive one who couldn't get enough of her? Well then, fine. He'd be that for a night. Give them both what they craved, and then they'd be free. The plan made total sense in his head, so he didn't dig deeper into what he was really doing. He didn't hesitate, because if he did, then he might abandon this whole thing.

He did feel out of control, but the kicker was, it felt damn good. He liked this pull in his heart, tugging him toward Jenna. It was exhilarating, like a drug. How had he lived without this for ten years?

He knocked on her front door, shifting his weight back and forth, realizing he hadn't changed out of these damn fancy clothes.

A light turned on inside the house; he could see it through the small oval window at the top of the door. He imagined—*hoped*, because that was safe—she was looking through the peephole at him. So he stared right back.

There was no sound. Nothing.

"Jenna," he said firmly, knowing his deep voice would carry.

Another pause, then the click of the deadbolt. He lowered his gaze and watched the doorknob turn. Then the door opened, and Jenna was standing in the doorway, light spilling out onto the front porch from behind her. She was wearing a short, thin blue robe. Her hair was piled on top of her head in a messy bun.

Her face was free of makeup, and she stood with one foot on top of the other.

She was so fucking beautiful, his chest hurt. He wanted to fall to his knees at her feet and beg forgiveness. He'd take any fucking scraps from her right now, as long as it was something, anything, to put him out of his misery.

Anything to make him feel, one more time, that he was worth something.

She licked her lips, and he tracked that pink tongue. "Cal?"

In one step he was inside the house. With his booted foot, he slammed the door closed behind him, blindly turning the lock. Then he grabbed Jenna's face in both hands and crashed his lips onto hers.

Her hands flew up, gripping his biceps, her little nails digging in through the fabric of his shirt. Cal wasn't messing around as he swiped his tongue over the seam of her lips, demanding entrance. But she kept her lips shut tight.

He should have known she'd make him work for this. He pressed kisses to the corners of her mouth, to her cheekbones, to that pert nose and her jawline. Then back to her mouth, nibbling her lips. "I'm sorry."

"Goddamn you," she huffed against his lips, and he took that opportunity to slip his tongue into her mouth.

She took the offensive now, opening her jaw, pushing against his tongue. She retracted her claws on his biceps and melted into his arms. He relinquished his grip on her face and skimmed his hands down her neck. When he broke the kiss, he leaned his forehead against hers, panting into her mouth. He turned them around, so her back was against the door. Leaning back a little, he eyed the gap in her robe, where the pale skin of a rounded breast showed.

He lifted his gaze to hers. She was breathing hard, chest rising and falling, so each time that robe slipped a little bit more. He wanted to rip it off. He was hard, cock straining against these pants that were too goddamn tight to begin with.

"Why are you here?" Jenna asked.

He answered as honestly as he could. "I want you."

And maybe that was it. Standing in front her now, Cal wasn't stupid to think he and Jenna could limit their interactions to just sex. There were too many feelings. Too much history. But yet, it was simple in that he wanted her, and her lust-filled gaze told him she felt the same. So even though this would inevitably crash and burn, the ride there would be worth it. At least he knew going in that it would end badly. At least he could prepare himself.

Jenna's mind must have been working the same formula. He waited, prepared to be told to go fuck himself. He'd taken this risk, knowing she could refuse.

But by God, he hoped she didn't.

She sawed her top teeth over her bottom lip. Then her eyes flickered, and her face set. With a stiff nod, she said, "Okay."

"Okay?"

She blinked and then her breath left her in a rush as she said four words that he'd take to his grave: "I want you too."

He cupped her cheek, resting his thumb at the corner of her mouth so he knew when she opened up to let him in. Their tongues dueled and their lips mashed. He wanted to inhale her into his lungs. He couldn't get enough.

He broke the kiss and brushed his lips over hers. "Open up your robe, sweetheart."

She sucked in a breath, a small gasp escaping. Her eyelids were heavy, and he thought she'd refuse. Then her hands came away from where they'd been pressed behind her on the door. She looked up into his eyes and slowly untied the knot at her waist.

She let the ends of the tie dangle so they touched the floor. She leaned her head back so it clunked on the door and raised her hands over her head, clasping her wrist in the other hand.

The sides of her robe moved with her movements, tempting him to open them like a curtain. She smelled like soap and spice and like everything he'd been missing for ten fucking years.

When he reached his hand toward her, it was shaking. With his index finger, he hooked the edge of her robe, slowly pushing it to the side. The fabric caught on her nipple and then gave way to reveal a full breast, thin waist, and flare into a gorgeous full hip, like half of an hourglass, while the other edge of the robe called to him to reveal his whole present.

Her red, swollen lips were parted, and her chest heaved. Her belly quivered, and he let his gaze fall between her legs, to that area of perfectly trimmed hair. One of her legs was bent slightly, resting on the ball of her foot and turned in, so he couldn't see all he wanted to see. He wanted to fall to his knees right there, spread her legs, and bury his face in her, cover himself with her, lick her up until she could say no other word but his name.

He hooked a finger on the other side of her robe and opened it as well. She was fully bared to him now, all that pale soft skin. She was more gorgeous than she'd been an eighteen. More rounded, more full. Her chin was lifted, eyes on his. He wondered if she knew that despite the fact she was naked and he was fully closed, she held all the power here. She always did.

He ran the back of his fingers between her breasts and over her stomach. A shudder wracked her body and goose bumps popped up in the wake of his touch.

He gripped a hip, digging his fingers into the softness, wondering if she'd welcome finger-shaped bruises tomorrow. He lifted his gaze to her. "Didn't think it was possible for you to look even more beautiful than I dreamed about."

She sucked in a breath and opened her mouth, but Cal didn't give her a chance to say anything back. He leaned in, and he took one of those pink nipples in his mouth and sucked.

The sounds that came out of her throat weren't words but moans. She gripped his hair and tugged. He thumbed her other nipple and rolled the hard bud in between his thumb and forefinger. He smiled, biting her breast gently, like she'd always loved. And she still did, if the bucking of her hips was any indication.

He pulled off her nipple, blowing on it, watching as her skin pebbled as his cool breath hit her wet skin, and then he moved on to the other one. She whimpered now, whispering his name, one hand tugging at his hair while the other tugged on his shirt, trying to free buttons.

"Cal."

"Not done."

"Don't want you done. Want you naked."

He huffed a laugh against her skin. "I'll get naked after you get off."

Her eyes widened. "Jesus."

He dropped to his knees. "Ball's in your court." A hand fluttered and landed on his shoulder. He kept his gaze on her face. "Spread your legs for me, Sunshine."

"Cal—"

He licked his lips. "Come on."

He swore he could see her pulse beating in her neck. Her breasts trembled with her breaths. He thought she'd refuse; tell him to get up off of his knees. He'd do it, but it'd kill him.

Instead, slowly, she lowered her other heel to the ground and then placed her feet about shoulder width apart. Cal finally lowered his gaze, taking in the trimmed patch of soft curls. He could smell her arousal, and she shifted her legs restlessly when he made no move to touch her.

He wasn't sure if he'd get this chance again, so he sure as hell was going to enjoy this while it lasted. He placed his hands above her knees and slowly ran his palms up her thighs. His calluses rasped over her soft skin, his hands permanently stained with grease while her skin was practically glowing clean. Hadn't it always been that way? He made her dirty, and she loved it. Did she still?

He lifted his gaze to her again and locked onto her hazel eyes. They were glazed over, unfocused, and he wanted to keep her that way, wanting him. He planned to drive her out of her mind.

He took one of her legs and lay it on his shoulder, and then he leaned in, running his nose along her slit.

She was wet already, the slick fluid glistening on her skin. When he spread her open with his fingers and applied the flat of his tongue in one long, slow lick, she went *wild*.

He'd always loved that about Jenna, the way she responded to his touch, his mouth, his cock. And she hadn't changed, not one bit, because she was bucking, grinding herself down onto his face, and he didn't care. He spread her open and braced her against the door and let her work herself on his tongue. He didn't give her everything, though; she was going to have to work for it if she wanted him naked.

A hand came down and threaded through this hair and then pulled. He grunted.

"Cal." Her voice was strangled.

He fucked her with his tongue, lapping up her wetness, but ignored her clit, flicking it occasionally with his nose, just enough to drive her insane but not get her off.

She twisted her wrist, and he wondered if she'd taken a hunk of hair with her as pain laced through his scalp.

"Cal." This time her voice was a growl.

He leaned back a little, so his lips still grazed her wetness. "Yeah, Sunshine?" He knew his voice was a vibration as she shuddered.

"You know." She gritted her teeth.

He smiled. "You wanna come?" He hated games, but this one was a little too much fun.

"You—"

"Tell me, Jenna." He moved his lips up and let his breath coast over her clit.

Her eyes were glassy. "I want to come," she whispered.

"With my tongue?"

She swallowed. "With your tongue."

"Wish granted." He dove back in, attacking her clit, sucking it, swirling it. Her hips rocked into his mouth and with one more painful twist of his hair, she was coming, pulsating against his face, crying out, her entire body shaking so that he had to sit back on his heels and catch her as her legs gave out.

Her entire body vibrated in his arms, the aftershocks of her orgasm rocking her. He ran his fingers through her hair, amazed he could still feel the softness through his thick skin and calluses.

He buried his nose in her hair, smelled *Jenna,* and closed his eyes, because nothing took him back like the scent of her as she lay in his arms.

Chapter Nine

JENNA SQUEEZED HER eyes shut, face shoved into Cal's neck. She needed a moment to get herself under control because Cal had completely taken her apart, limb by limb.

She'd let him. And she loved it.

This. Them. Together. It was the same as it was a decade ago, yet different. Their bodies had changed. There was a new learning curve, but this magnetic connection that had always existed still crashed them together. Cal's pull still tugged at her gut. Her heart ached, like it wanted to crawl out of her chest and into his.

He still smelled like Cal, clean with an underlying metallic tang. She nuzzled between the collar of his shirt and his neck, opening her mouth against his skin to sneak a taste.

He shifted beneath her, the rough fabric of his pants brushing the overly sensitive flesh between her legs. She sucked on his skin, adding some teeth, and he groaned, one hand sliding up to fist her hair, the other palming a bare ass cheek.

With a grunt, he pulled on her hair so she was forced to tilt her head back and look at him. His eyes, normally a light blue-gray, were dark and intense. "Jenna."

She licked her lips. "You promised me nudity."

He barked out a laugh. "Hold on, then." She wrapped her arms around his neck, and in one fluid motion, he gathered his feet under him and stood up, taking her with him. She wrapped her legs around his waist, loving the strength it took him to stand up—with her clinging to him—without even a wobble. He began to walk toward the stairs. "Bedroom," he said against her lips.

She didn't answer and instead focused on kissing him back.

He lost his footing on the stairs a couple of times, probably because she was attacking his face and throat with a million kisses. When they reached the top, she pointed to her bedroom, and they lumbered inside, crashing against a wall as she sucked on his tongue.

Despite her grip on him, he easily dislodged her and tossed her onto her back on the bed. She hit the mattress on a bounce, then raised up on her elbows as he undid a couple of buttons on his shirt, and then fisted it between his shoulder blades and pulled it off.

The room was dark, the only light supplied by the moon filtering in through her curtains. It set all the hard muscles and ridges on his abdomen in stark relief. God, he was fucking gorgeous. Bigger than he'd been at eighteen, bulkier. He had more hair now, a light dusting over his pecs and down his abs. Her fingers itched to grip it and pull until he grunted.

Cal pulled his belt through his pants and threw it to the side, the buckle clacking across the hardwood floor. One flick of a button and the lowering of a zipper, and then Cal dropped his pants.

He was commando.

Her robe was off now, pooled below her on the bed. She rose up on her hands to get a better look at Cal. She saw now why he could lift her so easily. His thighs were huge, veins coursing under the skin.

His cock was big and hard, jutting out from a thatch of dark hair. If she'd been standing, her legs would have buckled. She'd give anything to have that glistening tip in her mouth.

Cal stared at her, stroking his cock. His fist moved lazily over his shaft. He took a step toward the end of the bed. "Sit up."

His command sent a pulse of arousal through her belly. She scooted to the end of the bed, letting her legs dangle over the ledge. She fisted her hands on her thighs and looked up as Cal stepped between her legs.

He continued to stroke his cock with one hand while the other cupped her neck, his thumb rubbing her jaw. His tip glistened with pre-come and she would have leaned in to lick, but she waited for Cal's next instruction. She needed it. Cal had always been able to get her to shut off her mind and just feel.

"Open up for me," he whispered as he rubbed the head on her bottom lip.

Her eyes fell shut as she opened her mouth and took him in. She started with just the head, sucking on it, flicking her tongue over that sensitive vein on the underside. She could hear him breathing heavily and when she opened her eyes, he was holding his shaft tightly.

She gently brushed his hand away and replaced it with her own and then began to earnestly suck, bobbing her head with the same rhythm she pumped with her hand. He was thick, and long, and there was no way she could take him in all the way without gagging.

She lifted her gaze to his face as she ran her fingers up the back of his thighs to grab his firm ass. He was watching his spit-slick cock go in and out of her mouth. His eyes were slits, his teeth gritted. She closed her eyes again and worked harder, wanting to get him off, wanting to taste him.

He pulled his hips back, so his cock slipped from her mouth. She made a sound of protest, but then she was thrown up higher on the bed, and Cal's body was on top of hers, pressing her into the mattress while his tongue devoured her mouth. She moaned and wrapped her arms around his shoulders, her legs around his hips, and dug her heels into the back of his thighs.

He rocked against her, and that thick, hard heat rubbed through her wetness. She was empty. So incredibly empty. Her inner walls contracted against nothing, and she needed him before she lost her mind.

He tore his mouth from hers. "Want inside you."

"Then get inside me," she said, panting against the damp skin of his throat.

"Condom," he grunted.

Just like Cal to use as few words as possible. She reached over to her nightstand, pulled open the drawer, and rummaged blindly until a foil packet made its way under her fingers.

She held it up to him. "Might want to check the expiration date."

He raised an eyebrow as he kneeled between her legs to put on the condom. "That your way of telling me it's been a while?"

She bit her lip. "Maybe."

He didn't talk again until the condom was on and the heat of his body was back on top of her. His lips ghosted over her earlobe. "It'd be the same at my place."

She squeezed her eyes shut at the words.

And then with one smooth thrust, he was inside of her. She bit down on his shoulder, hard, and Cal shoved his face into her neck, his body stilled between her legs.

"Fuck. Jesus." He grunted like he was in pain.

She breathed hard, because she'd never been this full, never in her life. Not even the last time she'd been with Cal. Her heart beat against her rib cage, and Cal's echoed against the sensitive skin of her breast.

She didn't want him to move. Because when he moved, this would be one moment closer to being over. And that would be one step closer to the heartbreak that she knew was unavoidable, as it always was with Cal.

The tears threatened, and she clamped her teeth on him harder, sucking now, wanting to break skin, mark him, so he never forgot how good this could be, how much this mattered.

She squeezed him with her inner walls, and he moaned. "Killing me."

Jenna pulled away from his skin, admiring the mark she'd made. "Don't want to kill you. Want to finish you."

"Fuck," he growled into her neck. Then his hips snapped back, and he slammed into her. They both cried out, and then Cal was moving, thrusting into her like he was punishing her. Punishing himself. Punishing *them* for being apart for the last ten years.

He rose above her, one hand braced on the bed beside her head, the other gripping her face. His eyes didn't stop moving, roaming above her head, where her hair was spread out on her pillow, her eyes, and lips, her neck, and then to watch her breasts as they jolted with every thrust.

Another orgasm threatened, the sensation racing through her body. She reached down between them, where Cal's cock slammed into her again and again. He grunted a low rumble each time, and the vibration echoed in her own body. Jenna touched her clit, swirling, searching for it, needing Cal for just a moment longer.

And then, like a tidal wave, it crashed into her. Her legs clamped around his hips, she reared her head back and came. Her eyes slammed shut as it swept through her out to every limb.

Cal was still moving, and then his hips stuttered. With his face shoved into her neck, he came on a long moan, ending in her name, a whisper that was like a prayer.

He didn't move from inside of her. He rolled them gently onto their sides and hitched her leg over his hip. He kissed her softly, just a brush of his lips on hers, and the tenderness squeezed her heart. Then he slowly pulled his hips back and rolled off the bed on his way to the bathroom, which was attached to her room.

She watched the way his back muscles rippled under his skin, the way his thigh muscles flexed. He turned on the bathroom light and closed the door behind him. She watched his shadow in the light creeping out below the door as he flushed the toilet and ran the water in the faucet.

He hadn't said a word but that kiss…how a kiss like that could mean so much, she didn't know. But everything he couldn't say in words, Cal always said physically.

His shadow stopped moving. And she imagined him standing in front of the sink, his mind racing as hard as hers was right now. They were both naked, with only a thin, hollow door between them, but it felt like an insurmountable barrier.

She wondered if he'd come out, get dressed, and leave. It was what he'd done after they'd made out in his tow truck. He'd placed distance between them.

But last time, they hadn't gone this far. Maybe because Jenna was almost thirty, she was at the point where she knew emotions were rarely separate from sex. And especially with two people who had as much baggage in their past.

Like, enough to fill a Boeing 747.

The light shut off inside the bathroom, and then the door opened slowly. Cal leaned against the doorframe and crossed his arms over his chest. The moonlight glinted off of his pale eyes.

He was gorgeous, all hard muscle developed from years of physical work. He was a perfect picture, like in a magazine or calendar. Of course, if she told him that, he'd roll his eyes. Cal was the opposite of vain, even completely naked.

"Want me to stay?" He didn't look away to give her time to think or to cut down on the awkwardness. That wasn't Cal. He watched her face the whole time, squinting as if to see her in the dim light.

Jenna was on her side, and she reached out and ran a hand over the bare sheet beside her. "Stay is kind of a vague word, isn't it?"

The muscle in his jaw ticked. "Do you want me to sleep in that bed with you tonight?"

She swallowed. "What about after that?"

"I'm not talking about 'after that' yet."

He was so stubborn. "What if I want to talk about that?"

"Then talk. Doesn't mean I gotta talk too."

"Sometimes, you can be a real pain in the ass, Cal Payton."

His lips quirked up. "Sometimes?"

She rolled her eyes. "All the time. Now get in this bed and sleep with me."

He grinned and walked over to the bed. Once he lay on his back, he pulled the covers over them and tucked her into his side. She'd always fit there, just like a puzzle, and it surprised her how they slotted right together again.

She laid her hand on his chest, flexing her fingers into the short hair. "I like this."

"Chest hair?"

"Yeah, I like it."

His body rumbled with a short laugh. "Max makes a chili that my dad says puts hair on your chest."

"What do you do? Bathe in it?"

He laughed again, louder this time, and the hand curled around her shoulders tugged on a lock of hair. "Real men wash with chili."

"This is getting gross."

"You started it."

She tweaked his nipple, and he reached down and smacked her ass. Jenna turned her head and nuzzled into the skin of his chest, breathing him in. She hadn't realized how much she'd missed these silly conversations with Cal. They could slip from mature lovers to teenage teasing so easily. She wished she could enjoy the moment, but at the back of her mind, she knew this was going to end.

"This'll be it, right?" she said softly. "You'll leave again, and we'll chalk this up as a relapse?"

His body tensed under hers, and she raised her head to see his eyes narrowed on her. "That how you see me? Like a drug that's bad for you but you can't quit?"

Jenna reached up to cup his face. "Cal—"

"Why you think I stopped this that night in the tow truck? I was trying to save us this conversation."

She'd screwed this up. Not that he wouldn't have left in the morning anyway, but now he'd leave pissed. "Wait—"

He wrapped his fingers around her wrist and lowered her hand to rest on his chest again. "Go to bed, Jenna."

She blew out an irritated breath. "Will you quit interrupting me?"

His chest hitched as he inhaled. "I'm sorry. But I meant what I said earlier. Not talking about this. Not now."

She pursed her lips. "You're dictating the conversation just like that?"

"Guess I am."

She dropped back onto his chest with a thud. She was too tired to argue. "Fine."

His body relaxed once again, his fingers making small circles on her shoulders. "Night, Sunshine."

"Night, Cal."

Chapter Ten

CAL EXHALED THE smoke out the window he'd opened in Jenna's screened-in back porch.

It was a nice room, small, although the only furniture she had in there was a small table in the corner with some droopy-looking plant. He'd had to drag a chair out from the kitchen so he had a place to sit.

He'd woken up at two in the morning with Jenna's hot little body wrapped around him. He hadn't wanted to move. Lying there forever had sounded pretty damn nice, which was why he freaked out and hauled ass.

He'd found a pair of jeans in the saddlebags on his bike when he'd gone out to get his cigarettes and pulled those on rather than those god-awful pants he'd had on earlier. Although, he had caught Jenna looking at his ass, so they'd been worth the chafing.

He braced his elbows on his knees and held his head in his hands, his cigarette still burning between his first and second finger in his right hand.

Relapse.

Fuck, that word had killed him. It wasn't like he hadn't thought the same thing a time or two, that Jenna was like a drug, but the way she said it made his stomach churn. He didn't want to be her bad addiction.

If she made him feel like the sun was shining on him, how did he make her feel? Like he was dragging her into the shadows?

"Fuck," he whispered. "Fuck me."

He should leave, and he probably would, as soon as he'd sucked all the fucking carcinogens out of this damn cigarette that he could. His nerves were a mess. This was what happened around Jenna. He lost his damn mind. Had he really changed all that much from when he was eighteen? Maybe he'd just avoided all situations that mattered, that made him care.

Situations that caused *feelings.*

He didn't hear her until the wooden step leading down to the porch creaked. He closed his eyes briefly, then peered over his shoulder.

Jenna stood in front of the door as it fell shut behind her. She wore that blue robe again. The one he'd peeled off her body. He wanted to do it all over again. At the first spike of his returned arousal, he regretted not zipping up his jeans. He turned away from her, taking another drag on his cigarette and flicking the ash into a small bowl he'd placed beside his chair.

This wasn't her fault. It was his. He didn't trust himself to keep a cool head around her, to be the man he'd spent ten years trying to be. Around her, all he felt like was that head-over-heels-in-love kid.

And that kid had been a fuck-up.

He waited, listening to the rustle of her robe as she moved. A hand fluttered on his bare shoulder, and then she gasped.

He turned his head quickly, unsure why she'd made that sound. Her eyes were glued to his shoulder, her eyes wide, a hand covering her open mouth.

Shit.

He turned back around so he didn't have to see her face. He'd forgotten about the tattoo. He'd gotten it years ago, when he was a heartsick twenty-one-year-old who drank too much. He didn't hate it; in fact, he loved it. But he'd never intended for Jenna to see it.

Ever.

Her fingers reached out again, tracing the black-inked rays of the sun that extended down his bicep. The sun itself, on the cap of his shoulder, wasn't inked, but the black rays around it showed the circular outline.

He held his breath until those fingers left his skin.

"Cal," she whispered.

He inhaled the last of his cigarette, blew out the smoke, and stubbed out the butt into the bowl. "Got it a long time ago."

"It's a sun." Her voice shook.

"Yep."

She walked around and stood in front of him. He clasped his hands between his knees and stared at his bare feet.

"You tattooed a sun on your shoulder, *Cal.*"

"Told you it was a long time ago, *Jenna.*"

Her voice was quiet. "Are we allowed to talk about what's next now?"

He tensed his shoulders so they rose up around his ears. "Don't think there is a 'what's next.'"

She made a sound of protest in her throat, but before she could get a word in, he stood up, towering over her. "You said yourself you didn't mind coming back here to start a family. And that's great. I hope you get that white house and three-point-two kids or whatever the fuck, but that's not gonna happen with me. I don't want it."

There it was. Cal didn't see the point in continuing this when they wanted drastically different futures. Love hadn't been enough then, and it wouldn't be enough now.

Jenna eyes widened. "Are you kidding me right now?"

"No, I don't want—"

"Stop." She held her hand up, and he clamped his mouth shut. She crossed her arms over her chest, and her hazel eyes blazed up at him. "What the hell do you think? I came back here to find a guy ASAP and pop out some kids?"

He clenched his jaw. "You said—"

"I know what I said, but damn, if I'd known you'd take it so literally, I never would have said it."

"Well, do you want to get married and have kids?"

Her mouth opened, then closed, then opened again.

"See?" he demanded.

"I didn't say anything yet!" She straightened her fists at her sides.

He ran a hand through his hair in frustration. "This is why I tried to avoid this in the tow truck that night. Well, that and the fact that I didn't want to fuck you for the first time in ten years in a fucking tow truck."

She rolled her eyes. "Okay, so to be honest, yes, I want kids. But I want a family, not a sperm donor. I want to find the love of my life and marry him and then kids…well…hopefully they come next. But I'm not watching my biological clock and biting my nails. I didn't even have any intention of dating anytime soon, but you have a way of always messing with my plans, don't you?"

That was a low blow, the reference to their plans to stay together. He flinched. And she did too. "Shit, Cal, I didn't mean it that way."

He turned away from her, not wanting to look into those eyes anymore. "Nah, you did. And it's okay. I know I messed up the best plan I'd ever made."

She laid a hand on his bare back and slid it around his waist. Her other arm did the same, until she was hugging him from behind, her face pressed against the ridges of his spine. He was lost in thought until her voice said softly, "You don't want kids?"

"Been there, done that."

She paused. "You mean Max and Brent?"

Yeah, he meant them. He meant the messed-up family that they'd somehow managed to keep together with duct tape, car grease, and a prayer. They were all present, accounted for, and healthy, even if Max'd had a scary run-in with a couple of muggers on his college campus a couple of years ago. They'd put him in the hospital and scared Cal out of his mind.

Cal had raised his brothers. He couldn't abandon them like everyone else did. They were *his*. His family. His flesh and blood. So he did the best he could and took care of them—when he still needed caring for himself.

He sighed. "I already raised a family. Don't wanna get married and do it all over again. Filled my lifetime quota, I think. I like being responsible for myself, and that's it."

Her fingers played on his stomach. "You didn't always feel that way."

He didn't want the same things anymore. He wanted nothing more to do with that kid who'd had big dreams of a career, with Jenna and their family. "I don't want what you want, Jenna."

Her hair brushed along his skin as she moved her head, and he closed his eyes, relishing the heat of her body against his. She didn't deny it, because she'd already told him how she felt. So that was that. Impasse.

He could have let it go, but Jenna's presence always made him spill his guts. He needed her to understand. He needed her to believe why he felt this strongly. "Did I tell you Max got attacked and put in the hospital?"

She shifted around his body so she stood in front of him. "What?"

"Last year he was in college, some assholes were assaulting and robbing people. They had a gun when they got him, whipped him in the back of the head. He got away because he's a fucking hero and called the police before collapsing."

She gasped. "Oh my God."

"He's fine now. You saw him. He's happy. Engaged. But I swear to God, that took five years off of my life when I got that phone call and then another ten when I saw him in that hospital with a bandage on his head."

She wrapped her fingers around his forearm and squeezed. "I'm so sorry."

"So I know it may seem stupid to you, or...I don't know...immature or something. But I have rules for me. It's how I've lived for the past ten years, and I know it's what works."

She opened her mouth, but he shook his head. "Wish I could change, but I just don't think I can. Got enough people in my life right now that I worry about all the time. My dad and Max and Brent. I'm going to worry about you too now, even when this is over. I can't help that, because you're Jenna. But I can help putting myself into an early grave by taking on you and everything that would come with you."

She frowned. "I don't want you to change. And what do you mean, take me on? I'm not a project. You get back what you put into it. You think I wouldn't worry and be responsible for you too?" Her voice softened. "A relationship is give-and-take. It's not all on your shoulders."

He looked away, unable to see the hurt on her face. He didn't believe that. It'd been a long time since he'd felt like he was given anything. And that was fine; he wasn't bitching about it. But he wasn't throwing more of himself into anyone else either. He turned to walk back into the house.

"So that's the end of the conversation?" Jenna asked, her voice steady and a little hard. "You're just gonna walk away—"

He whirled to face her. "I don't have anything left!" His voice came out louder than he meant it, and her head snapped like he'd slapped her. He took a deep breath and counted to ten before he spoke again, keeping his tone low. "I'm tapped out. Drained dry. I'm not who I was back when we were together. And I'm sorry for that. I truly am. Wish I could be more, and I wish I could do this with you, but I can't."

Her eyes blinked rapidly, but he saw no tears. She swallowed and lifted her chin. "I don't believe that."

"Well—"

"I don't believe you're done for life. I think you can be recharged. I think someone has to show you that she can put in as much as she takes out."

He looked away.

"Is that how you think we were?" Her voice was soft, inquisitive. She wanted an honest answer. "Do you think I took and took from you?"

He stared out the window to the backyard and shook his head. "No, I think I took and took from you. Until you wised up and left me, like everyone knew you would."

"Cal—"

He turned to her. "You're back, and you're still shining, and that's the way it should be."

"So why'd you come here tonight?"

He hesitated, and then gave the only answer that he could. "Because after seeing you in that restaurant, I couldn't imagine being anywhere but here." Her face softened, and he shook his head. "But I shouldn't have. Selfish of me to—"

"I'm a big girl. I let you in that door. I could have said no."

He rolled his jaw. "Yes, you could have."

They both stared at each other, until she spoke again. "So that's it?"

"Don't know what else to say about it."

She stopped talking then and looked at him with eyes a little sad, a little regretful. He wished he knew what she regretted. Ever meeting him? Letting him into the house tonight? He guessed it didn't really matter. He should probably go now—gather what self-respect he had and get on his motorcycle and return to where he came from.

Jenna shook her head and took a deep breath, gathering herself in front of his eyes, something he admired, because he needed privacy, ten minutes, and a cigarette to pull himself together.

Jenna needed ten seconds and a toss of her hair. And then she smiled, even though it trembled a little. "Are you hungry?"

That was the last thing he expected her to say, so he paused before answering slowly. "Sure."

And then, with the ends of her robe brushing his legs, she grabbed his hand and led him back into the house.

Chapter Eleven

THEY ATE CORN Pops and Honey Smacks on the floor of her living room. Cal leaned against the couch, and Jenna sat cross-legged on the floor.

They'd done this so many times in high school, she could barely count. She'd lied a lot back then, telling her parents she was spending the night at Delilah's, when really, she was at Cal's. His dad didn't care when he'd stumbled out of his bedroom in the middle of the night to pee and caught them cuddling on the couch with bowls of cereal on their laps.

She didn't know what it was about cereal, but if she was having trouble falling asleep, all she needed was a bowl of carbs and milk, and she'd sleep like a baby. Of course, she'd always slept the best in Cal's arms.

Cal had finished his cereal, and the bowl sat on the coffee table. His legs were bent, wrists braced on his knees. His head was leaned back on the couch seat behind him, but his eyes were on her. He was still barefoot and shirtless, wearing the pair of old jeans he hadn't even bothered to button.

She didn't know what happened now. Their visions for the future were so different. Cal was resigned to a life of bachelorhood, and she wanted a life partner, a family.

It pained her to see how much his vision of the future had changed. At one time, that had been all they talked about, making a life together in Tory. Sure, they'd been eighteen, but they'd meant every word. She was sure of it.

And now, Cal couldn't be more adamant that he was fine with a life of bachelorhood. She didn't think it was necessary to have marriage and a family to be happy, but Cal had always been so family-oriented. And he'd talked all the time about starting a family with her. It'd been the one thing that was sure to put him in a good mood.

Their connection was still white-hot, but they were going to douse it in a bucket of ice themselves. Again. Was it possible there was another man out there who would make her want and feel and *crave* as strongly as Cal did?

Maybe that wasn't in the cards for her. She'd meet a nice man—husband and father material—who wasn't grumbly and wasn't stubborn. Hopefully, he'd still like to eat cereal in the middle of the night.

This didn't feel like enough, this time they'd had, half of it discussing the past and the future they'd never have. She wanted to live in the moment, the present, and enjoy a little time with Cal where they weren't reminded of all the reasons they couldn't be together.

"Do you have plans tomorrow?" she asked.

Cal's head slowly tilted forward until he pierced her with those slate eyes. His gaze flicked to clock overhead and then back to her. "Do you mean today?"

"Right, today, Saturday. You know what I mean."

"No, I don't have plans on Saturday."

"So spend the day with me," she blurted.

He didn't react.

"Just a day, Cal. A day where we don't think about everything we had and everything we could have, but we just…enjoy the now." He opened his mouth, but she cut him off. "I'm glad you told me what you did, about not wanting a family, rather than let us go on and raise my hopes. So all I'm asking for is a day. And then…that's it. We'll move on and coexist in Tory and that will be that. We'll remain history." Her voice cracked on the last word. He must have heard it, because he flinched slightly. His jaw tensed, the muscles moving beneath this skin.

He was silent for so long, she wondered if he'd fallen asleep with his eyes open. And just when she thought about reneging on the whole offer, he said quietly, "Okay, I'd like that."

So this was it. And while this attraction was still hot between them—hotter than ever—that didn't seem like it was enough anymore. They were two separate people who wanted two separate things.

But for now, for one day, they'd want the same things.

Jenna crawled toward Cal. He unclasped his hands and let his knees spread farther apart so she could wedge herself between them.

Cal's tan was uneven, a little redneck. But he'd always looked like that. This was Cal, a guy who didn't give a shit about tan lines while he was bent over the hood of his car.

She ran her fingers over that tattoo. Damn him. She'd almost swallowed her tongue when she'd seen it. "Were you angry when you got this?"

The dim light in the room made his pale eyes glow. "No." He paused for a minute, and she knew he was sorting the words out in his head, in that way he had. Cal didn't like to start talking until he knew exactly what was going to come out. "I was lonely and drunk."

"Cal," she whispered.

"It's done, and I don't regret it."

"It's hot," she admitted.

His laugh was husky. "Glad you think so."

She ran her hands over his skin, feeling the imperfections, the scars from high school football and accidents at the garage. Cal was so different than a lot of the polished executives she'd dated in New York.

Cal was…real.

Her hands drifted down to the open button of his pants. She lowered the zipper, and Cal's stomach expanded and contracted as he took deep breaths. She wiggled down onto her hands and knees and then peered up at Cal. He was watching her with narrowed eyes.

"You didn't let me finish earlier," she said, pulling out his shaft and stroking it slowly.

He shifted his body lower and his lips twitched. "I'll be a gentleman and let you finish now."

She opened her mouth and took him in. He grunted softly above her, and his hand rested on the back of her neck. But he didn't push, and she took her time, opening her jaws wide to take him in as much as she could and then sucked hard as she pulled off his shaft. She swirled her tongue around the head and performed every single trick she knew—most of them learned from Delilah.

A lot of girls complained about giving head, but Jenna wasn't one of them—if it was a guy she really wanted to give pleasure. She thought of it as a gift. Something she wanted to give, but she wasn't up for giving it out to anybody, because hell, blow jobs were work.

But Cal? She'd suck Cal for all he was worth. She intended to suck his brain out through his dick until he was half comatose, and if the writhing of his hips and soft curses were any indication, she was doing a hell of a job of achieving her goal.

And Jenna MacMillan had always been an overachiever.

She took a breath, opened wide, and took him down the back of her throat, swallowing around the head of his cock.

Cal came on a gasp and her name, shooting his release on her tongue.

Jenna rose to the sight of Cal's head thrown back on the couch cushions, his eyes closed. She leaned against his chest and curled her arms around his neck. He didn't move. He didn't hug her. A small moan escaped his lips. She grinned against his skin. "You okay?" He didn't answer her right away, and she began to giggle. "Cal?"

"I need…a minute," he croaked.

She laughed harder. "Wow, it must have been a really bad blow job if you can't even face me afterward. I'll make sure not to wake you up with one tomorrow or anything."

His head shot up. His eyes were glassy and a little unfocused. "What? Wait, what? You'll do that?"

"Well, if it was bad, then—"

He grabbed her head and smashed his lips into hers, licking into her mouth, tangling his tongue with hers. He pulled out of the kiss and rested his forehead against hers. "Best I ever had."

"Yeah?"

He leaned back so he could look her in the eye. "Well, actually, my high school girlfriend was really good at that."

Jenna huffed. "Oh yeah? Where is she, so I can go beat her up?"

Cal's smile slowly faded, but his features remained soft. "Ah, no need to do that. Didn't know it was possible, but I like you more."

Damn Cal and his honesty. His fingers teased the edges of her robe.

She shook her head. "How about we go to bed, because I'm about to fall asleep on my feet, and you owe me tomorrow."

His grin returned. "I owe you, huh?"

She nodded.

"Sounds like a win-win for everyone."

Jenna rolled her eyes and stood up. She reached for the cereal bowls, but Cal pulled up his pants and beat her to it. "You go on up. I'll take care of these, lock the door, and turn out the lights, okay?"

"Sounds perfect." And as Jenna walked up the stairs to the bedroom, she realized how domestic it all sounded.

She wondered if Cal had noticed. She wondered if he liked it.

CAL WAS HOT. He didn't remember ever waking up and it being this hot. He had central air conditioning, and he didn't have a damn dog. He was serious about that "not being responsible for another living thing" vow.

He inhaled and immediately smelled *Jenna*. His eyes popped open. He was lying on his side, his arm slung around a female waist, and her head was tucked right under his chin, brunette hair in a mass of waves on white sheets. And then he remembered—he was in Jenna's house.

He told himself to pull away, to roll out of the bed and walk away, but his body wasn't dumb. It was warm, and he had a naked woman pressed against him. A naked Jenna. This—he could get used to this. But this would lead to *that* and the *other thing* or a *couple of things* and *family* and *no*. Just no. He'd promised himself he wouldn't do this—that a life of bachelorhood was fine, and he'd dote on nieces and nephews.

But as her warmth seeped into his skin, he cursed himself. Because even though he couldn't give her a wedding or kids or anything long term—hell, he didn't even want to promise her Labor Day—he wanted her, needed her, for a little bit longer. He knew it would probably only increase the pain when this ended, but he was going to focus on instant gratification now and forget about next week. Because now, he had Jenna in his arms, her scent on his skin, and he wanted her there a little bit longer.

This had always been good between them. So he was glad they had one more day together. And it was still the morning. His dick was hard, pressing into the cleft of her ass. He had to grit his teeth not to thrust like an animal until he came all over the small of her back.

Good morning! I rutted against you while you were asleep. Sorry about that.

Plus, he owed her.

He grinned to himself and fanned his hand out on her stomach. She was waking up now, making small snuffling sounds. He nuzzled down to kiss behind her ear. She lifted her shoulder and made a sound of protest, because she was ticklish as hell. He always had to warm her up, because if she wasn't turned on, all she would do was giggle whenever he touched her. So he needed to work harder until she was aroused and no longer ticklish.

He slid his hand lower, until his little finger touched the top of the curls between her legs. She shifted her thighs restlessly and made a small whimper at the back of her throat.

When he ran his nose along the shell of her ear, she shivered. He trailed his fingers up her stomach to her breasts, flicking a thumb over her peaked nipples. She moaned his name and pushed her butt back into his groin.

He lowered his head to her neck and placed open-mouthed kisses on her skin. She didn't giggle or shy away, and he smiled, because she was ready now.

He lowered his hand again and dipped a middle finger into her slit, sliding it through the wetness. "Oh God," she said and curled an arm around his head, her hand clutching his hair.

"Give me some room," he ordered. And she did, immediately, separating her thighs by hooking one leg behind his.

And then, it was easy to work her. He dipped two fingers inside of her, plunging them in and out, while his thumb worked her clit. She gripped his hair harder and panted, riding his fingers. She had no inhibitions when she got going, no self-consciousness about how she looked or the sounds she was making. She just let go.

Her breasts rocked with their movements, and he could stare at them all day, those rosy nipples begging for his mouth. *Later,* he thought. He still had the rest of the day.

When she came, she came hard, crying out his name, grinding herself down onto his fingers. He left them in as the orgasm slowed, rubbing slightly until she angled her hips so they slipped out. Her hand that gripped his hair fell to the bed in front of her. "Jesus, Cal."

Then she reached forward, opened up a drawer, and pulled out a condom. She opened the wrapper and handed it to him over her shoulder.

He didn't question it. He slipped it on, rolled her onto her stomach, and kneeled between her legs. He opened her up wide with his knees and entered her from behind.

She bit her pillow as he thrust in and out of her sensitive flesh. He was so wound up from watching her come all over his hand that it didn't take long. He raised himself up on his hands and watched her face where it was turned so the light from the window highlighted her features.

He let his gaze fall, taking in her narrow waist and full hips. He loved those hips, and if he had the energy, he would have pulled her up onto her knees, gripped her ass, and rode her hard. What a fucking view.

He'd save it for later.

But even the thought had his balls drawing up tight, his spine tingling, and then he was coming on a soft exhale of her name.

He fell onto his stomach on the bed beside her. Her head was turned to face him. She was disheveled, and her face was clean of makeup, and he swore this was the most beautiful thing he'd ever seen.

He thought about what it would be like to wake up to her every day. Just like this, with her fresh face on the pillow next to his and her warm skin pressed against him.

But that was a fantasyland. Still, she needed to know just how much this meant to him. He brushed her hair off her forehead and pressed a kiss to her temple, letting his lips linger there. "There's not a cloud in the sky, but all the sunshine is right here in this bed."

He didn't wait for her reply. He stood up and walked toward the bathroom.

When he walked back out to the bedroom, he found she hadn't moved. He crawled back under the sheets and lay beside her on his back, his arm tucked behind his head. He really wanted a cigarette, but lying with a naked Jenna won.

"So we have today," she said, propping her chin on a fist on his chest.

"We have today," he echoed.

"It's better that way."

He didn't know who she was trying to convince. "Yeah."

She blew a stray piece of hair out of her face, and he helped her by smoothing the crazy strands over her head.

"I look a little Medusa-ish, don't I?"

He mimed freezing to stone, stiffening his body like a board, and she laughed, plunking her forehead onto his breastbone. He pulled her up, so they laughed together against each other's lips. She gave him a quick peck.

"Have you ever ridden on a motorcycle?"

She shook her head, eyes still a little lazy from sleep and sex.

"Why don't we pick up breakfast to-go and take a ride?"

She cocked her head. "Where do you want to go?"

He didn't know if River's Edge was off limits, since that was a place that held almost all their history, but he couldn't think of a single other place he wanted to take Jenna on his bike. When he was silent for too long, she reached up and squeezed his neck and then let her fingers trail over his tattooed shoulder. "Why don't we hike on one of the trails at River's Edge?"

"You reading my mind, Sunshine?"

"You don't hide your thoughts as well as you think," she said, rising from bed. "Give me ten minutes, and I'll be ready."

He watched her walk into the bathroom, shutting the door behind her. He thought he did a pretty good job of hiding what he was thinking. To everyone but Jenna.

Chapter Twelve

IT WAS MORE like a half hour before they were both showered, and Jenna was staring at him as he sat astride his bike. It was a hot day, but he'd still urged her to find an old leather jacket in the back of her closet. She'd loaned him an old T-shirt that was big on her, one she said she wore to bed sometimes. When he unfolded it, his breath caught, because it was his high school football T-shirt, one he remembered giving her after one of his games. She'd kept the damn thing for ten years, and the maroon fabric was faded, the lettering peeled, but he pulled it on. He was thankful he'd worn his motorcycle boots to dinner so he had them for the day.

Cal only had one helmet, so he settled it on her head outside as they stood in the driveway. It was too big, but it'd do in a pinch. She looked cute as hell with her eyes gleaming through the face mask, her brown hair billowing out around her shoulders below it.

He guided her onto the bike behind him, urging her to grip him tightly with her thighs and arms. Partly because it was safe and partly because he liked how it felt.

The only other girl he'd ever had on the back of his bike was Max's girlfriend, Lea. She'd asked for a ride, and he'd obliged, while Max stood scowling at them, his body quivering with nerves. Lea had loved it, but everything about her touch had been sisterly and platonic. Her thighs had grazed his; her little hands had stayed firmly over the top of his clothes.

Jenna's hands were already stealing under his shirt to touch his bare skin as he started up the engine. The rumbling cut through the humidity of the day, shaking up a crop of birds on Jenna's front lawn. She nestled closer into his back. He'd always thought he wouldn't like someone riding with him. Riding was something he did for himself, to get his mind off everything and just be, with the wind in his face and ruffling his clothes. But Jenna at his back felt good. Felt right.

And he knew it was because it was *her*.

He eyed her over his shoulder. She nodded, the helmet bobbing on her head. He chuckled, turned back around, and eased out of her driveway.

He took the bike slow throughout her neighborhood, so she got used to leaning with the machine through curves.

And then he headed right for the open stretches of road in Tory that he always did. His route was pretty damn sacred to him—not even Brent knew where he rode—but Cal wanted Jenna to share this with him.

Come Monday, they'd go their separate ways, but they'd have this memory together.

Her fingers curled into the muscles of his stomach, her pinkies resting along the waistband of his jeans. Her thighs were tight against his, and sometimes, a lock of hair would curl around and he'd catch a whiff of her scent in his nostrils.

They stopped at a little bakery on the outskirts of town, one that had just opened up, so the owners didn't know them. They wouldn't spread any gossip about Jenna MacMillan and Cal Payton riding around town on a Saturday morning.

Tory wasn't too small, but it was small enough that people talked. Which was why Cal had bought a house with a lot of land, so people couldn't look out their windows and see what he was doing. Christ, he was totally a hermit bachelor.

Jenna clutched their bag of muffins and pastries, and he secured a Thermos of coffee in his saddlebags, and they made their way to their predetermined breakfast spot.

At River's Edge, Cal parked his bike and cut the engine. He looked over his shoulder at Jenna, who was pulling off her helmet. She tried vainly to tame her mane, and he smirked as she huffed out a breath and pulled out a hair tie.

"Don't laugh at me. I'm going to shave my head."

He shook his head, stepped off his bike, and then helped her off. They gathered their breakfast and began to head toward the path that led to the many trails.

River's Edge was a popular state park with several walking trails running along the Tory Pine River. Cal pointed to the sign at the line that read FLANNERY TRAIL and was marked with a blue triangle. "They put a new one in a couple of years ago. There's a little clearing just up ahead with some benches where we can eat." When he looked at Jenna, she was biting her lip, and he knew she'd understood what he meant. Sure, he wanted to come to River's Edge with her, but not their trail, not their place. That was a little too much of the past. And today was about the present.

She looked at him and smiled, although it was a little strained, and nodded.

They took off on the path, with Cal's eyes on Jenna to make sure she didn't slip. They'd left the leather jacket back at the bike, so she was wearing a pair of jean shorts, a T-shirt, and old black motorcycle boots.

Cal didn't come here often; he was busy working or taking care of his house. But with Jenna at his side and the morning sun creeping through the filter of leaves above them, he knew he probably wouldn't be back again, no way. The whole place would remind him of Jenna now.

He shook his head. No "future" talk. No "future" thinking. He was here with Jenna now. Today. So he grabbed her hand, accepted the warmth of the smile she shot his way, and kept on walking.

JENNA HAD NEVER ridden on a motorcycle. At one time, she thought that would be her future. All Cal talked about as a teenager was getting a bike. It was his dream, so seeing him on the back of that red-silver-and-black beauty made her heart sing.

He'd gotten that dream, at least. They hadn't killed that one.

They sat on new wooden benches in a clearing on Flannery Trail to eat. A breeze rustled through the trees, which helped break up the humid air. She sipped her coffee and picked at her cranberry and orange muffin. "I'm so glad you got your bike."

Cal smiled at that and crumpled the empty wrapper of his chocolate-chocolate chip muffin. "Yeah I had an older model before this that I bought cheap. I saved up for the Softail so I wouldn't have to take a loan out. Insurance is outrageous, but it's worth it."

"Do you work on them at the shop too?"

His smile immediately twisted into something bitter. "You'd think, right?"

She propped a knee on the bench and leaned forward. "Wait...so you don't?"

He shook his head. "My dad's being stubborn about it."

"A Payton, being stubborn?" She gasped dramatically.

He chuckled a little at that and smacked her thigh lightly. "I prefer the term decisive."

"So what's going on with Jack?"

Cal crossed his arms over his chest and squinted up at the forest canopy above them. "I want to expand Payton and Sons to repair bikes, and he's being a stubborn bastard about it. He said he doesn't want to change the shop."

"Why?"

"Why does he do anything he does? He says he needs me for the cars. I told him Brent said we could afford another hire. But he's so committed to the way things are, he doesn't want to change. I went out and got the certifications to work on Harleys anyway. That was a fun fight."

Cal had loved bikes for so long that Jenna ached a little that he wasn't able to do what he really wanted to do. "So what's your plan?"

Cal was silent for a long time. "I don't want to leave him or Brent, but I might have to open up my own place if he keeps this up. I don't want to stop working on cars, but this town needs a certified bike mechanic in business."

"There isn't one?"

Cal shook his head. "I think the closest one is in Brookridge."

Jenna frowned. "And you told your dad that?"

"He doesn't give a shit."

"I'm sorry."

He shrugged and waved a hand. "It is what it is. I'll figure it out."

But it bothered her. A lot. And she wondered if there would ever come a time where she would no longer be emotionally invested in Cal Payton.

"So how's work for you?" he asked. And it didn't feel like small talk, like he was asking as a returning favor. His eyes were focused on her, those irises a little more blue than normal in the sunshine.

"Dylan's a dick," she said in reply.

He laughed.

She grinned at him. "Delilah still calls him Dill Pickle."

"With Delilah, I'm sure she says it to his face."

"She does. So anyway, I'm working on employee morale, since Dylan is close to running that into the grave." Cal didn't answer, and she eyed him. "I guess you heard about it?"

"Brent read the newspaper articles about the lawsuit. He likes the letters to the editor, especially."

"Yeah, so I'm planning an event for the employees. Like a big dinner—a thank-you. Maybe hold it at the country club."

Cal nodded slowly. "You could get the community involved—like give away local gift certificates or get businesses to offer free services. As a way of giving back."

She actually hadn't thought that far yet, but it was a great idea. "Like a raffle."

"Yeah. I'll donate a free inspection or tune-up or something."

"Really?"

" 'Course."

She smiled. "Wow, thanks. That's a great idea."

"I'm sure you would have come up with it on your own."

She shrugged. "Maybe, but you saved me the brainpower."

He laughed. "Don't count on that happening too often, Sunshine."

She reached out and laced her fingers with his, squeezing, as she held her tongue so she didn't bring up the future.

"Did you miss Tory while you were in New York?" he asked softly, his eyes on their clasped hands.

She thought about that. "Sometimes. I'm not sure it ever felt like home. I was kind of a long-term visitor. It was odd being back in Tory, but now that I'm here, I feel…more like myself again. Does that make sense?"

He nodded slowly, his gaze still on their hands, his thumb rubbing hers. "I do think it makes sense."

"And the older I get, the less I feel like pretending to be something I'm not."

He didn't say anything to that. His brow was furrowed, and she let him think. She took a sip of her coffee, felt the caffeine invade her system, and held Cal's hand like this wasn't the last day she'd get to touch him.

Like there wasn't a past. Like there wasn't a future. Only today.

Chapter Thirteen

THEY HAD LUNCH at an ice cream place that sold burgers, two for three dollars. High school kids worked there, faces flushed from the heat and the rush of a summer paycheck.

The umbrella over the picnic table shielded them from the sun as they ate the greasy burgers and dipped their hand-cut fries in ketchup. Cal told Jenna about Brent's latest hook-up, a woman who ended up being nineteen rather than the twenty-nine she'd told him, which Brent only learned about when her roommates tried to wake her up before the dining hall on the community college campus closed.

Brent wasn't amused.

Cal was. And Jenna laughed.

The Cal who sat across from her was a far cry from the tense man she'd seen at the garage that first week she'd been in town. This Cal smiled and laughed and didn't press his lips into a thin, irritated line.

They sat there for two hours, drinking Cokes with melted ice, as Jenna told him about the job she had in New York. He listened intently, and she believed he truly cared about her professional success. That's what she'd missed in New York. Hell, that was what she missed now—a partner who was as invested in her life as she was.

But as the conversation wound down, she pushed those thoughts aside. She'd be fine for a while. She knew how to be single and content. Or at least, she used to know how to be. Now, all she felt was this ache in her heart, this looming deadline when Cal would no longer be hers.

In one day, he'd seemed to erase the confidence she had that she was over him.

She'd never be over him, she realized. She'd have to learn to live with that.

When they hopped back on his bike, they didn't head toward the direction of her house, and she didn't ask why or what or where. She wrapped her arms around his waist and burrowed against the soft fabric of her own T-shirt that covered his back, and she enjoyed the ride, the vibration under her, the scent of Cal.

When they pulled down a dirt road, she raised her head, peering through the visor of the helmet he'd insisted she wear.

In front of her was a small two-story wood home. Cal's old truck sat in the driveway, and a warmth spread through her chest.

He'd brought her to his home. He wanted her to see it. When he stepped off the bike and helped her, he didn't meet her eyes, and she understood he was a little nervous to show her. She laid a hand on his forearm. "I like your house."

He squinted at it, like he was trying to picture it through her eyes. "Yeah, me too. It needs work, but it's private, and it's better than the apartment I shared with Brent."

He took her hand led her inside. The place looked utterly masculine, with beige walls and neutral furniture, but there were a lot of touches that were uniquely Cal—a series of family photographs in the hall, a cluster of vintage motorcycle prints along the wall in the living room. Cal explained to her that upstairs was his bedroom, a bathroom, and a spare bedroom.

When he was finished telling her about the house, he held out his arms. "I wanted you to see it."

"I wanted to see it," she said.

"You want a drink?"

"Water would be nice."

"Yeah, that's a good idea."

He rummaged in the fridge, and she heard the clinking of beer bottles before he pulled out two bottles of water. He gestured toward the back door. "We can sit on the deck unless you want to enjoy the air conditioning."

"Deck's fine," she said, accepting the bottle he handed to her. On the deck, she sank down on a glider and took in Cal's backyard. It was well kept, leading to a tree line that surrounded Cal's property. "How big is your property?"

"About an acre," he said, sitting beside her. He stretched out his legs and gently rocked the glider. His arm curled around her shoulders, and she rested her head against him.

She watched two squirrels chase each other, their tails fluttering wildly.

"You don't have to say it," he said quietly.

"Don't have to say what?"

"You know, 'Hey Cal, this could be us if you'd stop being stubborn.'"

She straightened. "That's what you think I want to say?"

He squinted at her. "Isn't it?"

"Maybe I'm thinking it, but I don't want to say it. I don't want to have to convince you to be with me. To want a family. I'm not going to pressure you into doing something you don't want and then have you resent me for it."

He was silent for a while as he mulled over her words. "You're probably right about that."

"But I do think you're stubborn. I think today was one of the best days either of us has had for a while." And if today proved anything to Jenna, it was that while she'd fallen hard for the eighteen-year-old Cal, if she let herself do the same thing for the thirty-year-old Cal, she'd never recover from it. The Cal of today was dangerous for her heart.

She glanced at her watch, saw it was close to dinner-time, and prepared to do what she'd been avoiding thinking about all day. "You should probably take me home now."

He whipped his head toward her. "But the day isn't over."

She sighed. "I know, but it's close, and...I'm think-ing maybe we should end this now. Before something triggers one of us, and we fight or get angry. I don't want to get angry, Cal. I want to leave here happy."

His face was stricken, every emotion clear as day. He wasn't even bothering to try to hide it. "But—"

She stood up. "I'll meet you in the house."

Five minutes later, she was standing by the front door when he joined her. He smelled like smoke. "Those'll kill you, you know."

His jaw tensed, his eyes flashed, and she wondered how she thought they'd ever be able to leave this whole situation intact. "I'm not your responsibility to worry about."

"Well, I'm sorry for caring."

He rubbed his hands over his face vigorously, like he was trying to scrub off his emotions, and then he lashed out an arm, curling it around her shoulders so she crashed into his body. She wrapped her arms around him, nestling her head against the soft fabric of his T-shirt, feeling the hard muscles underneath, as he buried his face in her neck.

"Sunshine?" His voice was muffled against her skin.

"Yeah?"

His fist tightened in her hair, his lips opened up on her neck, and he said everything with his body that he couldn't say in words. This was an embrace that wasn't meant to lead to anything else; this was meant to tell her something, that they'd always have this. It would never go away, and somehow, someway, they'd move on.

They'd get through it.

Even if they were breaking the same hearts, ripping open those same wounds that they'd worked so hard to heal for ten years.

And it hurt; it hurt like a knife to her chest.

She opened her mouth to do what she promised herself she wouldn't do, to beg for more time, to ask him to reconsider. But before any words came out, the doorbell rang.

And they both froze.

Locked in the embrace with Cal, Jenna worked on breathing steadily, because she was sure it wouldn't be anyone other than Brent.

And that was really the last thing they needed, because both of them were raw, flayed, and Brent would be like a dog with a bone, wanting to know why she was there.

Cal must have been thinking the same thing, because when she leaned back, his eyes were closed. "Come in," he growled in the direction of the front door.

Jenna braced herself.

But the doorknob didn't turn. A joking Brent didn't burst through the door with a wisecrack on his tongue.

Cal lifted his head and stared at the door. A tentative knock sounded.

With a jolt, he strode toward the door. "Jesus-fucking-Christ, Brent." He turned the doorknob and flung the door open. "Any other day, you—" His voice cut off. Just dropped off like someone had muted him.

Jenna slowly turned her head, wondering if this was going to get even more awkward because an old flame of Cal's was on his doorstep. But when she peered under the arm Cal had braced on the doorframe, her breath caught.

Because it wasn't Brent on that doorstep. It wasn't a woman. It was a kid. A teenage boy. He had a crazy haircut. The sides were shaved, but it was long on top, with the front combed forward so a lock of brown hair hung down his forehead, touching his eyelashes. He wore a pair of skinny jeans and a blue V-neck T-shirt. He was a little shorter than Cal. And he had a huge duffel bag thrown over his shoulder. And there was something familiar about him that Jenna couldn't put her finger on.

The kid was trying for bravado, Jenna could tell, but was having a hard time standing up Cal's scrutiny.

He had large brown eyes that stared up into Cal's face. The kid licked his lips. "A-Are you Cal Payton?"

Cal seemed frozen. Jenna wondered if she should speak, but then Cal's voice cracked on a "Yup."

The kid's eyes changed, getting even bigger and a little wet. He sniffed once, wrinkling his nose, and then he wiped his hand on his pants and stuck it out. "I'm Asher Weyland. I'm, uh, your half-brother, I guess. And I really need some help."

Jenna gasped. She couldn't help it. She clapped her hand over her mouth, but Asher's eyes darted to her anyway. He shifted on his feet. "Is that your wife?"

Cal ignored the question. "What are you doing here?"

Asher's eyes darted back to Cal. "I know this is kinda surprising and all, but—"

"Look, kid, I don't know who you are, but this isn't fucking funny. So I'll give you thirty seconds to get off my porch before I remove you."

The kid's face paled. "What?"

"I'm gonna start counting. Warning: sometimes I skip some numbers."

Asher looked physically ill. Jenna could see his fists clenched at his sides, and his slender shoulders began to tremble. She didn't know what was going on. She hadn't known Cal had any more siblings, and apparently, he didn't either, by the looks of it. But there was no way this kid was lying. He looked scared out of his mind.

"Cal—" she started, but the kid cut her off.

"Mom always told me you were her little man," Asher said.

And if possible, Cal's body turned to stone. But he wasn't playing now, like they had been in bed this morning.

The kid's eyes were huge, and he wrapped his arms around himself, as if it wasn't seventy degrees outside. "She said," he continued, "that she knew you picked up the slack when she left."

Cal didn't move. He didn't even blink.

"She talks about all of you. She's still not so good at the mom thing, but she didn't leave this time." He looked down and brushed a leaf on the porch with the toe of his Converse shoes. "I was the one who left."

"Your mom is Jill Payton." Cal's voice sounded like he hadn't used it for a century.

Asher bit his lip. "Yeah. Well, Jill Weyland. My dad's Bill Weyland."

Something clicked in Jenna's brain. His eyes. He had Max's eyes. Jill's eyes. And she was sure Cal noticed, because he hadn't taken his gaze off that kid's face. "What're doing here?" he asked quietly.

"I need a place to stay."

"You came all the way here from California?"

He shook his head. "We live in Virginia now. I took a bus."

Jenna's head felt like it was going to split open. This was no joke.

Cal swallowed, his posture not quite as defensive. "And why are you here?"

Asher gathered himself again, straightening his back and lifting his chin. "I need a place to stay. If you say no, I guess I'll go somewhere else. But we just moved. I have no friends. I have nowhere to go. I dug out your address from my mom's address book, and here I am."

Cal stared at him. "Why do you need a place to stay?"

That chin lifted higher, like the kid needed more courage to say what he was going to say next. "Dad's drunk a lot, and Mom's always making excuses for him. For a while, it was better, but since we moved to Virginia, he's gotten so much worse. He comes home at odd hours. He's driven drunk with me in the car, but this last time…he picked me up from the mall and almost ran off the road because he was plastered. I don't"—he swallowed and blinked rapidly—"feel safe with them anymore. I try to refuse to get in the car, but then he gets angry. So angry. And…I…I'm scared."

Jenna wanted to run to this kid and gather him in her arms. Get him a slushy and curl up with junk food on the couch, watching silly movies. No kid should feel unsafe with his own parents.

Cal hadn't moved, but the tenseness had returned to his shoulders. His fists were clenched. And Jenna knew him well enough by now to know he was *pissed*.

And then the kid threw his knockout punch. "Mom always said you were probably a better parent to your brothers than she could have been."

Jenna felt the tears. They were hot and they were prickly, and shoot, she was going to start bawling.

Because Cal still had that soft inside he always had. He hid it so well with his gruffness and his stares and scowls. But he'd shown her his belly this weekend. It was still there, just a little more scarred.

And that kid had gone right for it. *Freaking little genius*, Jenna thought.

"And you came here thinking…what? That I'd take you in? Be your parent?" Cal's words were harsh, but his tone was soft.

Asher blinked at him, and then his lip started trembling. But Jenna knew by the slump of Cal's shoulders that the kid had won this round.

"How old are you?" Cal asked.

"Sixteen." Asher wiped his nose with the back of his hand and sniffed again. "I just need a place to stay until I can figure out what to do." Jenna began to see some resemblance in the shape of their faces. Asher's body was more like Brent's—on the lean side—but those eyes were all Max and that face was Cal's. Unmistakably Cal's.

Cal jerked his chin toward the bag. "That all ya have?"

"Yeah."

He stepped away from the door. "Come in, then. Take off your shoes, because I don't want you tracking dirt in my house."

Chapter Fourteen

Jack Payton was going to have a heart attack. Because standing in the foyer of Cal's house, in a pair of faded Converses and a beat-up duffel bag, was a teenager staring back at Cal with Max's eyes.

With Jill's eyes.

Cal didn't know whether to laugh or cry.

How his sorry excuse for a mother hadn't informed her other three children that she'd had another child was a mystery. But yet, here he was, nervously licking his lips, looking like a mash-up of Max, Brent, and a third guy who must be his father.

Cal knew what it was like to be let down by someone he thought he could depend on. He wanted to drive to Virginia and beat the shit out of this kid's dad, but what good would that do? He thought the best thing to do would be to send the kid home. Asher wasn't his responsibility, but by the time he found the bus schedule and got the kid to the bus station, it'd be dark. And Cal couldn't bring himself to drop off a scared teenager at a bus stop to travel to Virginia at night.

He'd have to give the kid a place to sleep tonight, and then he'd call Jill in the morning to arrange a way to get the kid home. But it niggled in the back of his mind that it must be pretty bad at home for this kid to leave and show up on a stranger's doorstep.

Cal looked pointedly at the kid's shoes, and Asher hurriedly toed them off. He stood and looked around awkwardly. "Um, I like your place."

Cal didn't respond.

Jenna stepped forward. "Hi, I'm Jenna."

Asher eyed her. "I didn't know Cal was married."

"Oh, he's not. I'm just a friend."

Asher raised his eyebrows, like he didn't really believe that.

Cal ignored Asher's interest in Jenna. "You need food? Shower? A bed? Because I got all three, but I'll tell you right now—I'm not your servant. You'll clean up after yourself, or I'll shave off that ugly haircut in your sleep."

Asher's head jerked up. "What's wrong with my hair?"

"What isn't wrong with it?"

The kid's eyes narrowed. "This haircut cost me eighty dollars."

"Mine cost me ten minutes and a number-three attachment on my razor."

"Wow, you're a total dude."

"Last time I checked. You need food?"

Asher pressed his lips together. "I could eat."

Jenna stepped forward. "You said there's a spare bedroom upstairs, right? I'll go get it together. Why don't you two head into the kitchen and get something to drink?" She held her fingers out for Asher's bag. Cal looked at her for the first time since Asher showed up.

This was a lot for Cal to handle, this knowledge of a blood relative, this sudden responsibility, even if it was for the night. She offered him a smile, a reassuring one, and he clung to it like a raft in a storm. Thank God she was here, with her presence and her light. He could fall apart later, but for now, he could do this.

Asher handed Jenna his bag, and Cal cleared his throat. "Thanks, Jenna."

He led Asher into the kitchen and handed him a water bottle, keeping one for himself. Asher sat down at the kitchen table, rolling the bottle between his hands, while Cal leaned against the counter. The kid was jiggling his leg. Cal could see it from the corner of his eye.

"So," Asher said. "I can stay? I told my mom I was staying with a friend overnight."

"Thought you didn't have any friends?" Cal had barely glanced at the card his mom had sent, so he'd missed her change in address. It wasn't like he ever sent anything back to her.

"I don't. I made one up."

"And she didn't call the parent of this 'friend' to check before you spent the night?"

Asher shook his head.

Cal clamped down the anger and wiped his hand over his mouth. "You can stay tonight. I'm not putting you on a bus back home now. We'll call your mother tomorrow and figure it out then."

Asher's head was down, and he was making circles on the table with his index finger. Cal waited him out, until the kid looked up at him with those big Max-like eyes. "Okay, thank you."

"Plus, I think you're going to want to meet your other brothers. I'll call them tomorrow."

Asher looked like he was trying to hide his excitement. "Are they like you?"

"Like me, how?"

"Um, like, all…" Asher puffed out his chest and held his arms out from his body like his biceps were huge. "Don't dirty my house," he said in a false low voice. "Do what I say. Grrrr."

A laugh burst out of Cal before he could rein it in. "That's what I sound like, huh? Maybe punk kids who make fun of me get put back on a bus."

Asher held out his hands in alarm. "No, no, no! I'm sorry!" He grimaced. "Shit," he said under his breath.

Cal smiled. "Hey, I'm just kidding. Brent is, uh, a jokester. He'll tease you a lot and give you a hard time. Max will be your buddy. He's good at making friends."

Asher relaxed a little as Jenna came into the kitchen. She had her hair pulled up onto the top of her head in a messy knot, and everything about her posture showed purpose. "Okay, Asher? I got you set up in the spare bedroom. Your bed is made, and I put away your clothes."

Asher was in midsip of water and choked. "You put away my—"

"I put all your toiletries in the bathroom, and fresh towels are out," Jenna said.

Cal leaned back, watching her take charge. His woman sure knew how to get shit done.

And as soon as that thought went through his head, he wanted to kick himself. *His woman.* He'd always called her his girl in high school. Because that's what she'd been. But now? She was *all* woman now, and fuck it if his brain hadn't just skipped forward, still attaching that goddamn pronoun. That's what this weekend had done. She was no longer the girl he'd loved in high school. She was the beautiful, independent, smart woman that he could see himself falling for all over again. *Shit.*

Asher was blinking at her. "Thank you?"

She turned to Cal. "So, I'll just head out and let you two…catch up."

Cal frowned. "But I have to take you home—"

She waved a hand. "I'll call Delilah."

"You could take my truck. I still have my bike—"

Her smile was tight. "Cal, really, it's fine. Delilah's shop is closed by now. I'll just head on out to the road and call her."

This was it, and there'd be no embrace, no last-minute kiss, no nothing, because Asher was staring at them, and Cal's stomach was cramping from nerves.

But this moment…this moment could be something. He could tell her to stay. He could wrap her in his arms and tell Asher that Jenna was his girlfriend. And Jenna was giving him this decision, her hands clenched at her sides, her face a little hopeful.

But the anxiety crept up his spine, telling him that he couldn't get swept up in this temporary arrangement that was making him question everything he'd believed for the past ten years.

So he let the moment pass. And he nodded. And then he watched as Jenna's face fell, just slightly, before she slipped out the door.

He didn't have time to wallow, though, because he had a teenager in the house who probably needed to eat dinner.

He took a deep breath and began scrounging in his refrigerator for food.

CAL STARED AT his phone in his hands. The three cigarettes he'd sucked down before this phone call hadn't done much to steady his hands. And it wasn't even ten in the morning.

He'd slept like shit last night, and he didn't think the kid fared much better, since he now sat at the kitchen table wearing a pair of cutoff sweatpants, his hair sticking up at all angles, and sporting dark circles under his eyes. A plate of half-eaten scrambled eggs sat in front of him. "What do you think she'll say?" he asked, his voice way too tiny for a sixteen-year-old guy.

"It'll be okay, kid," Cal assured him, even though he didn't feel it himself. He didn't want to have to call his mother or hear her voice. He didn't want to have to tell her that her husband was such a drunk that his kid had run away from home. Rather than delay any longer, Cal typed in his mother's phone number that Asher had supplied and held the phone up to his ear as it rang.

Once.

Twice.

The third ring was cut off midtrill. "Hello?"

He hadn't heard her voice in…hell, he wasn't sure. She might have called him a couple of years ago, but he couldn't remember exactly. He cleared his throat. "Hey, this is Cal."

There was silence on the other end. It lasted so long that Cal thought she'd hung up. "C-Cal?"

"Yep." *You know, your firstborn son?*

"Oh, well, how are you?"

They weren't doing this dumb-ass small talk. No way in hell. He plunged right into the meat of his call. "Yeah, so I have Asher here in front of me." More silence. It stretched on and on until Cal had had enough. "For God's sake, you wanna act like you give a shit that your kid is in another state?"

"I do care!" she protested. "I'm just shocked. I thought he was with a friend—"

"He lied. He was on a bus to see his brothers—who didn't even know he existed, by the way, so thanks for that—because your drunk of a husband got behind the wheel, impaired, with Asher in the car."

"No one was hurt."

"Excuse me?"

"My husband said there was just a lot of loose gravel on the road—"

"Oh, really? Then why did Asher tell me that wasn't the first time?"

Silence. Just silence.

How in the hell was Cal going to be able to put this kid back on a bus to his hometown, knowing his dad drove drunk with him in the car and all his mom did was make excuses? How in the fuck was he going to live with that?

"Look, it wasn't—"

Cal was vibrating with fury now. "He was drunk. Asher knew it, and he was scared shitless. So scared that he put himself on a goddamn bus to seek protection from grown men he's never even met. Now what the fuck does that tell you?"

Silence. Then a small voice. "I can pay for his ticket home—"

"No, you fucking won't!" Cal roared. Asher's face was white as snow, his lips twisted in misery. "He's staying here until you guys get your shit together. I'm not sending him back so his dad can put his safety at risk."

"Bill's not going to like this."

"I couldn't give a fuck what Bill likes. He wants to come pry the kid out of my hands, he can fucking bring it."

"The police—"

"Would love to hear about his drinking problem, I'm sure. You've done some low things in your life, Jill, but it's the fucking lowest not to take this seriously. And thanks for the brother I never knew about."

And then he ended the call.

He couldn't stand to hear her make excuses for the husband she'd left his dad for.

Asher had his hands clenched on the table in front of him. He didn't speak.

And Cal thought he was going to throw up. He'd just accepted the responsibility of taking care of a teenage boy. That was what he'd done, right? He replayed the conversation and glanced at Asher. Yep, that was what he'd done.

Cal was officially crazy.

But he wasn't cruel. Asher was scared enough to run away, so Cal couldn't send him right back to where he didn't feel safe.

The bitch of it was that this was what Cal had worked for ten years to avoid. And now, here he was again, in the same position, with a kid named Asher who reminded him way too much of Max. Cal had fallen head over heels in love with little Max when he was born. He'd been a surprise to everyone. His mother had been pissed, having already checked out of their family, and his dad had been scared shitless. But Cal...well, he'd loved that fat baby more than anything.

He'd just laid into Jenna for his not wanting to be responsible for anyone or anything, and then Asher had showed up on his doorstop in a teenage package of irony.

Jesus. Fuck.

He threw his phone onto the countertop with a clatter. "I guess you're staying here for a while."

Asher's expression was so hopeful, it nearly broke Cal's heart. "A-are you sure?"

Not at all. "Yep. That woman is impossible."

"D-do you remember her much? Before she left?"

"Yeah, I do. Brent sort of does. Max doesn't remember her much at all."

"Do you know why she left?"

Cal sat down across from Asher and took a sip of the water he'd left on the table. "I think she doesn't know. She was a good mom for a while, and then she wasn't, and then she left. It's as simple and complicated as that. I think she might be a little selfish."

"So she's okay with me staying with you?"

"Well, I didn't really give her much of a chance to protest, but she didn't seem to have any intention of talking to your dad about his drinking. Until they can tell me you'll be safe, I'm not taking you back to them." Asher didn't cheer or even smile. Cal understood the feeling. Although the kid wanted to stay, he most likely wanted his parents to give a shit that he wasn't home. "Guess you're stuck with me for a little while then, kid."

Asher smiled then. "I think I can live with that."

Chapter Fifteen

JENNA HEARD THE voices first and closed her eyes, the Ultimate Fudge Brownie Mix box still clutched in her fists. She thought about hiding, but with her luck, she'd knock over a soup display or run over a little kid with her cart, so she stayed put as she waited for Cal and Asher to look up and see her in front of them at the grocery store.

She hadn't given Delilah any details last night when she'd picked her up. And for once, Delilah had shut up and hadn't asked too many questions. Jenna had gone home and nursed her wounds with a good book and a large glass of wine. Okay, two glasses. Okay, three-quarters of the bottle.

She rubbed her temples and then heard a "Jenna!" She lifted her gaze to see a grinning Asher walking toward her while a grumpy Cal leaned over the handle of the cart, steel eyes glowing from under the brim of his ball cap.

It reminded her of the night in his tow truck. She didn't *want* to be reminded of that night in the tow truck. "Hey, Asher," she said as the teenager drew close.

The kid looked tired but happy. "We're grocery shopping because I'm staying with Cal for a while."

She darted her gaze to Cal, who didn't react. She looked back at Asher. "Why's that?"

The kid talked to the brownie box in her hand rather than to her. "Cal called my mom and she didn't…uh, I guess Cal thought it was best if I don't go back there right now. You know…"

He was uncomfortable now, those brown eyes a little pained. Cal made a growling sound in the back of his throat. "Kid's safer here."

He'd spent the whole weekend telling Jenna he didn't want responsibilities and a family—hell, the man didn't even have a plant—and yet here he was, stepping up because the brother he never knew about needed him.

Yeah, she would have fallen in love with this Cal.

"Cal said he only grocery shops for milk and eggs. His food options are really pathetic," Asher grumbled. "And I get to meet my brothers tonight, so we need something to make for dinner."

Cal rolled his eyes. "We're here, aren't we?

Jenna smiled and tossed the brownie box she was holding into their cart. Cal looked at it like it was a snake. "What's that for?"

Jenna had already begun to push her cart away, Asher following her. "What did you say?"

He pointed to the box and grunted.

Jenna wasn't in the mood for his lack of conversation skills. She had a headache. "Brownies," she said dryly.

"I know they're brownies. What're they for?"

"They aren't *for* anything. It's just a box of brownie mix."

"If they aren't for anything, then why are they in my cart?"

Asher's head was shifting back and forth between the two of them. Jenna fought her irritation. "Because everyone should have brownie mix on hand. It's like Keeping House 101."

Cal leaned back and placed a hand on his chest. "Well, damn. No one told me that. I guess I've been failing Keeping House 101 for ten fucking years then."

"Can you not swear in the baked goods aisle, Cal?"

"Can you not throw random shit we don't need in the cart?"

She threw up her hands. "Fine, put the brownies back on the shelf. I don't care."

Cal studied the boxes in front of him and then placed the brownies Jenna had picked back on the shelf. She watched, arms over her chest, as he picked up a box labeled Chocolate Chunk and tossed that in his cart instead.

He looked at her with raised eyebrows.

She tapped her fingers on her elbows. "Really?"

He drew an imaginary check mark in the air. "Chocolate Chunk beats Ultimate Fudge. Just saying."

She pursed her lips, trying to hide a smile, because this all felt incredibly domestic.

Asher followed her over to the next aisle, where they checked out the cereal. Asher bit his lip. "I usually just have a granola bar with breakfast."

"What kind of granola bars?" Jenna asked.

"Whatever's on sale."

She smiled and placed a hand on his arm. "Okay, well, how about this—I have an amazing recipe for homemade granola bars. I swear, once you get Jenna-granola, you don't go back. I can make them and bring them over, okay?"

"Really?" Asher said, a huge grin on his face.

"Sure. They're easy, and I'm running low."

Asher turned to Cal. "She makes her own granola bars."

"I heard, kid."

CAL FOLLOWED BEHIND Jenna and Asher, watching as they discussed groceries and as his cart filled with food he wasn't sure he'd ever bought in his life. They were in the dairy aisle, talking about yogurt, and he wandered over to the pharmacy.

Asher had frowned at Cal's cigarettes this morning, and while the kid didn't say anything, the dislike was clear on his face. Jenna's "They'll kill you" echoed in his head on repeat. His relationship with cigarettes was long and uncomplicated. They were like a best friend in a way, one that was always there and soothed his nerves. And all they asked for in return was a couple years off of his life.

No big deal.

He picked up a brand of nicotine patches hanging above a shelf. He read the label: *To increase your success in quitting, you must be motivated to quit.*

Was he? They sure made him feel good. Brent was so used to his smoking that he hadn't said much when Cal headed out on their balcony to light up. But Asher didn't need to be around it, for the smell to seep into his hair and clothes.

So Cal threw the patch in the cart, and then grabbed the next patch in the plan, and then the next. And he felt like crying a little as he broke up with a best friend.

Good ol' Nico Nicotine. "It was good while it lasted," he mumbled to himself.

By the time they headed to checkout, Cal's only contribution to his own household's food was to add some more bags of frozen vegetables.

He'd tried to throw in some frozen meals, because the microwave was his best friend, but Jenna had shut that down. "Wow, you really are a dude," Jenna said, blinking at him.

"Why do you two keep saying that?" he asked. As they began laughing together, he added, "What the hell am I supposed to be?"

That made them laugh harder. He pushed the cart away, muttering under his breath about how he'd never participate in group grocery shopping again.

Out in the parking lot, he looked around, hoping to help Jenna load her groceries, but he didn't see her car.

So he drove home, Asher talking excitedly in the passenger seat about the steaks Jenna had picked out for the dinner she wouldn't even be at. And Cal wondered, not for the first time, what the hell he was doing.

BEING THE RESPONSIBLE one again was an odd fit. It was like pulling on a leather coat after it had sat in a closet all summer. The fabric was a little stiff on his skin but after a while, it warmed up, and he remembered how comfortable it all was.

Asher seemed like a decent kid. He had a little bit of a stubborn, defiant streak in him, Cal could tell. Stubbornness ran in the family, so that wasn't a surprise.

Every time Cal thought about Asher's father driving drunk with him in the car and his mother not sticking up for the safety of her child, Cal wanted to rage. But he kept a lid on it and instead, sorted the groceries with the kid.

He showed Asher his TV and the video game system he never used. Cal had pitiful games for it, and Asher teased him.

Cal stood out on his back deck, jonesing for a cigarette and scratching at the patch on his arm. He had to figure out what to *do* with Asher now. He didn't know how long he'd be here, and Cal didn't want him sitting around getting bored. Because bored teenagers got into trouble or got themselves hurt, and that wasn't happening on Cal's watch.

He heard a knock at the door through the screen he'd left open. When he walked into the house, Asher stood in the kitchen, bouncing on the balls of his feet, nearly vibrating.

Max was still in town, staying with their dad, so he'd been able to come by with Brent.

It'd been a dick move not to tell them about Asher when he invited them over. It was only fair, though; Cal hadn't gotten a warning, so his brothers wouldn't either.

Cal clapped Asher on the shoulder as he walked by on his way to the door. "Relax. I'm the scariest one, and you've met me already."

He opened up the door, and Brent rushed in ahead of Max. "If this surprise isn't a stripper, I'm going to be super-disappointed."

Max's eyes went wide. "Stripper?"

"For fuck's sake," Cal said. "There's no stripper." He held out his arm in the direction of Asher, who stood in the living room with huge eyes. "There's your brother."

Brent stopped abruptly, so Max slammed into his back. "What the—"

"Brother?" Brent said hollowly, staring at Asher.

"Brother?" Max echoed, peeking out from behind Brent.

"Brother," Asher confirmed in a shaky voice. "Well...half-brother."

Cal stood next to Asher. "Turns out Mom had another kid."

There was no sound. Nothing.

Brent's eyes had gone a little hard, and Max's face was blank. Asher began to tremble, and Cal knew he had to be the example. He was the big brother, and the younger guys had always followed his lead. He didn't always guide them the right way, but he knew he could in this situation.

He slung his arm around Asher's shoulders and faced Brent and Max. "Quit standing there holding your dicks and say hello, numb-nuts."

Nobody moved for a good ten seconds. Then Brent jolted out of his stupor and strode toward Asher. He grabbed Asher's face with both hands and held his gaze. "Fuck me; he's got Max's eyes." He looked over his shoulder. "Look at this—you actually look related to someone now."

"Fuck you! We look related!" Max shot back, but there was no heat in his words. Brent stepped back, and Max held out his hand. "Nice to meet you. I'm Max."

The kid shook it. "I'm Asher."

"Asher, huh?" Brent asked. "Why didn't I get a cool name like that? I always wanted to be, like, Jackson or Gage or something."

"Will you shut up?" Cal said.

Max ignored both of them. "So how did you find us?"

Asher opened his mouth and then looked up at Cal, clearly wanting him to make the explanations. He didn't want to put the kid through it again, so Cal explained, in as few words as possible, that Asher had an asshole father, and he was staying at Cal's temporarily.

Brent's face was red. "And your mom didn't do anything about it? What the fuck is wrong with that woman?"

Max bit his lip, his eyes sad. "That's horrible, Ash. I'm sorry. Damn, Dad's a total dick, but he's never done something like that."

Cal didn't miss the nickname, and he also didn't miss the way the tenseness had begun to leave Asher's body.

"I didn't know what to do," Asher said quietly. "Mom talked about you guys sometimes. I always wanted to meet you, but she put me off every year. I assumed I wouldn't be able to see you until I could drive or until I turned eighteen or something."

"Christ," Brent muttered under his breath, turning away to rub his forehead.

It was a cluster-fuck, Cal knew that, but he'd held them all together before when shit hit the fan. He'd do it again. "I have some steaks, so how about I grill 'em up, and we all sit down and eat together, yeah?"

Max nodded, his eyes on Asher. Max was a teacher now, so Cal thought he'd be one of the best to know how to deal with a teenager. "Ash is complaining about my video game selection, Max. Maybe you two can talk about what's popular now."

Max led Asher away toward the video games, their heads bent together, talking softly. Asher looked at Cal from over his shoulder, and Cal nodded. Ash smiled and continued to talk with Max.

Cal took a deep breath and walked into the kitchen, Brent hot on his heels.

"What the fuck, fuck, fuck?" Brent chanted under his breath. "Dad is going to lose his ever-loving mind."

Cal opened the refrigerator and grabbed the package of steaks. He dropped it on the counter and began to unwrap them. "I know."

"Like, in the looney bin after a heart-attack-slash-stroke kind of thing."

With the steaks on a plate, Cal grated pepper over the top of them. "I know."

"Like, lose-the-function-of-one-side-of-his-body kind of stroke."

Now that the steaks were seasoned, Cal grabbed a pair of tongs and walked out to his deck.

Brent, of course, followed. "So he came here? Not a friend's house?"

Cal had already preheated the grill, so he opened up the lid and began tossing the steaks on. "They just moved from California. He said he doesn't know anyone."

"How'd he get here?"

"Bus."

"Damn," Brent said, leaning on the railing with his arms crossed over his chest. "That's committed." He furrowed his brow as Cal lowered the lid of the grill, the steaks sizzling inside. "And not safe, man. He's sixteen?"

"Yup."

"Not safe at all to travel by bus by himself. You wouldn't even let me ride in Sam's truck until he'd been driving two years, remember?"

Sam had been a friend of Brent's in high school. "Yeah, I remember. Damn kid was a maniac. And I was right too. He totaled that truck after six months and broke his arm."

Brent chewed his lip. "Yeah, you were right."

"And I know it wasn't safe for him to the ride the bus alone, but can't do anything about it now. He's here, and I'll make sure he's okay."

Cal made to walk past Brent, but his brother shot out his arm and grabbed his bicep. "Hey."

Cal kept his eyes on the window of the back door, looking at Max and Asher sitting on the couch together inside.

"If anyone can take care of that kid, it's you," Brent said quietly. There was no joke behind his words. No smirk. "You dragged Max and me out of the muck, and you can do it with Asher."

Cal closed his eyes and let Brent's words sink in. He didn't want them to. But his tone slipped in all his cracks and plunged right into Cal's heart.

"I know that Max and I don't tell you enough that we appreciate what you did. But we do. And Asher is going to appreciate it too."

Cal didn't want that to make his heart beat faster, to make his skin warm. He wanted to resent Brent and Max. And then Asher, for putting him through this again. But he couldn't resent them. Because he'd do it all over again in a heartbeat. Seeing Max happy and hearing Brent's awful singing and bad jokes always reminded him that every sacrifice was worth it.

He'd been so focused on how people took from him that he hadn't realized all they'd given to him.

He didn't trust himself to speak, so he nodded. And Brent's hand dropped away.

Cal walked into the house. His head was spinning, his stomach rolling. He walked toward the door to his garage to be alone to smoke a cigarette, but Max's voice brought him to stop.

"Cal, I was just telling Asher about the Halloween that Brent and I dressed up as the Teenage Mutant Ninja Turtles. Remember that?"

Cal swallowed thickly and nodded as he heard Brent walk in from outside behind him.

"Oh, shit," Brent said. "I'd forgotten about that." He turned to Asher. "Max and I were into them. Dad gave us some money for costumes, but it was too late to find one. So Cal made them."

Asher's eyes went round. "You made them?"

They weren't a masterpiece or anything. He'd been twelve and had to buy that iron-on fabric in different colors and sewed what he could a little crudely. Army-green sweat suits did the trick. When he was done, he had three costumes. He shrugged. "They looked pretty homemade."

Max waved his hand. "Whatever. So Cal ended up getting sick, like the flu or something. And Brent and I felt bad, so at every house, we got extra candy and picked out the ones that Cal would like. He's got a thing for sweet-and-sour stuff."

Cal did remember that, now that Max brought it up. As soon as he was better, he'd had a whole pillowcase full of treats that they'd gathered for him.

Asher blinked. "Man, I always wanted brothers. Growing up as the only kid sucks."

Brent shrugged. "Sometimes we pissed each other off a whole hell of a lot. When it got ugly, it got real ugly. But when it was good, it made up for all of that."

Cal couldn't breathe. The tightness in his chest, the pounding of his heart. Was he having a fucking heart attack? Maybe he needed to lay off the takeout. And the smokes. He excused himself and made his way to the bathroom on stiff legs.

In the bathroom, he sat heavily on the toilet and put his head between his legs, clasping his hands on the back of his neck.

Deep breath.

In. And out.

One simple conversation with his brothers, and his whole world tilted.

All this time, he'd been like some fucking accountant, making checkmarks in columns—*I did this for Brent. What did he do for me?*

Jenna had tried to tell him all of this, hadn't she? That relationships could be balanced. It wasn't like he'd had any good examples. His parents' marriage had always been fucked up. So everything he knew, he'd learned…well, he'd learned from Jenna. She'd been the first person outside of family to love him.

He pulled his head up and dropped his hands onto his thighs. The sounds of brothers talking in the living room filtered through the closed door. Max's deep voice and Brent's loud tone and Asher's laughter. It sounded good to have his house full, to be surrounded by family.

It was romantic to say that love was enough, that love was giving without expecting anything in return. But in real life, with the stress of a job and money and putting food on the table, a little give-and-take was needed for the long haul.

He had to get himself under control. He tried to find the Cal he'd relied on for the past ten years, the one who didn't let his emotions guide his actions. But that was out of focus now, surrounded by…feelings. *Fucking feelings.* A pull toward Jenna and a protectiveness over Asher.

If he had any sense, he'd put Asher on a bus back to his parents. He could call Jill and smack some sense in to her. But what if that didn't work, and Asher was still unsafe? Cal couldn't live with that.

He blew out a breath. He'd stock up on nicotine patches and beer, and he'd get through this, taking care of his younger brother. And he'd do his damnedest to avoid Jenna until she stayed back in that little box he'd placed all the MacMillans in long ago. She had to stay there, because if not, he might just go insane.

Chapter Sixteen

"So, Cal's GIRLFRIEND is nice," Asher said, cutting into his steak.

Cal groaned as utensils clattered on a plate, and Brent's head shot up, those slate eyes burrowing into Cal. "Girlfriend?"

Asher looked confused. "Yeah, Jenna—"

"She's not my girlfriend," Cal cut him off. What she actually was, he didn't know. But girlfriend? Definitely not. She was something else. Another category that he was trying to forget about.

Asher frowned. "I know she said she was just a friend, but you both throw off more-than-friend vibes. And then you guys kinda argued over the brownie mix in a weird way."

Cal glared at him. "You are this close to being put back on a bus to Virginia."

Asher winced and then lowered his eyes to his plate.

Cal softened his words by nudging the kid with his foot and shooting him a grin, which Asher returned.

"Whoa." Brent's hands were waving in the air. He was a dog with a bone now. "Jenna was here? Yesterday?"

Cal drained his beer. It had been halfway full.

"I like Jenna," Max said conversationally.

"Spit it out, Cal," Brent said.

"Can we not discuss this in front of the kid?"

"Hey, I'm sixteen! I don't like girls anyway."

Max's fork fell on the floor. "What?"

Asher's face paled somewhat, but he turned to his brother. "I'm…gay."

The table was silent for a minute. Cal raised his eyebrows. He hadn't seen that one coming.

Brent pointed his finger at Asher. "Nice diversion with the gay news, but I'm way more interested in why Jenna was here."

Cal was done with this. "We spent the night together. She was here when Asher showed up, and that's the end of the discussion."

Asher picked at his napkin. "She was really nice to me. Got my room all set up, and then we ran into her at the grocery store. She made sure we got food that was healthy and easy to make because Cal isn't so good at that."

She'd also talked to Asher respectfully, like he was an adult. The kid was clearly craving some sort of parental unit, because he'd walked around the grocery store gazing adoringly at Jenna as she laughed with him and touched his forearm affectionately.

Brent was still looking at Cal through narrow eyes. "Yeah, she's pretty damn amazing, isn't she, Cal?"

"Brent—"

"You can't threaten to put me on a bus, so shut up."

"Look, it was one night, and that was it. Done."

Asher's head shot up, his face pale. "What?"

Cal frowned. "Look, kid, I don't have time to get into it, but Jenna and I have…history. A lot of it. But that's all it is. History. Past. Not present." *Not future either.* Maybe if he told himself that enough times, he'd actually believe it.

Asher looked heartbroken. "B-but I like her. I was hoping we could do something to thank her for today."

Well, shit. "Uh—"

Brent placed his chin in his hand. "I saw a box of brownies in your cabinet. Are they for something? Because if not, you should make those. And then take them over there and thank her in person. Women love that shit."

Those fucking brownies. Cal kicked Brent's shin, and his brother didn't even flinch but instead grinned at him.

Asher nodded eagerly. "Yeah, let's make her those brownies! Girls like brownies, right?"

"Of course," said Brent, still grinning.

"Everyone likes brownies," Max added.

Cal worked on breathing deeply so he didn't explode. Because this avoiding-Jenna plan? Well, he'd had it for about a half hour before it reached its first roadblock.

Fucking feelings.

"So what are you gonna do while you're here, Asher?" Brent asked. "You want to help out at the shop?"

Asher perked up, like a puppy. "Wait, could I? For real?"

"I'm not sure if cars are really your thing, but—"

"Do you work on bikes too?" he asked.

Cal wanted this entire dinner to end, because none of these conversations were happy places for him. "Not right now, kid, but I'd like to."

Asher's face fell a little. "Oh, I wasn't sure because I saw your bike, so I thought…" He shook himself and focused on Cal. "Would you give me a ride on it?"

Cal frowned. The kid would need a better helmet, and the thought of putting him on the back of the bike made Cal anxious. "How's this: you help out at the shop for a little bit, couple of weeks, and then I'll see about getting you a ride on the bike."

Asher made a fist pump. "Yessss."

"Hey, kid?" Brent said.

"Yeah?"

He grinned. "You start tomorrow."

JENNA SIPPED HER wine and tried to focus on the text of her e-reader. It was a good part too. The hero was groveling. And he needed to grovel after the shit he pulled. The heroine was making him work for it and normally, this was the part Jenna loved.

But it was hard to concentrate when her mind kept drifting to Cal. She wanted to forget about him, toss the thought of him out with her trash, but that wasn't possible. It was worse now, since he'd shown a little bit of the Cal she once knew. This Cal was harder, more cynical, and a hell of a lot more stubborn.

But he'd made it clear that he wanted to be alone. He didn't want a relationship, not with her, not with anyone.

And she had dignity. She'd been this close to begging, but she'd been saved by the doorbell, thank God. She wasn't going to chase Cal and try to convince him that she was worth it. It wasn't a matter of his not being able to see a future with her; it was that he didn't want to, she thought. And if he didn't *want* to, there was no changing that.

He was happy on his little island all by himself.

And so there'd he stay.

Which made her as miserable as it made him.

There was a knock at the door, and Jenna checked the clock. It was almost nine at night. She stood up, straightening her cotton shorts and tank top.

She glanced through the peephole of her front door and blinked. But nope, her vision was correct. Cal and Asher stood on her front porch, the light by her door illuminating their faces in the dark. Cal was staring right at the peephole, just like he'd done Friday night.

Asher held a foil-covered dish.

She wished she could read body posture better, but the peephole didn't allow for that. So she took a deep breath and opened the door.

Immediately, she smelled brownies.

Those damn brownies.

Asher held the dish higher, beaming ear-to-ear. "Hi, Jenna. I wanted to say thank you for today, so I made you brownies."

She smiled at him. "That's so sweet of you. Good thing you had those brownies on hand, huh?" She winked at

Asher, who laughed. Cal said nothing, his face frustratingly blank.

She stepped back. "Well, why don't you come inside. I bet you'd like some too, right?"

Asher's cheeks reddened. "Yeah, sure, if that's okay with you."

She ushered him to walk past her, and she pointed down her hallway. "Go right ahead through to the kitchen."

Asher trotted off, and she turned to Cal, who hadn't moved. She leaned against the door. "You want some brownies too?"

He stepped inside, brushing his boots on the mat inside her door. Another step and he was in front of her, the door shut behind him.

It'd been less than twenty-four hours since they'd woken up in the same bed, since he'd been *inside* of her. Her mind wanted to forget, but her body sure as hell didn't. Despite all the things they'd said to each other today, all the times he'd said he didn't want a future with her, she couldn't seem to slip her libido the memo.

He hadn't shaved today, and a hint of gray was mixed in the scruff on his jaw. Those piercing eyes were on her, studying her. "Hey," he finally said, his deep voice soft.

"Hi," she answered.

Cal wore jeans and a T-shirt, his uniform, but hell, no one wore it better than him. His gaze shifted down the hall and then back to her. "Asher, uh, he likes you a lot."

"I like him too."

Cal ran his tongue over his teeth. "I realize that staying away from each other would be ideal, but, uh, I don't know how that will fly with the kid. He's got a shitty mom and you're...well, you're just about the opposite of shitty."

"Such a flowery compliment."

Cal's lips tilted into a smile, and he scratched his head, a blush staining his cheeks. "Yeah, you know me. Poet."

"So you trying to tell me that you'll suffer through my presence to keep Asher happy?" She smiled, to take the sting out of the words.

"Should I pour some milk for us?" Asher called from the kitchen.

"Yep. Be there in a minute!" Cal yelled back.

"Cal—"

He stepped closer, right into her space. His chest brushed hers, the heat from his body seeping in to her skin. She sucked in a breath as those intense eyes locked on hers. "It's not easy to be around you. I'll be honest about that. Because you remind me of all the things I used to want. So yeah, it's hard to look at you and not see everything I failed at. But that's on me. That's not your fault. I'm not sorry this weekend happened, but I am sorry if I hurt you. Believe me, that's the last thing I want to do."

Each sentence, each word, each syllable was a wave crashing against her. She struggled to breathe as the meaning behind what he was saying soaked her to the bone.

He wasn't done. "And now, I got that kid out there who needs me, so that's what I'm focusing on. You're a part of what makes him happy, so I'm hoping you can stand being around me because of what it means to him."

That was a lot of words for Cal. A lot of words and a lot of honesty. Really, did she expect any less? Cal wanted to pretend he had a hardened heart, but she didn't believe that. Not one bit. Cal was tapped out? No more energy for someone else? That was all bullshit. The kid in the kitchen who'd stolen their hearts in one day proved otherwise.

She knew this was dangerous to slip into this surrogate parenting role for Asher. But how could she say no? "I'll do anything to help Asher. And you."

Cal nodded. He ducked his head and stepped back, hands on his hips.

"You guys coming?" Asher called.

"Yeah, coming now!" Cal called. He glanced at her, his lips shifting, and then he lunged forward, pressed a kiss to her forehead, and took off down the hallway. She was left staring at his back before she gathered herself together to join the guys in the kitchen.

Asher was standing over a plate of brownie crumbs. "I started without you guys. Hope that's okay. They smelled really good."

Jenna grabbed a plate and cut out a huge square of brownie. She needed chocolate. Like, yesterday. "So are you settling in okay?"

"I met my brothers!" This kid had the biggest eyes, and when he widened them, they took up his whole face.

"Ah, and how are Max and Brent?"

"They were really nice. And we had steaks and played video games. And they told me stories about how they grew up. And then Cal and I made you brownies to say thank you." Asher pointed to the dish proudly.

Cal shoved a brownie in his mouth and then leaned against the counter, his eyes on Jenna. She wished he'd look away, at Asher, anything but stare at her with those damn eyes.

Asher spun his half-full glass of milk. "I wonder if my mom will call again. To ask me to come back."

Jenna lifted her gaze to Cal, whose jaw had hardened. He looked away, and a muscle in his cheek ticked. "We'll stay in touch with her and make sure when you do go back, you feel safe."

The look of hero worship on Asher's face as he gazed at Cal made Jenna's chest ache.

This was dangerous, she knew, but in that moment, any other option seemed wrong. Asher wanted to feel safe and cared for, and the kid probably wanted a damn friend too. She could make excuses, tell them she was busy at work—which wasn't a lie—but why crush the kid? He was already attached.

She met Cal's gaze again over Asher's bent head. He blinked once, those long dark lashes fanning his cheeks. Damn him, because no matter how much she knew that they didn't have a future, that wouldn't keep her from thinking all the dirty thoughts about him that she wanted, now that she had a vivid memory of what it was like to be with him. The man Cal, not the boy.

His eyes darkened a little, like he could read her thoughts.

She shoved another brownie in her mouth and turned away.

Chapter Seventeen

CAL PARKED HIS truck behind the garage on Monday morning and turned to look at Ash. The kid was staring out of the window at the Payton and Sons building.

"Kid."

Asher turned to him, biting his lip.

"My dad's name is Jack. And he's…a little scary, okay? He's pretty much a miserable bastard, but he means well. Kind of."

Asher looked even more uncertain now. Cal sighed. "Just do what I say and don't expect any warm fuzzies from the guy, all right? He barely tolerates us, and we're his kids." Cal opened up the door of the truck.

"Is he gonna hate me?" Asher's voice was weak.

Cal froze on his way out of the truck. "What?"

"Is he gonna"—Asher fidgeted with his hands in his lap—"resent me or something?"

Cal blew out a breath. "Nah, kid, he's not going to hate you or resent you. But you're going to remind him of his ex-wife, and that's not going to go well. It's not about you, though. You just gotta remember that, okay? Don't take it personal."

Asher looked a little more confident at that. "Okay."

"All right, then. Let's head in."

Cal walked ahead of Asher. The shop hadn't opened for business yet, but Brent and Jack were inside, getting the place set up.

Last night, Brent had called Jack to give him a heads-up. Cal had figured that was the best way to handle the situation. Of course, Jack had only grunted into the phone at the news and hung up on Brent. So…there was that. But at least they weren't springing this Max-like kid on their father.

Cal joked about his dad dying, but he didn't actually want it to happen.

He looked over his shoulder. Asher walked slowly, his head down, eyes on his bright green Converses. The kid hadn't packed many clothes, but he still looked put together as hell, with his hair doing that flip thing. His father might flip more at the kid's clothes than his genes.

Brent greeted them at the door and ruffled Asher's hair. The kid looked a little miffed but seemed to appreciate the supportive gesture for what it was.

Cal heard his father's boots first and looked up. Jack rounded a car and stood in front of Asher, taking him in.

To Asher's credit, the kid didn't back down. He stood firm and waited silently.

Finally, Cal's dad stuck out his big, callused hand. "I'm Jack."

Asher shook it. "Asher."

Jack grunted, squinting his eyes. There was silence for a full thirty seconds before he talked again. "Don't get in the way around here. I don't want you getting hurt, because then my insurance rates will go up." And then he turned around and walked away.

Brent placed his hands on his hips and pulled down his lips, tilting his head. "Huh. That was actually decent for Jack."

"Agreed," Cal said.

Asher looked at them like they were crazy.

Cal barked a laugh and clapped him in the back. "Let me show you around."

After the short tour, they walked out to the garage to get back to work when Gabe's voice boomed from the parking lot. "How ya doin', guys?"

Gabe Acosta was all of five foot six, Puerto Rican, and loud as hell. Cal liked him because although he could be a little shit sometimes, he did his job and was generally fun to be around. He had a kid trailing behind him as he stepped into the garage. Well, a teenager, Cal would guess, probably around Asher's age.

"This is my brother, Julian. He goes to Tory High School."

Gabe and Brent talked about the new construction to the high school, but Cal was focused on the two teenagers. Julian and Asher had locked gazes, and neither was looking away. Like a game of chicken, but Cal thought there was something going on that was more than a simple teenage game. He clapped Asher on the back, who stumbled a little. "This is Asher. Long story, but he's our half-brother. He's in high school too. He'll be helping us out here for a little while."

"Cool!" Gabe said, paging through the schedule, completely oblivious to his brother's huge blue eyes locked on Asher. "I was gonna have Julian hang around a little because he was interested in learning more about the shop."

Asher made a small sound in his throat.

Cal wasn't sure if this was a good idea to have these two teenagers in close proximity or a completely horrible one.

Asher stepped forward and held out his hand to the other teenager. "Hey."

Julian's eyes got even bigger. "Hi."

Asher motioned to the back room. "You wanna soda or something?"

Cal shoved him a little. "Yeah, that's a great idea. You two go get something to drink. And maybe clean up back there too. Sweep or something."

The kids walked back together, leaving more distance than necessary between them. When Cal took his eyes off their retreating backs, he met Brent's gaze.

Brent raised his eyebrows. Then he waggled them.

Cal snorted.

"What's so funny?" Gabe asked.

"Your mom," Brent retorted.

Gabe rolled his eyes. "You're an idiot." He turned to Cal. "Hey, uh, you got a minute?"

Cal glanced around. Their father was in the far bay, bent over the hood of an SUV, and Brent had gone into the office. "Yeah, sure. What's up?"

"Well, I just bought a '95 Harley from a friend of mine. I need to get it checked out. I think it's all right, but it doesn't ride real smooth. Anyway, you got time?"

Cal wished he had time to work on it right now. "Can you give me a week or two? Asher's with me now, so that's keeping me kind of busy. Are you in a hurry?"

Gabe waved his hand. "Nah, man, that's cool. Whenever. Just let me know, and I'll bring it over."

"Wish I could work on it here in the shop, but…" He gestured toward Jack.

Gabe grimaced. "There's no one in town that I trust other than you, so it sucks like hell that Jack won't think about expanding."

Cal shrugged. "I'm working on it. Anyway, I'll let you know."

Julian and Asher walked out of the back room, closer together this time, shoulders brushing.

Asher's cell phone was in his hand, and he slipped it back into his pants.

"So it's cool if I bring Julian around?" Gabe asked.

"Yeah, no problem," Cal said. "We can always use some help."

When Gabe and Julian left a half hour later, Cal caught Asher peering around the opening of the garage, watching their truck drive away.

Chapter Eighteen

JENNA GLANCED AT the container on the passenger seat of her car and tightened her grip on the steering wheel.

She'd put this off all week, but it was Saturday; no more excuses. She'd promised Asher granola bars, and so she must deliver granola bars. He'd called her earlier in the week to chat, and she said she'd swing by over the weekend.

How was it possible to both dread and crave something at the same time? She didn't know, but it certainly was possible, because there was no other way to describe the churning of her gut, sweaty palms, and lightheadedness at the thought of seeing Cal again.

During the workday this past week, she'd been okay because her brain was busy. But once she got home, all bets were off. She wondered what Cal and Asher were eating for dinner; she wondered how they were getting along. This was territory Cal had been avoiding; it was the reason they didn't have a future. Yet he'd taken the kid in despite his vow of solitude.

When Jenna lay alone in bed, she remembered the heat of Cal's body, the rasp of his callused palms on her skin, the sound of his whispered *Sunshine* in her ear. It'd been one freaking night, and he'd ruined her. Oh hell, who was she kidding? He'd ruined her long ago. She'd never been fixed.

She pulled into Cal's driveway, and with one look at what was going on in said driveway, she almost turned back around.

Cal must have heard her car coming, because he stood with one arm braced on the side of his parked truck, the other on his hip. He wore a pair of jeans and boots, and that was it. That was *freaking* it. Sweat glistened on his bare chest, his jaw covered in a five-o'clock shadow, his posture relaxed. Jenna was about two seconds away from throwing her car in reverse and peeling rubber to get as far away from the six feet of male temptation as she could.

Cal had never been vain. He wore his hair short so he didn't have to mess with it. If he had stubble, it was because he didn't feel like shaving. And his muscles were from labor. He wore it all with an unassuming confidence that was ridiculously sexy.

The damn man.

If the single ladies in town knew he was out here in the middle of nowhere, working on his truck, shirtless, he'd be able to sell the real estate around his house for millions.

He watched her with those light eyes as she parked behind his truck and stepped out of her car. She shut the door and leaned against it, crossing her arms over her chest. She wore a simple cotton sundress and sandals, and as his gaze dipped down her body and back up, she wished she'd worn more clothes. Like a parka. Anything to prevent seeing that spark of heat that was now in his eyes.

He didn't talk, so finally she straightened and took a step toward him. She gestured toward her car, where the container of granola sat on the passenger seat. "I brought some granola bars for Asher, like I promised."

His gaze flicked to her car and then back to her. "Appreciate that."

She cocked her head. "Is he here?"

He shoved his hands in his pockets, so the muscles in his biceps and forearms flexed. "Nah, he's with a friend."

"A friend? Here? Wow, he moved fast."

Cal chuckled and ran a hand through his hair. "You know the kid I mentioned? Who works for us?"

"Yeah."

"His name is Gabe, and he's got a younger brother, Julian. He and Asher met at the garage and seemed to…uh…hit it off, I guess."

"Well, that's really great. Asher doing okay, then?"

"He's getting settled. He said he likes it here, that it's quiet. He and Brent get along real well. I guess because Brent's still basically a fifteen-year-old kid."

Jenna smiled. "Yeah, I guess he is."

Cal looked away, squinting into the sun. Jenna stared down at her painted toenails. Her car's engine dinged. A bird chirped. How much more awkward could this be?

Just give him the damn granola and leave, Jenna, she told herself. But instead, she stood there, unable to get her feet to move. Cal didn't seem eager to do it either. She wondered how long they could stand five feet from each other without making eye contact.

She glanced up, noting the hood of his truck was up. "Something wrong with it?"

"Huh?" He finally met her gaze, brows drawn in.

She gestured to his truck's hood, and he glanced behind his shoulder before turning back to her. "Ah, no, nothing's wrong. I don't drive it much in the summer. Usually ride my bike. But with Asher...I wanted to make sure everything was okay with it, now that I know he'll be in it with me."

Did he even listen to himself speak? He was spending his Saturday off from his job of fixing vehicles *to fix his own vehicle* to ensure Asher rode in something safe. Her throat tightened and her eyes stung. God, if only Cal could see that he had so much to give. If only he wanted to. If only he was willing to see how much he was getting back.

But he didn't, and the sooner she got that through her thick skull, the better they'd all be.

She turned around. "I'll just get the granola..."

A truck turned down Cal's driveway, rumbling on the stones. Three people sat inside, a man and two teenagers. The driver waved at Cal through the windshield, and then the passenger door opened. Asher hopped down, leaned back inside to say something, and then shut the door behind him.

The truck made a sloppy three-point turn and then headed back the way it came. Asher walked toward Jenna, his smile bright. He wore a pair of red Converse, shorts, and a T-shirt. "Hey, Jenna!"

"Hey, buddy, I finally got around to bringing you the granola bars."

"Sweet! Thanks!"

Jenna reached inside her car and handed the container to Asher, who looked at them eagerly. "Check it out, Cal."

She turned to look at Cal, but his eyes weren't on her or the granola; they were zeroed in on Asher, and he didn't look happy. "What's that on your neck?"

Asher's head shot up, his color draining, and he clapped his hand around his throat. "What?"

Cal took a step forward, his posture stiff, head tilted. "What's that on your neck?"

Asher's eyes darted to Jenna, but she was confused. "Cal, what—"

"Is that a hickey?"

Asher's mouth dropped open. "Cal—"

"You said you were going over there to play soccer with Julian and his friends." Cal's voice was getting louder. "So how the hell did you get a hickey?"

Jenna began to sweat. So apparently this day could get more awkward. Really, the possibilities were endless with Cal around. "Cal, how about you guys go inside—"

He turned to her. "Do you not see that on his neck?"

She squared her shoulders. "Actually, no, I didn't notice, but I think confronting him in the driveway might be a little much."

The front door to the house slammed, and Jenna and Cal both turned to look at it. While they'd been arguing with each other, Asher had taken the granola and run into the house.

Jenna sighed. "Cal, for God's sake…"

He speared his fingers in his hair and then ran his hands down his face. "Shit."

"Are you sure it's a hickey? If he was playing soccer, then maybe—"

"Asher's gay, Jenna."

She clamped her jaw shut and blinked. She turned around, eyeing the dust that was still settling from the truck that had just left. Then she turned back to Cal. "Okay, I think I'm missing something."

Cal pointed in the direction that the truck had left. "I'm pretty sure Julian is too. He and Asher…I don't know, there's something there. And that's fine; they're friends. Whatever. But he's known him for a week, and he comes home with a hickey?"

"I get that you're concerned, but they're teenage boys. I mean, think about what we did when we were teenagers."

Cal's face turned white. "Oh, shit."

Jenna just barely grabbed his arm and prevented him from stomping into the house. "Cal, calm down." He tugged in her grip but not as hard as he could. She held on, and while the tension remained in his body, he at least wasn't currently banging and yelling on Asher's door. "Stop. Please talk to me."

He looked at her, eyes full of concern. "They can't get pregnant, so I guess that's a good thing. But there's…other stuff, right? He needs to be safe. And I've only known

Julian for a week. I don't know what kind of kid he is or if he'll hurt Asher, and—"

"Cal—"

"Isn't there a PFLAP thing I can join? I need to Google that."

"Pretty sure you mean PFLAG—"

"And if he breathes one word about River's Edge, I'm going to lose my fucking mind—"

"Cal, *shut up!*"

He shut up, and Jenna blew out a breath, tired of bracing herself to keep Cal from running into the house. She didn't know anything more about this than Cal did. Hell, when they were teenagers, they couldn't wait to get alone. And they'd been so in love, so quickly, it hadn't taken long before Cal was buying the value pack of condoms to keep in his truck.

God, those were the days.

Jenna shook her head. "Can I talk to him? Please?"

Cal looked at her, biting his lip.

"Do you trust me?" she asked softly.

Cal nodded. When she let go of his arm, he stayed standing.

"Why don't you smoke a cigarette and calm down?" she said over her shoulder.

"I quit," he grumbled.

She stumbled and held her arms out for balance. Slowly, she turned around. "What did you say?"

He pointed to a flesh-colored patch on his arm she hadn't noticed earlier. "I'm doing this to help me quit. Got 'em at the grocery store the other day."

He quit. *Quit.* He'd smoked since he was sixteen. "Are you serious?"

"Unfortunately."

"Why did you quit now?"

He shrugged and kicked a stone with the toe of his boot. "Felt like it was time."

She didn't know what else to say. She settled on, "Well, I'm glad," and then continued walking into the house to talk to Asher.

So maybe he'd overreacted.

Just a little.

As Cal stood in his driveway, wishing he had a damn cigarette, he tried to parcel it out in his head. He hadn't been that uptight with his brothers. Was it because Asher was gay?

But that didn't seem right either. It had nothing to do with Asher's being a guy or being gay or anything, really. It had to do with Cal now realizing how much that first love mattered. How much it could hurt when it all went downhill.

And maybe he wanted to save Asher the heartache. He wanted to keep him in this house where nothing could make him feel unsafe or unloved.

Jenna had been inside for fifteen minutes. Cal finished with his truck, and so he figured it was time to venture into the house. He took a deep breath and walked inside, swiping his T-shirt from the bed of his truck and pulling it over his head. Best not to face whatever was inside half-naked.

When he opened the front door, voices drifted in from the kitchen. He made his way toward it and then stopped in the doorway, eyes on Jenna and Asher. They sat at the kitchen table, eating bowls of cereal. Both looked up when he walked in. Jenna looked calm, comfortable, while Asher was clearly anxious, watching Cal.

Cal licked his lips. "Hey, kid."

Asher blinked. "Hi."

Cal clenched his jaw and then figured he should get this out of the way. "Sorry, uh, about that. For how I reacted."

Asher's smile was tentative. "It's okay."

"Nah, it's really not. I acted like an asshole, and I'm sorry."

"You weren't an asshole—"

"I yelled—"

"At least you care."

That shut Cal up. Fast. He swallowed around the lump in his throat. And why were his eyes hot all of a sudden? He rubbed them with his thumb and forefinger. He had to remember who had raised Asher, what the kid was used to. He took a deep breath and glanced at Jenna. Her head was bent, swirling her spoon in the milk left in her bowl. Cal turned to Asher. "I do care."

"I know."

"Do you want to talk about the…" Cal gestured toward his own neck, all the while thinking to himself, *Please say no, please say no.*

Asher ducked his head. "I mean, if you want, but I talked to Jenna about it."

Thank fuck for Jenna. Thank fuck. "So…"

"So I'm okay…um…not talking about it again. Right now."

The awkwardness. Cal needed a shower. "Okay, that's fine. But I'm here if you change your mind."

Asher smiled. "Thanks a lot." His phone rang, the corresponding vibration rattling the table. His cheeks colored when he glanced at the display. "I…um…this is Julian."

Cal waved him on, and Asher hopped up, answering the phone with an excited hello as he raced up the stairs.

Cal picked up Asher's bowl and placed it in the dishwasher. When he turned around, Jenna was watching him.

He leaned against the counter and crossed his ankles. "Thanks for talking to him."

"I didn't mind. He's just lonely. He left his friends when his parents moved, and then he came here. And he found a cute guy who's into him. I think…a hickey isn't such a big deal. And that's all it was, Cal."

He kept his eyes on his boots. "I know. I started thinking about all it leads to. More worried about his heart than his body, I guess."

A chair scraped. Footsteps. Jenna's shadow fell in front of him. "What do you mean?"

He couldn't look at her, not while he said this. "I worry about him getting attached too soon and too…" He scrambled for the word, wishing he'd just kept his mouth shut. "Permanently."

She stepped closer now, enough that he could smell the sun on her skin. "Like us?"

He squeezed his eyes shut. "Like us."

She didn't speak for a long time, so long that he thought she might have left. But then her voice came softly. "You think we're attached permanently?"

He raised his head then, even though it took monumental effort. "If we aren't, then it shouldn't be this hard to be around you, knowing I can't have you."

Her lips parted, and a small sound escaped. "That was your decision not to have me, Cal. I was willing to give this a shot. To try."

This time, when he closed his eyes, he kept them closed. And he didn't open them until he heard his front door open and close. Until he heard Jenna start her car and back out of his driveway.

And even then, when he opened his eyes, he didn't really see anything. All his reasons for keeping Jenna away were crumbling. And all the reasons for keeping her remained, like an unshakeable foundation.

For the first time, Cal wasn't sure which he preferred.

Chapter Nineteen

Jenna slipped her feet out of her heels under the table, groaning as the pressure eased from her cramped toes.

Delilah raised her eyebrows at her from the other side of the table. "You going to take your bra off in here too? I mean, make yourself at home."

Jenna balled up a napkin and tossed it at her. "Shut it. I had a long day. You?"

"Long, but I don't feel the need to undress in the restaurant."

The waiter's appearance saved Jenna from having to think of a witty comeback. He took their drink orders, and Jenna flipped open the menu. Delilah had picked her up after work for a dinner date, which was a deviation of Jenna's regular routine of somehow finding her way to Cal's house every night this week.

Not that she intended to go there, but Asher would call her, or he and Cal would stop by her place on their way running errands. Asher would talk excitedly while Cal maintained a stoic expression.

Well, he tried to be stoic, but Jenna caught his eyes lingering on her when he didn't think she was looking. He wasn't as sneaky as he thought. The whole thing messed with her head because in her heart, there was still hope—just a little bit of hope—that this Cal would take a chance and give them a try.

Stupid hope.

"So let me get this straight," Delilah said after they ordered their food. Today, Delilah wore her hair in a tight bun, her eyeliner in a perfect wingtip, and her lips rosy red. "The Paytons have a half-brother they never knew about?"

"That's pretty much it."

Delilah whistled. "That's going to go around the Tory rumor mill faster than when Cindy Edgar slept with those twin professional football players."

"How is Cindy?" Jenna asked.

Delilah shrugged. "Good, I guess. She's married now to some insurance agent in town and has two kids. She came in recently and bought a dress for their anniversary."

"Good for Cindy."

"So, the kid?"

Jenna took a sip of her wine. "Asher's a good kid. Sweet. Really cute. He dropped his phone in the toilet the other day, and you should have seen his face when I told him to shove it in rice. It worked, though. Phone is functional now."

Delilah was staring at her.

"What?"

"Nothing," Delilah kept her expression blank, but Jenna wasn't buying it. "Go on. Tell me more about him," Delilah prodded.

"Um, he's gay and has a crush on Gabe's little brother. Do you know Gabe? Works at the garage?"

Delilah nodded and twirled her wine glass.

"Okay, so Asher came home with a hickey, and there was a whole thing with Cal losing his mind over it, but it's all right now. I talked to Asher, and Cal apologized, so that's that."

Delilah sat silently.

"Oh, come on, Delilah. What?"

Her friend shrugged. "I just think it's hilarious that you said Cal wants to avoid the whole relationship and family thing, yet he's doing exactly that with you and his brother without getting the benefit of you in his bed."

Jenna opened her mouth, then closed it, and then opened it again. "But this is temporary. It's not the same thing."

Delilah cocked her head. "I guess it's not, but if the idea of a family makes him break out in hives, then he sure has a funny way of showing it. Since he's pretty much shacking up with you."

"We're not shacking up. I don't sleep there."

"Which is my point. If he'd quit acting like a brick wall, he'd at least get laid out of it."

Jenna narrowed her eyes. "Look, it's not that simple. I don't know if I'm willing to do this either, you know. I thought maybe…but there's so much history there. That breakup nearly broke me. You know that. So thinking of doing all that again…"

Jenna knew her friend understood. Delilah had been on the receiving end of Jenna's phone calls during freshman year in the college. The year Jenna didn't eat. She didn't socialize. She almost dropped out of school and came home because the ache of missing Cal was a constant hunger in her gut.

The only reason she pulled through was because she didn't want to go home with her tail between her legs.

Even though she was ten years older now and much more secure in who she was, it scared the hell out of her to think what Cal could do to her heart again. She took a sip of her wine and shook her head, unwilling to talk about this further.

Delilah, like the good friend she was, sensed that Jenna wanted a change in subject. "So how's work?"

Now that was something Jenna did want to talk about. "Oh, I'm glad you asked. I'm getting a company party set up—kind of an employee appreciation thing—and we're going to have a raffle for prizes for charity. I wanted to know if you'd donate a gift card or something from your store."

"Of course! I can put a little gift basket together, maybe with some accessories, along with a gift card."

"That would be perfect."

Delilah leaned back in her seat with her drink. "Other than that, how are things?"

Jenna had an odd pang in her right shoulder, probably from sitting hunched over her keyboard and holding her phone in the crook of her neck. "Good but exhausting.

It's a lot of work to plan an event and set things in motion for publicity. It's a difficult job because a lot of what I do doesn't yield immediate results, you know? I can't point to a specific line item and say, 'I brought in X amount of money.' So, it's hard, because people don't always think we actually do anything. Which is the point, really. If everyone could easily pinpoint all the little things I did to improve the reputation of the company, I probably wouldn't be doing my job." By the time Jenna finished speaking, her back was aching, and now her head hurt.

Delilah's eyes were wide over the rim of her cup. "You need a vacation."

"I've only been there a week and a half," Jenna said with a laugh.

"Then you need a nice bath and some wine and a dirty book."

Jenna smiled. "Now, that I agree with."

"And a man who gives you orgasms."

Jenna scowled.

Delilah smirked.

CAL AND JENNA fell into a routine that next week.

Cal wasn't even sure how it happened, but it did. Jenna was just there, all the time. He thought maybe it should bug him, that he should feel pressured. But all she ever did was spend time with Asher, and instead of it bugging him, it made his chest tight, his eyes hot.

Cal's new normal was Jenna's notes on his kitchen table, letting him know dinner was in the refrigerator. It was finding a shirt of hers mixed in with his laundry. It was her bright smile in his kitchen and her laughter in his living room.

Cal's new normal was feeling the stretch of his own rusty smile on his face, the ragged sound of his laughter in his ears.

The tension around him and Jenna eased a little, but it was always there, this low simmer that sometimes sparked if their skin met or they had to make eye contact.

Asher asked Cal one day if he and Jenna would ever date.

"We tried that already," he'd said in response.

Asher's eyes were big. "You did?"

"Long time ago. About when we were your age. We're just…friends now, okay?" The word *friends* felt odd and bitter in his mouth, but what other word was there for what he and Jenna had?

Asher looked like he was going to ask more questions, but instead, he frowned and turned away.

It was Friday now, and Cal was on his way home from work. When he pulled up in front of his house, Jenna's car was there. He smiled to himself. Because he could imagine what this conversation was going to be like after what he'd done yesterday.

When he walked inside, he heard music from Asher's bedroom and the sound of dishes in his kitchen. He headed toward the latter.

Jenna stood at his counter, sprinkling something over a bowl of popcorn. She wore an oversized T-shirt, and a pair of cutoff shorts peeked out from under it. Her feet were bare, the toes of one foot scratching her other calf.

"Hey."

She looked up, her face clear of makeup, her hair piled on top of her head. "Hey."

He waited, knowing what was next.

"My car?"

There it was. He walked over to the refrigerator and grabbed a beer. He popped the top off and took a gulp. "Yeah, what about it?"

"I can change my own oil, you know."

He smiled. She'd been out with Delilah, and he'd snuck over to her place and checked out her car. He was worried since that asshole who'd sold it to her had screwed her over with the nonexistent spare tire. Cal had left her a note so she'd know it was him messing with her car. "I know that."

"Okay, so then why did you do that?"

He braced a hand on the counter and leaned toward her. "I didn't do it because you can't do it. I did it because you're working your ass off, and then you still come over here and spend time with Asher. Plus, he's in the car with you sometimes. I wanted you both to be safe."

She stared at him with wide eyes, her full lips parted. She didn't say a word, just blinked.

He took another sip of beer and turned to walk out of the kitchen. "I need to shower—"

"Thank you."

Her voice was soft, so soft he barely heard it. He looked at her over his shoulder. "You're welcome."

"That was nice. That you noticed. And that you care."

He chose his words carefully. "I'll always notice when it comes to you, and I'll always care."

When he got out of the shower and threw on a pair of old jeans, he walked into the living room to find Jenna and Asher on the couch.

"We're having a John Hughes night," Jenna said. "You want a vote on which one to watch first?"

Both of them were looking at him expectantly. All he wanted to do was drink a beer and fall asleep watching baseball. "I don't know what movies he's in."

There was a gasp, and Asher clapped his hand over his mouth. Jenna covered his ears with her hands and hissed, "Don't say things like that in front of the children!"

Had they both been at the sauce while he was in the shower? What the—

Jenna's hands dropped from Asher's ears, and he turned to her, clasping her hands. "It's okay, Jenna. It's going to be hard, but I think I can overcome this."

Cal threw up his hands. "For God's sake—"

"John Hughes is not an actor." Jenna's voice wobbled, like she was speaking at his funeral. "He's only one of the greatest filmmakers of all time."

"*Breakfast Club...Ferris Bueller's Day Off...Weird Science!*" Asher's voice cracked at the end.

They were both still clutching each other, staring at him like he had leprosy. He rolled his eyes and stalked into the kitchen for another beer. "You guys are ridiculous."

"We'll pray for your Hughes-less soul!" Asher shouted.

BY THE TIME the credits to *Ferris Bueller's Day Off* rolled down the screen hours later, Asher was asleep between them on the couch. His head lolled on Cal's shoulder, his legs stretched out in front of him on the floor.

Cal leaned his head back on the couch and turned it to face Jenna. "Okay, so consider me educated on the body of John Hughes's work."

Jenna laughed, the hair on top of her head bobbing. "And what do you think?"

"I really liked that last one." *Pretty in Pink* had not been his favorite, but that Ferris guy was cool as shit. "Remember our Senior Skip Day?"

Jenna smiled but looked at her hands in her lap. "You were such a bad influence."

He reached across the sleeping teenager and tugged a piece of hair that had escaped from her bun. "That day was worth it." They'd been eighteen, so close to graduation they could taste it. And in love. They'd spent the whole morning at River's Edge, hanging with friends, and then spent the rest of the day in Cal's bed, wrapped up in each other until Jenna had to go home.

They'd talked about the future then. How Jenna was going to go to college and come back when she graduated. He'd wanted to propose then, claim her, keep her from leaving him for some smart, rich guy. But she'd assured him she'd come back, that they'd get married and buy a house and have those kids they'd always talked about.

And then, two weeks later, those dreams were gone with one punch to her brother's face.

Cal rubbed his eyes, wishing he didn't remember all of it. But he did. He looked at Jenna again. She wasn't smiling anymore; now she was watching him, her lips parted, her eyes a little wet. "That day *was* worth it."

His arms still rested along the back of the couch, his fingers brushing her shoulder. He didn't want to move, didn't want this moment to end, because in a minute, Jenna was going to get up and go home. She was going to shatter this brief illusion of family, this glimpse at what Cal's life could have been like.

Could it still be like that?

Jenna blew a breath out and lowered her feet to the floor. "I should go—"

"You could stay." The words were out before he could stop them.

She froze and stared. "What?"

"You could stay. It's late and...I can sleep on the couch. You can sleep in my bed." And wasn't that just a trip down memory lane? Last time she'd been in his bed, they'd had sex.

Her eyes widened. "I...don't think that's a good idea."

Shit. Shit. No, it wasn't. So he watched as she stood up, as she fixed her hair, as she slipped her feet into her flip-flops.

When she walked behind the couch, her fingers brushed the back of his head, the touch prickling his scalp. "Good night, Cal."

Then his front door opened and shut. Asher grumbled in his sleep, snorted, and then quieted.

Cal's heart ached.

Chapter Twenty

WHEN JENNA AND Asher pulled into the parking lot of the garage, Cal was leaning on the wall outside, hands in the pockets of his overalls, something white dangling from his lips. Jenna thought at first that it was a cigarette, but then he gripped the stick and popped a lollipop out of his mouth.

Even with a red lollipop, Cal looked effortlessly cool.

Jenna took a deep breath, wishing that it would get easier every time she saw him instead of harder. Cal worked one Saturday a month, and Asher had suggested they bring him lunch. The kid had already hopped out of the car, bag in hand from the local deli. "We brought you lunch!"

"What the hell did you do to your hair?" Cal's voice boomed across the parking lot.

Jenna grinned and stepped out of the car to follow the newly blue-haired Asher.

Cal was staring at the kid's head with utter horror.

Asher ran his hand over the longer hair on top. "Jenna dyed it for me."

Cal's eyes cut to her, but she'd long ago learned not to wither beneath the steel of his gaze. She shrugged. "He wanted to dye it."

"Yeah? And if he wanted to get his tongue pierced, you'd let him do that too?"

"I actually do want to get my tongue pierced," Asher said.

Cal's eyes widened. "Yeah? I'll pierce your mouth shut before I sign to let you get your tongue pierced."

Jenna laughed and smacked Cal's chest with her hand. "Calm down. It's just hair."

"It's fucking blue," Cal muttered.

"He likes it, and there's no harm."

"Fine," he said and then pointed at the teenager. "But no fucking piercings!"

"Who's talking about piercings?" Brent's voice called from inside the office. He strolled out, wearing a pair of jeans and a faded gray T-shirt. "Because I've got—"

"No one wants to know," Cal growled. "Swear to God, Brent, no one wants to know."

Because Jenna never learned not to poke the bear, she turned to Cal. "I kinda want to know."

Cal's jaw clenched, and Brent winked at her. "I'd let you find out if I didn't think Cal would cut off my balls."

"I'd do more than cut off your balls," Cal said.

Brent raised his eyebrows. "See?"

"So…" Asher lifted up the bag of sandwiches. "Anyone hungry?"

That effectively shut down the conversation, which was a good thing, because Cal was glaring at Brent, and Brent seemed positively delighted about it. They walked to the back room, and Brent went with them, humming under his breath.

"Don't you have things to do other than hanging around the garage on your day off?" Jenna asked Brent.

He shrugged, and his slate eyes, so like Cal's, shuttered. "Just getting some paperwork done."

"Do you need help?"

Brent waved her away. "You and your *boyfriend*"—he winked at her—"have a nice romantic lunch together."

"Brent!" Cal said over his shoulder. "Quit being a pain in the ass."

"Can't." Brent tipped an imaginary hat to Jenna. "It's when I stop being a pain in the ass that you gotta worry. Later, kids." He walked into the office and shut the door behind him.

Cal's gaze kept straying to Asher's hair as they ate. Then he'd shake his head and look back down. Jenna figured he'd get over it in time. His lips were stained red from the lollipop he'd had in his mouth, and he looked infinitely kissable. She needed to think about something else. "So how's business?"

Cal shrugged. "Good. Busy."

"You talk to your dad any more about working on bikes?" Jenna asked.

Cal spoke after he'd swallowed the bite of his sandwich. "I haven't said anything yet, but I'm getting ready to put my foot down. I hired a realtor, and I've been checking out some places I can rent to open up my own shop." He glanced around and then spoke quieter. "I hate to do that, because I don't want Brent to get caught in the crosshairs of the fight, but why should I let Dad make all the decisions? He a stubborn son of a bitch."

"He's not that bad," Asher said softly, crunching on a pickle.

Cal raised his eyebrows, but before he could respond, Jack's voice came from the garage. "Where's the kid?"

"Back here!" Asher called, and Cal's eyebrows rose higher.

"Doesn't your dad have off today?" Jenna asked.

Cal stared at the doorway, his tongue touching the corner of his mouth. "Yup."

"So what's he doing here?" she asked.

"I'm sure he'll tell us."

Jack strode into the room. She'd only seen him briefly at the restaurant that night all hell broke loose, so she got a better look at him now. He was a huge man, easily six foot four, and stocky. His face was craggy, probably from all the time he'd spent in the sun and all the cigarettes he'd smoked. He'd never been friendly to her, but then he'd never been outright hostile either. He saved that for his sons. Max always got the worst of it. Jenna had always thought Jack had a soft spot for his oldest son, even though he rarely showed it.

"Cal." Jack's voice was a crack.

"What's going on?" Cal asked.

"Need the kid."

"The kid?"

"Did I stutter?"

"Why do you need the kid?"

Jack was staring at Asher now like he had two heads. "Why the fuck is your hair blue?"

"Dad, why do you need the kid?"

"Airport. And seriously, why is his hair blue?"

"What are you talking about?" Cal sounded incredibly confused, and Jack looked pissed off that he had to explain anything. Jenna wondered how they got anything done where communication was essential.

Jack turned to Cal and huffed out a breath. "I'm taking the kid to the airport."

Jenna looked at Cal's face, which was frozen in shock. "The Tory airport?"

"Where the hell else? You think I'm taking him to LaGuardia? We're going to eat at Smithy's. Let's go, kid. Should probably stick a hat on you so you don't give the old men there a heart attack. Jesus. Blue? Why blue?"

Cal stared. "Wait, why—?"

"Quit with the fucking twenty questions. Now come on, kid, so we can get there before they run out of the rib special!"

Asher's eyes were huge, a chip raised halfway to his mouth. "You're taking me to the airport?"

"Did I not just say that? You got dye in your ears? Let's go."

Asher stood up, gathering his trash.

Jack's gaze then focused on Jenna, like he'd only just noticed her sitting there. "So you're back, huh?" The man talked like he was raised by wolves.

"Yes," Jenna said. "Good to see you, Mr. Payton."

"Jack," he grunted with a scowl.

"Jack," she amended.

He squinted at her, his eyes not dropping below her neck. "How long you sticking around this time?"

"Dad—" Cal started.

"I'm here for good, Mr.—Jack."

Cal laid a proprietary hand on her forearm. Jack's eyes dipped to that and then honed in on his son. "Well, that clears that up."

"What?" Cal asked.

"Thought maybe girls didn't give you those feelin's anymore. Wondered if you were the kid's way."

Jenna had to turn her head so she didn't burst out laughing.

Cal wasn't amused. "I like women, Dad."

"I'm just sayin'."

"You don't date, so who're you to talk?"

"I'm too fucking old for that shit."

Jenna was still stuck on Jack's taking Asher to the airport. "Does Asher like planes or something?"

Cal turned to her. "Dad's into 'em. We all chipped in and bought him flight lessons, but he hasn't done it yet, even though he hangs around that airport with fucking puppy-dog eyes—"

"Now, see here—"

"And now he's got another kid who will maybe share his obsession, since none of us give a shit."

"Hey, I like planes," Jack protested. "They fucking fly!"

Jenna cocked her head. "You like planes," she said to Jack, "like Cal likes motorcycles."

Both men fell silent.

"Never thought of them bein' compared like that," Jack muttered.

"And if you do let Cal work on bikes here—"

"Gettin' her on my ass about this too?"

"I can help," she continued. "I have marketing experience. I could drum up some business."

Jack was scowling at her, while Cal looked like he was going to kneel at her feet.

And then Brent broke the silence, his voice warbling from inside the office as he belted AC/DC.

Jack rolled his eyes. "That boy."

"Dad—"

Jack waved his hand. "We'll talk later."

"That's what you always say."

"Well, I need my ribs. I'll have him home by dinner." He nodded to Jenna and then waved to Asher to walk ahead of him.

The kid turned around and waved. "See ya later."

"Thanks for bringing lunch," Cal said.

As they walked out, Jack called over his shoulder. "Quit lollygagging and get back to work!"

Jenna waited until she heard Jack's truck start up in the parking lot before turning to Cal. "He's spending time with Asher?"

Cal was staring at the doorway. "That's weird as shit."

"About him and Asher?"

"Hell, yeah. They're like…night and day." He chewed his lip.

"What?" Jenna asked in response to his troubled stare.

Cal shook his head out of his trance. "Nothing, I…well, I guess I'm just surprised. The airport was always my dad's thing. He rarely took any of us." Cal huffed. "Getting paternal in his old age or something."

"Think he'll ever cave about the motorcycles?"

Cal blew out a breath. "Hell if I know. Thinking now maybe I need to stick Asher on the case."

"Sounds like maybe you're not the favorite anymore," Jenna teased.

Cal snorted a laugh. "I think I'm all right with that."

CAL WASN'T EAGER to get back to work after they finished lunch. He stood, drinking his water at the sink, while Jenna talked about what she'd done with Asher that morning. Her hair was down in soft waves around her face, and the green of her tank top brought out the green in her hazel eyes. Her cheeks were flushed from the heat, and since it was the best damn sight he'd see all day, he wasn't in a hurry to get away from it.

"I washed Asher's hair in the sink, so I didn't stain your bathroom, by the way," she said.

"Appreciate that."

"And there's barbecue in the Crock-Pot for dinner. I have plans with Delilah."

She'd brought him lunch and made him dinner. "Okay."

"And Asher needed a new pair of sunglasses. Remember, you sat on his and broke them? So I ordered some online. They'll be there in two days."

She'd spent time with his half-brother today and saw that he got what he needed. "Sounds great."

"And he wants us to go see that new Sam Andrews movie. It's out on Thursday. I went ahead and ordered tickets, but if you can't go, then I'll cancel them—"

"Jenna, what are we doing?" he asked softly.

She stopped talking abruptly and stared at him, eyes wide. "What do you mean?"

"This." He gestured between the two of them. "What is this?"

Caution. That was the emotion creeping over her features. Caution. She stood up and walked toward him until she stood a foot away, arms crossed over her chest. "I'm not sure what you mean. This is me, being a friend to Asher, just like I want to be and like you asked me to be. This is us, being friends and only friends, because that's what you wanted, Cal. And that's what's best for us, since we want different things. That's exactly what this is."

She was everywhere now, like air. She was in his head and his life. It had only been a couple of weeks, yet Cal had a hard time remembering how life was without her. And his attraction to her? It hadn't faded, not one fucking bit. Because even now, with her features hardened, he wanted her.

He'd always want her.

His fingers itched to grab her waist, to bury his nose in her hair. He wasn't content to remain in her presence anymore, soaking in her light.

He shook his head. "I don't understand what's happening."

"I understand," she said softly, taking a step toward him until their hips brushed. He sucked in a breath. "What's happening is that you don't see what's right in front of your face. You didn't want a relationship or a family...well, what exactly do you think has been going on for the last couple of weeks?" She stepped back then, and he almost went with her. She fisted her hands at her sides. "Think about that, will you?" She tossed the rest of her lunch in the trash and walked out.

HE COULDN'T SAY what he did for the rest of the day. He worked on autopilot. He did his job, but his mind was elsewhere. Jenna's words swirled in his head, and even though he tried hard to drown it out with the radio, nothing was working.

He'd thought for so long that he didn't have it in him to be a relationship man, a family man. At one time, that's all he wanted to be, to prove to himself that he wasn't like his dad, that he wasn't like his mom.

But that had been ten years ago. He'd spent the decade since then convincing himself he didn't want that anymore. But if he was honest with himself, he hadn't been this happy since...well, since he could remember. He and Jenna had fallen in to this weird give-and-take relationship, and he hadn't even noticed until now.

Cal didn't do anything unless it meant something. If he went all-in with love, then everyone's money needed to be in the kitty in the center of the table.

His brothers had been all-in this whole time; Cal had held up a martyr complex as a shield, rather than face the truth.

And that didn't fucking serve anyone.

Was he really going to keep up this lone-wolf act forever? It was exhausting. And now that he remembered what it was like to step outside of his little circle, to let his emotions guide him, it had felt damn good. He missed that, the drive to be with someone so badly he ached.

He hadn't felt like that with anyone, ever, except Jenna. He was still unsure about being…enough. He didn't know if he had it in him to do this all over again. If he still had the drive to care and protect. But Jenna's return and Asher's presence had stirred something in him that made him think maybe…maybe he could. Which just showed that his reserve of emotions and those damn *fucking feelings* went deeper than he thought.

He owed it to himself and to Jenna to give this relationship with her a chance. He wasn't ready to propose or commit to two-point-five kids, but what kind of coward was he that he wasn't willing to try?

That's all Jenna had asked for, after all. The chance to try.

When Cal closed up the shop for the day, Brent was still in the office. His brow was furrowed as he bent over the file of invoices, his pen tapping on the glass counter.

"You about ready to head out?" Cal asked.

Brent's head went up. He wore a pair of reading glasses when he worked, and Cal liked to tease him about them. Brent must have seen Cal's smirk, because he whipped off the glasses and threw them onto the counter. "Yeah, I'm at a good stopping point. Let me get this stuff put away, and I can help you lock up."

Cal straightened up some magazines and turned off the TV in the waiting room while Brent shuffled papers.

"Nice of your wife to bring you lunch today." Brent shoved the accordion file under the counter and straightened.

The word *wife* felt thick and heavy. Too heavy. "We're friends. No need to rent a tux yet."

"Uh-huh. Right. Because I'm sure you and Jenna will be *just friends* by next week."

"Well, maybe—"

"Why did you look like I cut your brake lines when I said 'wife'?"

Cal crossed his arms. He wasn't sure exactly. Maybe he'd spent so damn long shoving that word into a corner until he was sure it was on permanent timeout, that now he couldn't stop the knee-jerk reaction when he heard it. "Maybe that word just freaks me out."

"Spouse?"

Cal shuddered.

"You have…" Brent waved a hand. "What's the word? Negative association. Yeah, that's it. You have a negative association with the word 'wife.' Might wanna get over that if you ever plan on marrying her. Would look weird if you threw up every time you introduced her to people."

"I wouldn't throw up," Cal retorted.

Brent raised an eyebrow.

"It's just a lot to take in. My life…didn't move. It was status quo for ten years. I settled in and dug the grooves so deep into my routine that I didn't think I'd ever get off track. I got knocked when Max went into the hospital, but I righted myself. Then Jenna came back and Asher showed up on my doorstep. And my life…" He shook his head. "My life isn't what I thought it'd be, and maybe I'm just trying to adjust the best I can."

Brent's expression was composed. "Sure. I get that."

Cal pointed a finger at him. "Don't patronize me. You're in a rut too, and you just wait, man. Some girl is going to knock you flat on your ass, and then I get to be the one who smirks and nods while you're hurting."

"You seem pretty sure of yourself there."

"Bound to happen sometime."

"I don't have a rut. That's the whole point of what I do." Brent's shoulders tensed defensively.

Cal enjoyed having the upper hand again. "What're you talking about? You totally have a rut. Just because the girl changes every time doesn't make it any less of a rut. When you have to deal with the same woman all the time and actually work at it, then you'll see how it keeps you on your toes."

Brent sniffed. "Well, whatever, then. I like my rut." A smile curled his lips. "You only wish you had my rut."

"Quit saying that word."

"I rut well in my rut."

Cal turned on his heel and walked out the door without looking back.

"Keep your eyes out of my rut!" Brent called after him.

Chapter Twenty-One

CAL COULDN'T STOP chewing the inside of his cheek. The skin was ragged, but at least it was hidden, where no one could see the evidence of his nerves.

Asher was humming happily to himself in the passenger seat of the truck on the way to pick up Jenna to take her to the movies. The kid had talked Cal's ear off for the first ten minutes about the movie budget and the cost of the special effects and a million other things that went over Cal's head. But he was good at nodding and murmuring at appropriate times in the conversation without really listening. And it's not that he didn't care about what Asher had to say; it was that he couldn't stop his mind from replaying the last couple of weeks with Jenna and all that it meant.

Despite his worries about Asher and the sexual tension with Jenna, he'd been happier than he could remember being in a long time. His house wasn't silent; his meals weren't alone.

Everything was full, nearly full to bursting, in a way he'd avoided but now craved.

Cal was a decisive kind of guy. The last time he changed his mind about something important was ten years ago, when he vowed to avoid a long-term relationship that would lead to a family.

But now...he was wondering if that was the one single thing that eighteen-year-old kid had right.

He didn't know how to do this or what to say to Jenna. They'd set an expiration date on their relationship, and the timer had run out. But now he wanted an extension. A trial period.

He parked in her driveway and muttered to Asher, "Don't forget the flowers," before stepping out of the truck. He let Asher lead the way, a bouquet that had cost a fucking fortune clutched in his hands.

When Jenna opened the door, her eyes met Cal's first before lowering to take in Asher and the flowers he held proudly in front of him.

"These are for you, Jenna."

She beamed brightly, and Cal thought to himself that flowers had the right idea, tilting their blooms toward the sun. Because that was him right now, basking in the sunshine that Jenna radiated, like always.

They followed her inside so she could stick the bouquet in water. Cal wanted to grab her around the waist and tug her to him, take her mouth until both of them forgot about leaving the house for some stupid movie.

She had her hair pulled up on top of her head somehow, with a piece in a swoop over one eye. She wore a pair of tight jeans, flat shoes, and a light-blue tank top. "You look nice, Jenna," he murmured softly in her ear and then pressed a kiss to her temple. She froze. He knew he'd avoided touching her with any sign of affection since Asher had showed up. Which was dumb. So fucking dumb. He should have been giving her flowers every day. He should have been kissing her and touching her and doing everything he could to show her how he felt.

She stared at the flowers and started arranging them in the vase.

He didn't move his head, so his lips still brushed the shell of her ear. He could still back away; he could blow off the closeness with a laugh. But Jenna knew him, and he was touching her with intent. He knew it and she knew it. This was his night to show her that he could be boyfriend material again, that he could treat her like she deserved. He was a little rusty, but he figured he'd go with his instincts. They'd never failed him before.

Jenna didn't move, and then slowly she turned her head so their lips were inches apart. "What are you doing?"

There was so much he wanted to say, but all the words banged around in his head, clogging until they were a jumbled mass. So he didn't speak. He brushed his lips against hers and then stepped back, offering her a smile he hoped said what he couldn't speak. He hoped Jenna spoke this language of kisses, because right now, that was the only thing he was fluent in.

She blinked, her lashes fluttering. Then she heaved a breath and stepped back, grabbing her purse off the table.

Her hands shook as she pulled out a tube of lipstick and coated her lips. He should have felt guilty, but instead, he was so fucking relieved that he still affected her. And that she hadn't slapped him. That had been a real possible outcome in Cal's mind.

In the truck, he let Asher sit between them. After everyone's seat belts were secure, he began the drive to the movie theater.

Casually, he draped his arm behind Asher's back and let his fingers rest along the back of Jenna's neck. She didn't pull away, like he thought she might. He ran his thumb along her skin, feeling goose bumps and the hitch of her breath.

At the theater, Asher walked ahead of them in the parking lot, still chattering about the movie. Cal walked beside Jenna, a hand on her upper back.

In the lobby, a big screen was showing previews of movies, so Cal left Asher and Jenna there to watch while he bought the tickets.

When he found them again, standing near a display of movie posters, he had a huge bucket of popcorn and a soda for Asher and another for Jenna. "Dr. Pepper," he said, handing it to her. She smiled, somewhat hesitantly. She'd always loved that soda. He'd never liked the taste of it, but he sure did love the taste of Dr. Pepper and Jenna.

He hoped he got a chance later.

CAL WAS KILLING her. And confusing her.

It was the little touches. The compliments. The hand-delivered Dr. Pepper, like no time had passed.

She dissected his actions and words in her head on the drive to the theater. While Cal was buying tickets. While she sucked on the straw of her Dr. Pepper. If Cal meant to give this a shot, it would change everything, and she wasn't sure she was ready for it.

So she tried to ignore the touches and the compliments as they took their seats in the crowded theater. She couldn't count the number of times she'd been to a movie theater since dating Cal back in high school, but there was something special about *this* time. Maybe it was Asher's presence, as he soaked up their attention like a sponge. The kid was desperate to spend time with adults who cared about him, who paid attention to him. And even though Jenna's mind was occupied with Cal, she still made sure to listen to Asher.

"So, I read," Asher was saying, sitting on her right in the dimly lit theater while the previews played, "that Sam Andrews broke his arm at the end of filming, so they had to do a lot of tricky camera work to cover it up."

Jenna winced. "Ouch. Did he break it during filming?"

Asher munched on his popcorn and shook his head. "He was jumping on a trampoline or something with his nieces and nephews."

"Oh wow, poor guy."

Cal shifted in his seat on her left, his jean-clad thigh brushing hers. She didn't move away.

"And," Asher continued, oblivious to the heat that was curling in her gut, "one of the stunt guys got third-degree burns on his chest from a mistimed explosion."

"Oh my God!"

Asher leaned forward. "Thanks for the popcorn. I think it's fresh because it's really crunchy." Then he sat back in his seat and took a sip of his drink.

Teenagers and their attention spans.

Cal placed his arm on the armrest between them. Jenna stared at it, then lifted her gaze to Cal's face. He was staring straight ahead at the trivia game on the screen.

"Drew Barrymore!" Asher crowed in response to the question, Who played Gertie in *E.T.*? He dropped his soda in the cup holder. "I'm going to go to the bathroom real quick. Is that cool?"

Cal nodded and Asher left, walking quickly down the aisle.

Jenna bit her lips as another trivia question came on, but her attention wasn't on the screen. She wouldn't have been able to tell anyone what it was about if asked. Her mind was on Asher and how Cal treated him. She lowered her gaze to her lap and ran her fingers along an imperfection in the denim of her jeans. "You're really good with him," she said softly.

Cal grunted. "Eh, it's like riding a bike."

She faced him again, and this time, he turned his head and met her gaze. "Something changed, didn't it?" She hoped he didn't make her explain further right now.

"Yup," Cal said.

She turned her head, but strong fingers gripped her head and forced it back. Cal's jaw was set, and his eyes were narrowed, glowing like liquid silver as they reflected the colors on the screen in front of them.

He looked like he was going to speak, but instead he pressed his mouth to hers in a kiss that wasn't so chaste, because he moved his lips, and there was his tongue, and by the time he was finished, she was a puddle in her seat.

And with that, he let go of her chin, dropped his hand into her lap, and laced his fingers with hers. Then he turned his face to the screen. *"Pirates of the Caribbean!"* he shouted in response to the trivia question.

ASHER CAME BACK, but Cal kept up the touches throughout the movie, rubbing the skin between Jenna's thumb and forefinger with his thumb. Sometimes his fingers strayed a little to her inner thigh, which scrambled her brain and made her lose track of the plot of the movie.

The back of his fingers brushed her jaw and neck as he slung his arm over the back of her chair. The warmth of his leg against hers infused her whole body with a searing heat.

At one point, she fanned herself with her hand, and Asher looked at her strangely. "Hot flash," she said in explanation, and with a look of alarm, Asher focused back on the screen and asked no further questions. Boys did not want to talk about girl stuff. Always a good defense.

By the time they left the theater, Jenna was tucked into Cal's side, and his arm was around her shoulders. She didn't protest, because frankly, it felt so good to be in Cal's arms, while Asher jumped up and down about how the movie was *so cool*, and the lead actor was *so hot*, and he *couldn't wait* for the DVD to come out so he could see all the bonus scenes.

On the way to her house, finally free of Cal's touch, Jenna thought maybe she should be resisting this. Maybe she should tell Cal to go to hell. But her heart didn't want to. That hope that had been a low simmer was now a rolling boil.

She could be strong and resist Cal, but the effort seemed futile. If she dug deep in her heart, she didn't want to avoid him. She'd never stopped loving Cal, although she'd certainly stopped being in love with him.

And now, the more time she spent around him, the more she could see that she was following that same path, where she tumbled head over heels in love with Cal Payton. These past couple of weeks had been just a taste of all they'd dreamed about when they were kids. She wanted more.

When they pulled into her driveway, Jenna unclipped her seat belt and turned to Asher. She smoothed back his hair, kissed his forehead, and then wrapped him in a hug. "Thanks for the flowers and for inviting me to see the movie with you."

Asher ducked his head after she pulled out of the hug. "Thanks for coming with us. I had a really nice time."

"Me too."

As she placed her hand on the truck's door handle, Asher spoke up again. "When am I going to see you again?"

Asher's face was hopeful, his dark eyes luminous in the yellow light above her garage door. She let her gaze drift past him, meeting Cal's steel stare. He said nothing. He gave her nothing. She looked back at Asher. "Soon, buddy. Okay?"

Asher smiled. "All right. Bye, Jenna."

She hopped down out of the truck and wasn't surprised when deep murmurings came from inside before she shut her door. A door shut behind her and booted footsteps followed her to her front door.

She didn't turn around, even though her hands were trembling as she stuck her key in the lock and let herself into the house.

Cal's heat was on her back, and she didn't bother shutting the door. Cal did it for her.

She stayed facing the hall, schooling her face until she felt under control, until she could focus on her thoughts rather than her body's reaction to the only man who had ever made her feel alive.

When she turned around, he stood in front of the door, hands on his hips, eyes on her. He didn't look away, and she wondered what he was thinking. And if he planned to talk first.

Ten seconds later, he answered both of those questions.

"Remember what happened last time we were standing right here?"

She swallowed. Not trusting herself to speak, she nodded. Her hands itched to touch him, to run her fingers through that thick hair, to brush the stubble on his jaw.

He paused again, and when he finally spoke again, his voice was gravel. "You opened that robe for me. You let me in. I can't stop thinking about that night."

His voice was killing her. Because although it was gravel, she knew if she dug hard enough, it'd be soft velvet underneath.

He took a step toward her. Just one. Like he was waiting for her to back up a step. But she didn't. She held her ground and waited for Cal to come to her. He took another step. And another, until he stood in front of her with a hand on her hip. His fingers rested on the top of her ass, and his thumb slipped under the hem of her tank top, teasing the sensitive skin.

"Thought I'd come here that night and steal a ray of that sunshine. Then walk away, hoping it would keep me warm for a while." He was whispering now, barely audible. His breath smelled like mint, because he'd been popping them the whole movie. "But damn if you didn't catch me in a day, sucking me back in, making me feel like if you weren't by my side, I'd die of frostbite."

Cal wasn't poetic. Cal didn't use flowery words. And there was a simplicity in this analogy that only Cal could pull off. But he'd thought this through. He'd worked it out in his head what he wanted to say to her. And it made her throat tight. It made her belly warm. It made her lick her lips because she wanted a taste of Cal. She wanted to warm him up.

She placed a hand on his chest and walked her fingers up to where she knew the sun tattoo lay beneath his clothes.

He reached up and covered her hand with his own. "I know I don't deserve this, but I'm asking anyway. Be patient with me. I'm opening my eyes, Jenna. I swear I am. But it's taking my eyes a while to adjust in the light, all right?"

His words—oh, his words—were seeping in all her cracks, and they were heating her body from the inside out. She didn't know whether her patience with Cal was a strength or a weakness, but right now, she didn't care, not when he was in her foyer, baring his heart the best he could.

She couldn't take his voice anymore. She dug through the gravel, felt the soft velvet on her fingers, and crashed her lips to Cal's.

He was mint against her Dr. Pepper, and she gripped his shoulders with both hands, tugging him closer, walking backward until her butt hit the wall behind her. Her head would have cracked into the drywall, but Cal's hand was there, cushioning the blow. And that simple touch sent her heart into freefall.

She dug her nails into his skin and moaned into his mouth. Cal echoed the sound, and just when she thought she'd die from the kiss, he pulled back and rested his forehead against hers. His breath coasted over her face, and she nudged his nose with hers. "See?" she said. "I can speak in kiss too."

His eyes fell closed, and then he dropped his head to her shoulder. She threaded her fingers through his hair.

When he straightened, his eyes were a little red, his lips wet, but he looked happy and more relaxed than she'd ever seen him. "I gotta get back out to Asher. I'll call you, Sunshine."

And then he was walking out her door.

Chapter Twenty-Two

"DIE, YOU UGLY motherfucker!" Brent hollered from the living room where he sat on the couch with Asher, playing some game that had a lot of guns and blood.

Cal sat at the kitchen table, paying bills, which was something he did most Saturday mornings. Best to get it out of the way so he could enjoy the rest of the weekend.

Although usually, he did it in silence. Today, Brent and Asher were hollering at the TV screen, and Jenna stood at the kitchen sink, finishing up the dishes from breakfast.

He licked the envelope for the electric bill and paused to take her in. She'd turned on the small radio he'd mounted under the cabinets and swayed to the beat of a classic-rock song. She wore a pair of short-as-hell jean shorts and a button-down shirt of his over a tank top.

Her hair was down, a mass of brown waves, which he'd run his fingers through last night. And again this morning. And every chance he got in the last two weeks since that night in her foyer when she'd agreed to be patient with him. They'd both been busy, so he hadn't had much time with her. She hadn't slept over yet, because although they were in this unspoken, odd trial period, neither was ready for the emotions that arose between them when they slept together. And even though he wanted to—God, he wanted to—he knew they weren't ready for that again yet.

Kisses, though? They were allowed. And some heavy petting. Along with heavy breathing. He kind of felt like he was in high school again, where a boob-grab was like winning the lottery.

But this was good, kind of like dating, and Cal was finding he liked this Jenna even more than the high-school Jenna. It made him wonder, if they had stayed together all those years ago, if they would still be a couple. The separation might have been what they needed for Cal to get his head on straight and for Jenna to grow into her independence.

As far as life with Asher, things were calm. Asher worked at the shop and hung out with Julian in his spare time. Cal had called Jill one more time last week, but when she started sputtering more excuses for her drunk husband, Cal hung up on her. He didn't have the time or patience for that shit.

Cal still hadn't taken Asher out on his bike. It'd been almost a month, but he still needed to get Asher a helmet that fit him. He'd promised him soon. Things had been a little busy lately, since Jenna was getting ready for the big event for the employees of MacMillan Industries. An event Cal was going to attend, as Jenna's date.

Normally, he'd never be caught dead at Tory Country Club, but he knew how much work Jenna had put into the party, so he agreed to go in support of her. He wasn't thrilled, but this was where the *trying* thing came in. He was trying. So that meant going to this fancy party.

Jenna wasn't paying attention to him now, as she danced a little around the kitchen. When she got close, he snaked an arm around her waist and tugged until she fell in his lap.

She made an oomph sound and frowned at him. "Hey."

He snuck his hand under her shirt and tank top, so his palm rested against bare skin. "Hey, yourself."

She sagged against him and placed her hand on his arms. He wasn't wearing a shirt, and her thumb rested on the edge of the sun on his shoulder. He leaned in and pressed a kiss under her ear. She shuddered in his arms. "Cal, I gotta leave soon."

He ignored her. Apparently, Jenna had a meeting at the country club for the party that was next weekend.

When he ran his tongue down her neck, she moaned. "Your brothers are in the other room."

"They're busy," he mumbled against her skin. He couldn't get enough of her taste, the feel of her in his arms. The way she melted into him with a simple touch. He was gone for her fifty times over, more than he ever had been as an immature teenager. It was weird how love evolved in his head as he got older. *Love?* Was that what this was, all over again?

She pouted. "I'm going to be late."

With a sigh, he pulled back and slapped her denim-covered ass. "Fine, then get out of here."

She stuck out her tongue at him and hopped off his lap. He smiled and picked up his pen to do more bills.

JENNA HAD BEEN gone a half hour when his doorbell rang. "Can you get that?" Brent called from the couch. "Shit, fuck, this damn fucker—I'm kinda busy here!"

Cal rose from the table where he was finished with the bills and walked past Asher and Brent in the living room, still playing video games.

When he opened the door, a tiny vision in red with huge black sunglasses shoved her way past him into the house.

Delilah Jenkins pushed her shades onto her head and gave him a once-over with her dark eyes. She wore a bright red dress and strappy shoes with a purse that was bigger than her head. He'd known Delilah as long as he'd known Jenna. She was the tiniest woman he'd ever met, but she was still too much for him. Too much personality, too much color, too much everything. He thought maybe she and Brent would hit it off, but they'd hooked up once years ago and left it as friends.

Delilah was good people, though. She was smart, owned her own business, and most of all, she loved Jenna. So Delilah was aces in his book.

Brent took his eyes off of the screen for one minute to lean back in the couch. "Hey, D!"

She waggled some fingers at him. "Hey, B. Not here for you, so you can go back to killing pixels."

" 'Kay!" he answered.

Delilah turned back to Cal. "Well," she said, her gaze lingering on his bare chest, "as much as I'm enjoying the view, you're going to have to get dressed, because no shirt, no shoes, no service and all of that."

He blinked at her. "Come again?"

She waved a hand at his body. "I need to take you shopping for this shindig Jenna is throwing."

All these words were foreign. "You need to take me *shopping*?"

He didn't shop. He didn't know how to shop. Most of his clothes were holiday gifts from Brent, because his brother was vain as hell and *did* shop.

Cal? Not so much.

Delilah wasn't having his attitude, apparently. Her expression told him he was trying her patience. "Yes, shopping, you big grease monkey. Now get a shirt on and let's go."

"And where are we going exactly?"

"The mall."

He swore his neck started to itch, like hives were forming. "This isn't funny."

She placed a hand on her hip in a flourish. "Does it look like I'm laughing? Jenna asked me to do this, so if you wanna keep her sweet ass in this little ol' house of yours, I suggest you get dressed and then get it my car."

Okay, he drew the line there. "I am not getting in that fucking car."

She scowled. "Don't you dare insult Daisy—"

"Oh, Jesus, you named that damn thing?"

"She's reliable and cute and—"

"I will go shopping with you on the condition that we take my truck."

Delilah's nostrils flared. "Is it clean?"

Cal scrunched his lips to the side before replying. "I'll put a towel down."

Delilah shuddered a little. "Fine, now just go get dressed."

It was a small victory, but he'd take it.

HE DREW THE line at a tie. He accepted the navy dress pants, white cotton shirt, and tan sport coat. But no way in hell was he going to be able to deal with all the assholes at this party with a noose around his neck.

Delilah wasn't thrilled about his refusal but seemed happy with all his other purchases, including a pair of dress shoes that he knew he'd burn in an elaborate funeral pyre when this was all over.

He wasn't a dick, though, so he offered to buy Delilah lunch. She'd taken time out of her day to argue with his sorry blue-collar ass. The least he could do was buy her a burger.

Of course, Delilah didn't want a burger.

They found a restaurant near the mall that Delilah liked, and while Cal ate his burger, Delilah dug into her salad. It was huge, the plate taking up nearly a quarter of the table, and she was eating it all.

Cal didn't know where she put it.

"So," she said after taking a sip of her water, "you're probably going to hate this party."

He swirled a fry in ketchup. "Yep."

"But you're doing it for Jenna."

"Yep."

Delilah shifted her lips to the side. "You know there are some women in town who are really sad you're off the market."

"Was never on it," he grunted.

"Brent's on it."

That made him grin. "He loves it."

Delilah smiled too. "Lovable asshole." Delilah stabbed a cherry tomato with her fork. "So Jenna said you want to work on motorcycles at the shop."

"Trying to convince Dad. But he says we don't have enough manpower."

"Are you able to hire someone else?"

"I had Brent crunch the numbers, and we could hire another mechanic if he was willing to take base salary."

She crunched her tomato and swallowed. "I know someone."

That brought his head up. "Yeah?"

Delilah studied him carefully. "Yep, a friend of a friend kind of thing. She's really good and is looking to get her foot in the door."

"She, huh?" He chuckled. "You trying to slip that past me?"

"No."

"Well, I'm still working on Dad. Have her send me her résumé, will ya?"

"Sure."

"And…uh…thanks for today. I don't really care what I look like, but I don't want to make Jenna look bad."

She touched the back of his hand where it rested on the table. "And you won't. You could walk in there in sweatpants and a T-shirt, and Jenna wouldn't give a shit."

"Ya think?"

"I know. But it'll make her family happy. And I must say, you look quite handsome in those clothes."

Cal popped an imaginary collar, and Delilah laughed.

JENNA HAD DONE a lot for MacMillan Investments since she'd been hired. She'd reworked their mission statement and was partnering with a graphic designer to update the company logo. She'd improved communication among staff and management. Hell, she'd even bought a damn Keurig for the break room, which she liked to think might have been the best thing she'd done yet. And she was currently in the midst of planning the biggest event the company had ever sponsored.

But all her brother could do was bitch about how Cal was coming to the country club as her date.

"You'll be busy coordinating anyway," he said, glaring at her from behind his desk. "Why do you have to bring a date?"

"Why do you care?" she shot back, drumming her nails on the arm of the chair. He'd called her into his office under the pretense of asking her a question about the party, but it was easy to see that all he wanted to do was be a pain in the ass.

"This is a MacMillan employee party," he said.

"Each employee is allowed to bring a date. A significant other. And Cal is my significant other." *Significant other-ish*, she amended in her head. Because it was kind of unspoken, what they had. "He has been for about a month, even though all of you want to act like he's not." The division in this town between the haves and have-nots was ridiculous and antiquated.

Plus, she happened to think Cal had a whole lot of haves.

"I don't see why this whole party is even necessary," Dylan complained. "The company morale is fine."

Jenna raised her eyebrows.

Dylan opened his mouth like he was going to speak but then shut it and looked away.

Jenna wished she had the type of brother who would simply support her. Who would clap her on the back and tell her she did a good job. She'd told Dylan plenty of times over the years that she was proud of the work he put into their father's company. And now, when she came back to help, all he could do was sneer at her ideas and her date.

She twisted her fingers together, gazed at her lap, and thought about Cal, who took in a half-brother he hadn't known, cared for him, and supported him. And she could barely get the brother she grew up with to acknowledge that she was his coworker.

It's not that she needed his approval. But she sure as hell would have liked it.

His chair creaked, and she looked up to see him leaned back, an elbow propped on the armrest, his chin in his fingers. His gaze was unfocused over her shoulder, his jaw hard. "If you insist on bringing Cal, then I guess I don't have any say."

"You don't have any say at all, Dylan. I'm almost thirty. Who I date is not your concern, and I don't need your approval."

"Guess I thought you got that rebelling thing about of your system when you were a teenager."

She leaned forward, pinning him with a sharp look. "That's what you think this is about? Rebelling against…what, exactly?"

"Your upbringing…your family—"

"My God, Dylan. Initially, sure, Cal was a rebellion. When I was freaking sixteen years old. And then it quickly became about love, and I can tell you right now, today, being with Cal has nothing to do with my family and everything to do with how he makes me feel."

He tilted his chin up, stubborn to the core. Why were all the men in her life stubborn? "I don't trust him. He can be violent, you know."

Jenna rolled her eyes. "He was an eighteen-year-old hothead when he hit you. Get over it already."

"He broke my nose."

"I think it was an improvement to your face."

Dylan's eyes went wide. Then his lips began to twitch, fending off a smile. "I had a regal nose before, and now it's a bump."

Jenna snorted. "Regal, my ass."

Dylan did smile then, one that she knew was meant to appease her, to end this aggressive conversation. So she smiled back. She hoped this was some sort of truce. Although with Dylan, she could never be sure. They didn't have enough in common to be friends. Jenna had always wondered if it would improve when they got older. So far, it hadn't.

She sighed. "Look, I don't want to fight with you about this. Cal's in my life, and I'm sorry, but you'll have to accept it. I don't want to be at odds all the time."

Dylan nodded. "All right."

"All right?"

"Yes, all right."

She stood up and smoothed her skirt. "I can get back to work now?"

"Yeah, I have to as well."

When she had her hand on the door, he called her name. She looked over her shoulder.

His eyes were unreadable. "I hope everything goes well at the party."

She gave him a nod and walked out, with an odd feeling prickling her spine.

Chapter Twenty-Three

"SO," JENNA SAID, her heels clicking smartly on the pave-
ment of the country club parking lot, "we need to get
in there and make sure the tables are set up correctly. I
said ten to a table, not twelve, but something about the
manager makes me think they are going to try to squeeze
twelve to a table—"

"Jenna," Cal's voice came from her side, but she was
on a roll.

"Twelve is just too damn many to a table. And don't
you hate it when there aren't enough trash cans, and you
don't know where to put your hors d'oeuvres napkin? So
I want to make sure there are plenty of trash receptacles."

"Jenna." His tone was firmer now.

"And I gave them the recipe for a signature drink, but I
swear they'll mess it up, so I want to taste it first—oooh!"

She was pushed up against a brick wall, and a hot body
was pressing her into it. Cal's hands rested on her face,

and she thought about telling him he was messing up her makeup, but she was too lost in those slate eyes. "Sunshine, you're gonna stroke out if you don't take a breath."

She struggled weakly, "Cal, I can't—"

"Breathe."

She scowled at him.

His lips quirked. "Take a deep breath. In and out. There, that's it."

While following his mandated breathing exercises, she glanced around to see where they were. He'd managed to shuffle them into an alcove along the side of the building not visible from the parking lot or entrance. There were rows of tall hedges blocking them in. So no one would see them.

The tight band around her chest loosened. This event was going to give her a heart attack. She wanted the employees to be happy and impressed and have a good time. Her dad had been skeptical about its being effective, and everything about her wanted to prove to him how much this could improve company morale.

But she admitted she'd been acting a little nutty. If she went in there with all cylinders engaged, she might make enemies.

Attract more bees with honey and all that.

She raised her arms and gripped Cal's waist as his hands slipped down to grasp either side of her neck. Cal looked, well, pretty damn amazing. His straight-leg navy pants made him look taller, while accentuating his strong thighs and absolutely amazing ass. His white buttondown shirt was open at the collar and set off his tan skin.

The color also made his eyes blaze. His hair was a little on the longer side, and he hadn't done much with it, so the messy hair with his crisp clothes gave him just about the sexiest look she'd ever seen. Clean-cut with an edge. She'd take Cal in a pair of jeans and a T-shirt—or nothing at all—any day, but she didn't mind this look on him either.

Her hand drifted down and squeezed his ass. He grunted softly and leaned in, teasing her lips with slight brushes of his before she squeezed his ass again. They hadn't had sex again, not since that weekend they'd spent together before Asher arrived. She ached for Cal like crazy, but what they had now was fragile, so fragile they didn't even talk about it. And with the way they were in bed, she knew it would make everything come crashing down on their heads.

They'd have to face it soon, though. Their families were talking and asking questions. And most of all, Jenna was falling for Cal the man way harder than she'd ever fallen for Cal the teenager. So she had to know if he was falling too, because if not, she was in for a rough landing.

Cal broke out of the kiss. "You look beautiful." His lips traveled down the column of her throat. She should push on his chest and tell him to step back, that they had to get to the party, but damn, it had been so long, and his lips felt so good. And his words…his words were even better. His strong fingers gripped her hip, his mouth brushing the shell of her ear. "Everyone'll take a little piece of sunshine tonight, but I know you save the best for me."

She smiled, loving the heat of his body seeping into hers. The tension left her muscles, and she swore she could have melted into him right there.

"So you need to relax," he said. His mouth sucked lightly on her collarbone. "No one will notice the little things. You've been working your ass off on this, and it will show, okay?"

She nodded.

He stepped back and slowly righted her clothes, putting her back together. Then he raised an eyebrow. "You feeling better now?"

She felt like liquid. "Yes, thank you."

He pointed at her with an expression of mock severity. "We'll finish this later."

She hoped so.

THE TORY COUNTRY Club was eye-roll-worthy, in Cal's opinion. Over-the-top and flowery, and man, all he wanted to do was put his feet up on the coffee table in the lobby, grab a beer, and watch a baseball game.

Or he'd rather be home, playing video games with Asher. He knew the kid would have been fine by himself all night, but Gabe had said he could spend the night at his house with Julian. Cal figured that was a better idea, so Asher didn't have to rattle around in his house all by himself. Cal would still rather be home with him.

Cal kept those thoughts to himself, though. He shook hands when Jenna introduced him to her colleagues, and he smiled. He even made small talk about the weather, which was painful. But Jenna beamed at him, her smile lighting up the entire place.

He managed to escape to a corner of the room with a vodka tonic clutched in his hand. Jenna worked the crowd, her dress swishing around her legs. He crunched the ice in his glass with his molars, shifting uncomfortably when the thought of his hand up that skirt made his pants tight.

"You might wanna simmer down on the eye-fucking," a voice said next to him.

He looked down at Delilah, who sipped from a martini glass and peered at him over the rim. Her hair was down, black and straight and so long it touched her elbows.

"Didn't know the kid's department sold dresses that tight." He gestured toward her purple dress.

She scowled. "It's called petite, jackass."

Cal grunted and let his eyes drift to Jenna, who had her back to them, round ass in view. "I like a good handful."

"Don't be a pig."

He snorted.

She plucked at his shirt. "I did pretty well, didn't I? Jenna like your clothes?"

He grinned wolfishly. "Yeah, she liked 'em so much, she—"

"Oh, shut up."

He laughed. "So what are you doing there?"

She waved a hand into the crowd. "I came as a plus-one."

"With you?"

"Some guy named Marshall."

"Marshall?"

"I just want my name in the raffle. Some great stuff is up."

"So you seduced a guy so you could get invited?"

She winked at him.

"You're a bad influence on Jenna."

She pushed his shoulder gently. "You have nothing to fear. That woman is gone for you."

He didn't answer that, because he sure hoped so. He was gone for her. If he thought about it, he might have been gone for her again the second he saw her standing outside his garage next to that Dodge Charger. He didn't know how Jenna felt. Of course, he caught her watching him, a small smile on her face. She was attentive and caring, but that wasn't the same thing as falling in love with him. He'd avoided talking to her about it the last two weeks, but it was time now, time for them to finally put into words what they'd been communicating with kisses.

He didn't have time to think about it now, though, because Jenna was walking toward them. She hugged her friend, and they chatted for a minute about clothes and stuff Cal didn't care about. Then Jenna announced it was time to sit for dinner, and Cal *did* care about that.

It was worth it too. Slices of rare roast beef and garlic mashed potatoes and roasted broccoli. Must have cost the company a pretty penny. Jenna's eyes flitted around the room during dinner until he placed a hand on her thigh. "Eat."

She looked a little guilty, but she dug in and cleaned her plate. They sat at a table with her brother and his date, her parents, and some other higher-ups in the company. Cal kept his head down and his mouth full, so he wasn't asked to contribute to any conversations. He let the voices carry over his head.

Dinner was fine until Dylan finished off what had to be his third drink and looked at Jenna with a gleam in his eye.

Cal's backbone stiffened.

"So you think this event will actually have a lasting impact?" Dylan asked, propping himself up with an elbow on the table.

Jenna's face was composed, and Cal knew if they were in private, she'd probably light into her brother. But not in public. "I do think it will. Something had to be done."

It was a reference to the damage her brother had inflicted on the company. No one at the table missed that. Dylan's eyes narrowed. "Thank God the brilliant Jenna was able to come back into town to fix everything. Never mind that I've been working my ass off at this company for ten years, helping to build it to what it was—"

"No one is saying you don't work hard, Dylan," Jenna's father said sternly.

But Dylan was on a roll. "So now you're back to play the hero and to finish this white-trash fairy tale you got going on." He waved in Cal's direction.

Jenna sucked in a sharp breath, and Cal curled his hands into fists under the table. He told himself Dylan was drunk. He told himself to ignore the words, that he didn't care what Dylan thought of him. Because he didn't. But this was Jenna's night, and he didn't want Dylan embarrassing her.

"Dylan," Jenna said in a firm voice, "enough. Why don't you switch to drinking water?"

Her brother stood and sloppily smoothed his tie. "I think I'll get another drink. We have to get our money's worth out of this open bar we're paying for, right?"

Cal stared at the man's back, wanting to go after him and get in his face. Instead, he reached over and slipped his fingers into Jenna's. She shot him a wobbly smile.

The night went pretty fast after that. Cal stopped drinking because the last thing he wanted to do was embarrass Jenna.

They listened to the raffle and clapped when Delilah squealed about winning an all-expenses-paid ski trip.

Then Jenna dragged Cal on the dance floor to slow dance, because Cal didn't do any other kind of dancing.

The strains of "Wonderful Tonight" by Eric Clapton came through the speakers set up by the DJ booth. Jenna's arms were on his shoulders, her fingers twirling in the hair at the base of his neck. He curled his hands around her waist, so his fingers rested on her lower back and the top of her ass. Most other couples kept it a little more PG, but Cal was tired and wanted Jenna as close as possible.

Her hazel eyes peered up at him in the dim light. "You were amazing tonight."

"Me? I didn't do anything. This was all you."

"Yeah, but—"

"You planned this event. I heard people talking about how nice it was and how much they loved it and how proud they were to work for MacMillan."

She blushed slightly.

He squeezed her waist. "That was all you."

"Thank you. I'm just saying that I know this isn't your thing, but you've been amazingly supportive all night."

"Wouldn't have thought to be anything else."

He'd spent a long time with his head down, working hard within a small circle of family. He'd found a place to rent to open up his own cycle repair shop, so once he told his father about it, he'd have his dream job. And in one summer, he now had a half-brother and a woman at his side who made his heart pound. He'd spent so long trying to separate himself from the kid he'd been that he hadn't realized that kid might have actually known a thing or two.

Eric Clapton's lyrics filtered into his brain, and with Jenna's upturned face full of devotion, all he wanted to do was say what was in his heart. This would change it all, he knew, this final acknowledgement of what had been steadily growing between them since she got back to town.

He had to take the plunge, because he trusted Jenna to be there at the bottom. He trusted himself to make it there. He raised his hand and brushed her hair off her temple. "Love you, Sunshine. Not sure I ever stopped. But what I felt for you at eighteen is nothing compared to how I feel for you now."

Jenna's mouth dropped open, and her hazel eyes were wide. She didn't blink. She didn't speak. Her fingers still clung to him, and so he focused on that, on her body against him, and waited for her to process his words.

She licked her lips, and her eyelashes fluttered.

And then she smiled.

But not just any smile—no, this was *the* smile, the one that lit up her entire face, made her glow, made her *shine*. Cal didn't want to move from this spot, not for a long while, as he basked in the warmth and absolute beauty of his Sunshine.

She opened her mouth, but whatever she was going to say was stopped by his cell phone ringing in his pocket. He normally would have ignored it, but he wanted to check to make sure it wasn't Asher. When he pulled it out of his pocket, Gabe's number was on his screen. It was the only thing that could tear him away from this moment.

"Jenna, it's Gabe, so I gotta—"

She waved him off, her hand trembling. He hated to leave her there on the dance floor, at this moment, which seemed crucial, because he didn't know if he'd breathe again until he heard what she was about to say. But what if something was wrong with Asher?

He put his phone up to his ear, but he couldn't hear over the music. As he headed back down the hallway of the bathrooms, the call disconnected. He frowned at it and called back, getting Gabe's voicemail. "What the hell?" he muttered, staring at his phone so intently that he wasn't looking where he was going and nearly walked into someone. He pulled up abruptly and lifted his gaze to the hazel eyes of Dylan MacMillan.

The guy didn't look like he wanted to move either. He was listing slightly to the right, a consequence of the rum-and-Cokes he'd been sucking down like water. But his arms were crossed over his chest.

And his eyes were cold as hell.

Cal straightened his back, already thinking of an endgame, a way to avoid a conversation and get the hell away from Dylan.

He wanted to answer this phone call, get back to Jenna, and find out what the hell she was going to say.

The way Dylan's lip was curled, the way he looked down his nose at Cal, chafed Cal's skin like sandpaper, but he held firm.

"So how will your relationship end this time, huh? Because we all know it will."

Cal sighed. *This conversation is already starting off well.* "I'm not doing this with you." He made to walk past Dylan, but the guy sidestepped to block his path. Cal clenched his fists and counted to ten.

Dylan was so close, Cal could smell the rum on his breath and a hint of his expensive cologne.

"It's so easy for her," Dylan snarled. "All she has to do is come back to town, wave a wand, and everyone falls for her. She gets the job and the man."

Cal tried to let the words go in one ear and out the other, but his blood was beginning to boil. He didn't care what Dylan thought of him, but he did care if he was disrespectful to Jenna. "Did you ever think about how that happens because she deserves it? Because she works hard and people notice?"

Dylan's nostrils flared. "And everyone's talking about you coming here on her arm, how sweet it is that you two are back together. Everyone forgets the Paytons don't belong here, especially not at the country club."

Cal threw his arms out to his sides. "Honest to God, Dylan. What the fuck is your problem with me? I couldn't care less about you. I don't care that you exist, so why the fuck do you give a shit about me?"

Dylan turned blazing eyes on Cal. "I'm tired of everything always being about her!" He shoved Cal in the chest with both hands, and since Cal was unprepared, he stumbled back a foot.

Cal clenched his fists and rolled his jaw, because what he really wanted to do was take Dylan's block off, put a fist through his face. Break his nose just like he did ten years ago.

"I wish everyone could see what you're really like." Dylan's voice was full of barbs. "And then they'll see she's not so perfect."

Cal's shoulder twitched, his whole body wanting him to throw a punch, but he thought back to half an hour ago, when Jenna danced in his arms. They weren't eighteen anymore. Cal wasn't a hothead. He'd walk away, because punching this guy at the country club would only make everything worse.

"Cal?" Jenna's voice filtered through the music.

Dylan's eyes widened. He glanced over his shoulder, and then he turned back to Cal. In two strides he was in front of the bathroom door. And Cal watched in horror as Dylan pushed the door open, then grabbed the handle, and slammed the door back into his own face.

"What the *fuck*?" Cal roared.

And Dylan screamed a high-pitched wail as he held his nose, which was now gushing blood.

Voices came closer, reaching the end of the hallway, as Cal watched Dylan bend at the waist, howling like a banshee.

Everything was in slow motion then. Jenna's dad was screaming for security. His wife, with a blanched face beside him, looking like she was going to faint. Dylan clutching his bleeding face, pointing at Cal. "He hit me! The asshole hit me!"

There were men around Cal, jostling him, grabbing his arms. He stared at his knuckles, scarred from labor, and wondered how the hell he was going to prove he hadn't touched Dylan. Who was going to believe him over the son of the company's owner?

Time froze when Jenna appeared at the top of the hallway. She was backlit from the lights on the dance floor, so her hair was a dark wavy mass around her face. Just a moment ago, he was there, floating on a high in her light. And now, not five minutes later, everything was back to fucking black. The contrast stung his eyes and pierced his heart. Cal stared at her, shaking his head, unsure what to say. "I didn't—" he began, but Dylan started wailing louder, drowning out Cal's assertion of the truth. Cal could probably take out the guys holding him with a couple well-placed elbow jabs, but how would that look? That would only make him look guiltier. So he didn't fight. He'd have to explain later, if he even got the chance. He allowed himself to be dragged down the hallway toward a back door.

Away from Jenna.

She stood there among the chaos. Motionless. Staring at him.

He hadn't known the knife of disappointment could flay him alive. He knew now.

FIVE MINUTES LATER, his mind wasn't on what had happened in that damn hallway of the country club. Because his phone rang again, and Gabe was hysterical with apologies, and Cal was doing ninety on the way to the hospital, thinking he wasn't sure he'd make it through seeing another brother lying on one of those beds.

Chapter Twenty-Four

THIS WAS DÉJÀ VU to Cal. It was Max all over again—when he'd been attacked on his college campus, pistol-whipped in the back of his head.

Cal had nearly gone out of his mind when he saw his youngest brother on that hospital bed, a bandage around his head.

And now…well…now it was happening again. Except this time, it actually *was* his youngest brother, the one he didn't know existed, lying on the white-sheeted mattress, a bandage on his head, his broken arm in a brace. The nurse said they'd cast it later.

Cal had shown up at the hospital to find a crying Julian and a hysterical Gabe, who apologized profusely. Cal hadn't said a word as they led him to Asher's room. Their words were nails hammered into his brain—how Gabe had given Asher a ride on his motorcycle around the yard. The bike had backfired, and Asher had fallen off, cracking his head on the driveway and breaking his arm.

Jesus fuck. He'd kept Asher in Tory to keep him safe. And he'd done exactly the opposite, suffering through a fucking party he didn't even want to be at, while the kid fell off a bike and landed in the hospital.

He'd been so busy with Asher and Jenna, he'd completely forgotten about fixing Gabe's bike. It just…slipped his mind.

Asher had been sleeping when Cal arrived at the room, so Cal talked to the doctors to find out that Asher was mostly fine, but he was being monitored for a concussion. While feeling like he was going to vomit in the fake plant outside his brother's room, Cal had called his mom to tell her what happened. The hospital needed insurance information. Cal had expected a guilt trip from her. He'd expected something, but all she'd said was to have Asher call her when he woke up.

Fucking ridiculous.

And now he sat on a bench outside Asher's room while the kid slept, telling himself to breath. In through the nose. Out through the mouth. He had his head between his legs, his hands laced behind his neck.

This is exactly what he'd wanted to avoid. This was why he'd spent ten years shutting himself down. Because this fucking hurt, to be so worried about someone else, to not have control. It made him want to gather everyone he cared about and stick them in a bubble where he could watch them and protect them all the time. He'd told himself he'd try this whole family thing all over again, and it hadn't taken long before it all got fucked up. Hadn't taken long before Cal realized he wasn't strong enough to deal with all of this again. Even right now, he was sick to his stomach, one step away from a mental breakdown. He'd tried this—the whole responsibility thing—and he'd failed.

His fists clenched, his chest constricted. He needed to get his shit together before Asher woke up.

He kept his phone off, having told Jill to call Asher's phone if she wanted to get in touch. Because he didn't want to hear the disappointment in Jenna's voice that would mirror that look on her face—the same one she'd give him a decade ago.

So he was done. He didn't want to hear it. He didn't want to see it. He didn't know what he'd been thinking, reaching for this elusive dream of Jenna and a family.

Because right now, while Asher slept, his face pinched in pain, Cal couldn't remember why it was worth it. Not now, while Jenna's disappointed expression ghosted in front of his eyes everywhere he turned. Not now, when his vision was blinking between Asher and Max, injured.

Maybe he wasn't strong enough. Maybe he'd reached the limit now. The reserve was gone. He was dry.

He was that eighteen-year-old kid again, wishing for things that would never happen. Fuck this shit. He was done. Life wasn't complicated back when he lived alone and kept everyone away with a scowl. He wanted that back.

He needed a shower. He needed a drink. He needed anything to get rid of these bugs crawling under his skin.

And he really wanted to burn these clothes.

Footsteps sounded in the hallway, and Cal looked up, expecting a doctor or nurse, but instead it was Brent. Cal frowned. "How'd you get here?"

Brent held two cups of coffee and two muffins. He handed one of each to Cal. "I drove." He sank down on the bench beside Cal and took a sip of his coffee.

"I mean how'd you find out about Asher?"

"Gabe called me. Said he thought you looked homicidal."

"I'm not homicidal."

"Well, he said you needed me, so here I am." *You needed me.* Cal filed those words away to deal with later. "Doctors say he'll be okay?" Brent asked.

"He'll be okay." Cal rotated the cup of coffee in his hands and watched the tendrils of steam lick the air. He told himself to keep his mouth shut, but Brent's quiet presence beside him loosened his tongue. "I feel like I failed him."

"Who? Asher?"

"I told him he'd be safe here and—"

"Don't be stupid."

Cal glared.

"No, seriously. You're pulling that martyr shit again, and I'm not listening to it. It was an accident, Cal. Both Gabe and Asher knew better than to ride that shitty motorcycle around their house."

"I should have remembered to fix Gabe's bike. I shouldn't have put Asher off and taken him for a ride already. I told him I'd take him tomorrow, and so I know he was excited—"

"Right. Asher was excited. And he's a teenager and made a shitty decision. Gabe's just an idiot all the time."

Cal snorted.

Brent leaned down so he caught Cal's eyes. "Don't do this. You've done so much for that kid."

"I'm worried he'll blame me." Would he even want to stay here after this?

"He's not going to blame you."

Cal fell silent. He stood up and peeked through the window of Asher's door to see large round eyes in a pale face staring at him.

"He's awake." Cal pushed the door open, with Brent following at his heels. Cal went right to the bed, peering down at Asher's dark hair flopped on the white sheet. "How ya feeling?"

Asher's stared at him for a minute, and then his lower lip trembled. "I'm so sorry."

"Hey, no need to cry."

Small sob sounds spilled from Asher's chapped lips. "I'm so sorry, Cal!"

"Whoa, whoa!" Cal pressed on Asher's shoulders, stilling him, because the kid was squirming and probably making his head and arm ache more. "It's okay. Don't get yourself worked up."

"I shouldn't have gotten on the back of Gabe's bike, but he said he wouldn't tell anyone and that he wouldn't go fast. And then the bike jerked, and I wasn't holding on tight enough, and—"

"Kid, take a fucking breath," Brent said in exasperation from the other side of the bed.

Asher stopped talking, but his eyes were wet, with small tears trickling from the corners.

Cal sank down into a chair beside the bed. Asher's eyes followed his every movement. Cal gripped Asher's good arm. "Take it easy. I'm disappointed you got on that bike, yeah. And I'm going to fucking kill Gabe. But you know it wasn't the right thing to do. So I'm not going to nail ya for it. Lying in a hospital bed is punishment enough, yeah?"

Asher nodded, and color returned to his face. "Yeah." He turned his head to Brent and then back to Cal. He licked his lips and tried for a small smile. "Thanks for being here."

" 'Course," Cal said.

"I hope I didn't make you leave the party early."

Cal snorted. "Nah, you didn't."

"Really?" Brent asked.

Cal waved an arm at him. "I'll tell you later." To Asher, he said, "Look, I called your mom so the hospital has your insurance information. She wants you to call her."

Asher swallowed. "She's not coming, then, I guess?"

Cal gritted his teeth. "Don't think so, buddy."

Asher shrugged, but it was forced.

Cal stood up. "Brent and I'll wait out in the hallway. Why don't you give her a call?"

After placing Asher's phone in his hand, Cal followed Brent outside of the room, and then Cal proceeded to tell him everything about the fight with Dylan.

Brent's eyes were huge. "So he's just jealous of his sister?"

Cal ran his tongue over his teeth. "I think…it's a lot about his pride. And that, for a man like him, is something he can't get over."

"That is fucking crazy."

"Yep."

"He actually smashed his own face against the door."

"Yep."

Brent started laughing.

"It's not funny, Brent."

His brother was doubled over, hands on his knees. He raised a finger as another gasp of laughter overtook him.

Cal crossed his arms and glared. Brent finally raised his head with watery eyes. "He smashed his own face! What fucking lunatic does that?"

"Can you stop swearing? We're in a fucking hospital!"

And that sent Brent into a whole other gale of laughter. When Cal realized what he'd said, he began laughing too. Although he sobered quickly when he remembered Jenna scolding him for swearing in the grocery store.

When Brent caught his breath, he said, "What did Jenna do?"

That sobered Cal up quickly. "Believed him, I guess. I don't give a shit."

Brent frowned.

"It's my word against Dylan's, and it was in front of her whole company. What choice does she have?" His heart felt like it was being tugged out of his body, piece by fucking piece. He'd had her for a whole month. A month that had been the best of his life since she'd left him the first time. He wished he could go back to that time on the dance floor, when he told her he loved her, when he'd handed her his entire heart. "If she still thinks I'm just like that eighteen-year-old kid, then what the hell are we even doing being together, you know? Maybe I should have just punched him."

"You think he'll press charges?"

Cal ran his hands through his hair. "Shit, didn't even think about that. I won't let her bail me out this time. I can afford to defend myself."

"Don't worry about that now. Let's get Asher taken care of, first."

Cal pushed the MacMillans to the corner of his mind, back to where he couldn't see them and where they couldn't affect him, and he opened the door to visit his brother in the hospital bed.

JENNA'S WHOLE BODY felt numb.

Dylan was whimpering about how Cal had punched him in the nose. Her mother was fanning herself on a chair someone had brought over as she twisted her necklace nervously, eyes skittering around the room like a hunted deer. Her father was comforting Dylan, checking his eyes, nose, and teeth like her brother was a stud horse.

The employees who had heard the commotion were standing around talking in hushed whispers, trying to hide their pointed fingers and accusing looks.

This party had been perfect. It'd been the culmination of hard work and perfect planning and in one fell swoop, the walls had crashed down around her.

The country club employees were ushering people back into the main room, and Jenna could only hope that most of them had imbibed enough for this whole thing to be a little fuzzy.

She swallowed, took a deep breath, and walked toward her brother.

Her mother's feeble voice called her name, but Jenna ignored her, her eyes on the two men in her life who screwed everything up once, but over her *dead fucking body* would they do it again.

She'd seen the blood smear on the bathroom door, but she wasn't sure if her father had seen it or had chosen to ignore it.

She'd also seen the look in Cal's eyes. The flare of defiance before a grim acceptance.

What she didn't see were cut knuckles. What she didn't see was the look of a Cal who'd lost his temper. Cal had changed. He wasn't the same man he'd been back when he'd broken Dylan's nose. He was passionate without the anger. He had more control. She had to believe that, because if not, they didn't have much of a future.

And dammit, Cal loved her. He *loved* her. She clung to that like a life preserver.

Then there was the mystery of how her brother had a bloody face. Cal, she believed in. Her brother, she did not.

Dylan must have heard the click of her heels, because he raised his head and narrowed his eyes above his swollen nose. "Look what your white-trash boyfriend—"

She slapped him. Right across the face, his skin blooming white at the impact.

Her palm stung, and she shook it before wiping it on the side of her dress.

"Jenna!" her father said, a hand on Dylan's shoulder but eyes blazing at her. "What on earth—"

"What really happened, Dylan?" She refused to look away from her brother, wanting to be witness to the guilt washing over his face.

"I told you, he—"

"See, no. I don't think Cal had anything to do with what happened to your face."

"He punched me before. You think he wouldn't punch me again?"

"Tell me why there's a smear of blood on the bathroom door."

Her father strained his neck to look at the door behind him, but Dylan kept his eyes locked on hers. "What are you, CSI?"

"Dylan."

"Well, he shoved me—"

"You said he punched you."

"H-he did both."

The fire in her belly was starting to rise up her throat. "Try that lie again without stuttering."

Dylan's eyes clouded. "You think I—"

"I'm not sure what to think. What's going on in my mind is pretty disgusting. So how about you tell the truth?"

Dylan stayed mute.

Her father turned to his son with a furrowed brow. "What's going on?"

"Tell me how your nose got bloody. Tell me, Dylan. Because I don't think Cal did it."

Dylan opened his mouth but then shut it again.

Her father dropped his hand from Dylan's shoulder and stepped back, eyes wide. "Tell your sister the truth."

"I'm going to ask one more time," Jenna said. "Did Cal hit you?"

Dylan swallowed. She expected him to start up the accusations again, but something flickered in his eyes, a little bit of regret mixed with embarrassment. And then, he shook his head, just once, confirming what she already knew.

"Dylan!" her father said sharply.

"Did you injure *yourself*?" Jenna asked.

Dylan clenched his jaw. "The truth doesn't matter. Everyone thinks he did it, and that's what matters. Now everyone sees you're not so *perfect*."

He hissed the last word, and it made Jenna want to rip her last name up into tiny shreds between them like bathroom tissue. "You did this whole thing just to make me look bad? You're a grown man, and all you did was make yourself look like an idiot. You want me to believe he did it so I'll dump him, because I'd have no other choice. I couldn't work at MacMillan and stay with the guy who punched my brother at a company party." She took a step away from them. "Well, this time, you're wrong. Because if that's my choice, I quit. Find something else to focus your energy on rather than competing with me, because I'm done."

She turned away from her gasping brother and father, past her mother's soft protests, and walked back out into the ballroom. She held her head high, despite the whispers. Because she'd done nothing wrong. Cal had done nothing wrong. But at the moment, she didn't care one bit about the rumors. All she cared about was getting to Cal.

After grabbing her purse, she ran outside, pausing to take off her shoes, not caring about the stones in the parking lot.

But Cal's truck wasn't there, and she could see the marks of his tires, showing he'd taken off like a bat out of hell.

She called his phone, but it went right to voicemail. She texted him: *Call me.*

Her phone stayed silent. So she called Delilah, who'd left the party early, hoping her friend could pick up her stranded butt from the country club.

Chapter Twenty-Five

CAL CALLED JILL again the next morning to tell her
Asher was being discharged.

He held the hospital phone to his ear while Asher was
in the bathroom. "What did you say?"

Her voice trembled. "I left my husband."

Cal swallowed, and he stared at his boots. "Okay."

"I guess it was the news that Asher was hurt that made
me think…that made me realize what was happening, letting his father put him at risk. I don't want my son hurt."

Cal clenched his jaw and rubbed his forehead. Asher
hurt. Like he had been under Cal's watch. "Glad to hear
that."

"Don't tell Asher yet, though, please. I need to get
some things sorted here, and then I'll be in touch, all
right?"

To take him home. Where he belonged. Which wasn't
with Cal. "Yeah, okay."

"I'll call soon."

Cal hung up the phone. So that was it. This fantasy family was vaporizing in front of his eyes. Wasn't this what he wanted? To be alone again?

And if so, why did this hurt so much?

ASHER WAS STILL a little pale as Cal helped him into his truck. The kid had been discharged earlier that morning after a night in the hospital. He was now the owner of a bright, lime green cast and a fresh set of stitches on his scalp. They were on the shaved side of his head, which irked Cal because he had to see them.

Asher was smiling, albeit weakly, and said he just wanted to get home and play video games. Apparently the non-high-definition television in the hospital room wasn't to his liking.

Cal glanced at his phone in the center console of his truck. He'd left it off overnight and hadn't bothered to turn it on. It all could…wait. Yeah, just wait.

Asher turned to him when they were halfway home. "I'm sorry."

"You already said that. And it's okay."

"Yeah, but I don't think it is. I just…you said you'd take me for a ride soon, that I'd earned it, so I didn't think anything of letting Gabe drive me around for a little…"

"So what exactly happened?"

Asher sighed. "Gabe said his bike had been acting up, so he got some shop to fix it. It's a couple of towns over, because there's no one in town that's certified to fix bikes."

That stung, because Cal could have fixed it if he'd remembered. Instead, Gabe had gone to someone else, who might not have known what he was doing. *Fuck*.

"So," Asher continued, "he said he wanted to test it out."

"At night?"

Asher bit his lip. "It was just around the house."

The stupidity of the whole situation was incredible. "Go on."

"So he was going slow, and I wasn't holding on really tight. Over the driveway, he gunned it a little, and...I don't know, something happened. It didn't sound right. And next thing I knew, I was in the air and landing on the ground." Asher put a knee to the bench and turned to look at Cal. "I feel like I really messed things up between us."

Things were messed up, but it wasn't Asher's fault. "You didn't."

"You sure?"

The kid would be relieved when he found out his mother had made the right decision and he could go back home. For now, though, he had to heal. The rest would all come later. "Positive."

Once they were parked in Cal's driveway, he helped Asher out of the truck and then grabbed the kid's bag of clothes out of the back that Brent had brought to the hospital.

He was halfway to the open door when he heard Ash yell, "Jenna!"

Cal froze. He heard her voice from inside the house, talking to Asher, and the boy's excited tone, laced with tears.

Part of him wanted to get back in the truck and drive away. Far, far away. The other part of him wanted to tell Jenna to go the hell home.

And the other part...the one he didn't want to acknowledge...wanted to rush inside and wrap her in his arms and tuck his nose into her neck, breathing in her scent and feeling her hands massage his back.

His feet carried him to the door, and he stood in the entrance, watching a fresh-faced Jenna fawn over Asher. She was wearing a pair of jean shorts and oversized T-shirt.

Asher was on the couch now, a pillow under his head, the video game controller in his hands. He was smiling up at Jenna like she...like she was the sun. And Cal's heart sank down into the toe of his boots.

She was here for Asher. She must be. The girl had a huge heart. She cared about the kid as much as Cal did.

When the sound of yelling and swords clanging came from the TV and the fast clicking of buttons from the controller, Jenna straightened up, blowing a stray lock of brown hair out of her face that had slipped from her ponytail.

They stared at each other. Cal hadn't moved from the doorway. He was still wearing the clothes he'd worn last night. He was sure he looked like hell. Because he felt like hell.

She motioned toward the kitchen with her head. He dropped Asher's bag on the floor, shut the door behind him, and followed her.

"What're you doing here?" His voice was harsh from the stale air of the hospital.

She had a sponge in her hand and was scrubbing the sink. *Scrubbing the sink?*

"I'm cleaning."

He leaned against the counter beside her and crossed his arms over his chest. "You're cleaning."

"Yes. Why don't you go take a shower? And maybe a nap?"

She was telling him what to do now? "How did you get in here?"

The look she shot him could freeze hell. "You gave me a key." She said it slowly, like he was an idiot.

That didn't explain what she was doing. "I don't—"

She sighed, really heavily, like every muscle in her body hurt. "Cal, please. Just go take a shower and lie down. I'll bring you some food." She paused and bit her lip. "Then we'll talk."

He bristled. "Not sure—"

"We're talking, Cal." Still with that stern look. "Go. Wash. Your. Body."

He huffed and turned on his heel sharply.

After making sure Asher was okay (he was) and that he didn't need anything (he didn't; Jenna had already given him water and food), Cal went upstairs.

He stripped on the way to the bathroom, leaving his clothes where they lay. He took a five-minute shower, wrapped a towel around his waist, and then crawled into bed. He was out seconds after his head hit the pillow.

THE SOUND OF a clattering on his nightstand jolted him awake. The sun outside his window had begun to descend. "Shit." He rubbed his eyes. "What time is it?"

"Six," Jenna said from somewhere behind him. He heard a rustle of clothes and then the sound of them hitting the bottom of his hamper.

"I slept that long?" he asked.

"I didn't wake you. Figured you needed the sleep. There's a sandwich on the nightstand for you."

He squinted at it. "Peanut butter and jelly?"

"Glass of milk is there too."

It was. And this small talk was painful.

"Jenna…"

The bed dipped beside him. "Asher's been asleep for about an hour. Do we need to wake him?"

Cal shook his head and sat up, reaching for the plate. "Doctor said no. They don't really do that anymore for concussions."

Her hazel eyes blinked. "Okay."

As he took a bite of the sandwich, he was acutely aware that he was wearing only a towel. And Jenna's hand was right next to his naked thigh. "So…"

"I quit."

So there it was, the closure. The *I can't do this*. The *I can't believe you punched my brother at my company party*. The *I don't love you back*. At this point, did he even want to dispute the facts? It would be so much easier to let her think he did it. To let her go.

"I can't do this again." Her eyes were on her fists clenched in his comforter. The peanut butter sandwich plastered to the roof of his mouth tasted like sawdust. "Last time was bad enough, but what happened this time was…way, way worse."

Last time Dylan had stood in front of him, bleeding, they'd at least been in private.

"I'm sorry," he said hoarsely, dropping the half-eaten sandwich on his nightstand and gulping down milk.

"I'm sorry too," Jenna said. "I mean, Dylan and I were never close, but now…well, I think I need to cut ties completely."

Cal's head shot up. "What?"

"Did he mean to hit his face on the bathroom door?" Jenna fidgeted with the ends of her ponytail. "Or was it an accident?"

Cal's head was spinning. Did Dylan tell the truth? There was no way.

"Cal?"

"What're you talking about?"

She frowned. "Dylan. He tried to say you punched him, but when I called him on the lie, he finally 'fessed up."

Cal blinked. "You called him on it?"

Jenna was doing that thing again, where she was looking at him like he was an idiot. "I knew you wouldn't hit him, Cal. Not—" Her eyes grew wide, impossibly wide, and then she shot to her feet and narrowed those eyes to slits. "Oh my God. You thought I believed Dylan, didn't you?"

He couldn't suck enough air in his lungs. "I…I…yeah. I did. What was I supposed to think? You stood there in the hallway with that fucking look of disappointment on your face."

"Hell, yeah, I was disappointed, Cal! I couldn't believe this was all happening again. And maybe for five seconds, I thought you punched him. But then I saw your face and...I knew you didn't do it."

"But last time, you chose—"

She shook her head, hair flying in her face. "I chose you!" She swallowed and then lowered her voice, sinking back onto the bed. "You have to know that, right? I chose you when I made that decision, even though it didn't seem like it. If I hadn't loved you, Cal, I would have let you take that hit. I would have let you fuck up your future. I loved you, so I chose you. And that meant I had to let you go."

He needed water. And alcohol. And a bath in nicotine patches.

"But this time, I don't have to let you go," she said. "I quit, because I won't work with my brother who uses you to carry out some stupid vendetta against me. Who won't accept you. So that's it."

He reached for her, but she pulled her hand away. "You told me the first time I saw you again that you weren't the same eighteen-year-old kid. And I believed you. So why can't you believe that I'm not the same eighteen-year-old girl?"

He didn't know what to say. His head was foggy, and his stomach still cramped from everything that had happened last night.

Jenna stood up, her on hand on top of her head. "Why aren't you saying anything right now?"

Maybe if Asher hadn't gotten hurt. If Cal hadn't failed at that. If Jill hadn't gotten her act together, he could have done this again. But his heart was raw, and he'd already begun building up that iron wall that had protected him for ten years. He didn't belong in Jenna's world, in her future. Cal didn't belong in anyone's future. He swallowed. "I don't know if this can work."

She blanched. "What?"

Now this pain, this was real, but if he could just get through it, he'd be back behind that wall that had served him so well. He had to walk over hot coals to get there but then never again. "I tried with Asher, Jenna, and I failed. And it would just be a matter of time before I actually fucked us up too. I thought I could do this again, thought I could dream for the things I once did. But I can't. I'm not the same guy I was at eighteen, and I don't want to be. No matter how much I try to pretend. It's been too long, and I'm too used to keeping everything on lockdown, surrounding myself with things I can control. And I can't control this. Any of this."

Jenna stood frozen; the only indication she was alive was the rise and fall of her chest. "You can't be serious right now."

"I have never felt so hopeless as I have in the last day. Between your brother and Asher..." He clenched his fists. "I'm dry, Jenna. My well has run dry. I got nothing left, no reserves. I've reached my limit. I thought I could give you what you need, but I can't."

She didn't move. Her eyes were huge in her face, and *fuck*, Cal was getting burned, scarred. Why couldn't this all be over so he could suffer in peace?

"And I'm not enough?"

He jerked his head up. "What?"

"That's what you're saying, then. That I'm not enough to give you what you need. To fill you back up."

He didn't know how to answer that, not at all. So he stayed silent.

She blinked rapidly, and her lips trembled. "So everything we've done—the late-night talks, my bringing you lunch at the garage, the movies, everything—that wasn't enough to get you through some hard times?"

The last month flipped through his mind, but right now, none of it was getting through to him. It couldn't cover the searing pain tearing through him now. "It's not your fault, Jenna. You're always enough. I just got a leak I can't fix."

She turned away, her ponytail flying around her face. When she reached the door of the bedroom, she stopped and said over her shoulder, "Thanks for being honest. Just so you know, I do think you're good enough. But I'm done trying to convince you of it."

And then she walked out.

Chapter Twenty-Six

"WE GOT MATCHING scars." Max grinned and touched his head to Asher's. "Head-trauma power!"

Asher laughed.

Cal didn't find any of it funny. "You each took about five years off my life, so I'll thank you not to make a joke of it, assholes."

The whole family was over at Cal's house to see Asher as he recovered. Max had driven down with Lea. Gabe and Julian were there, even though Cal spent most of his time glaring at Gabe, who stood in a corner looking uncomfortable.

Julian sat on the couch with Asher, their shoulders touching, and Julian looked so genuinely broken up about Ash's injuries that Cal decided he'd let the brothers live.

It'd been three days since Asher got home from the hospital. Three days since Cal had managed to fuck up his relationship with Jenna again. When he finally got his head together, he replayed the conversation. Over and over and over again. And each time was another cut in his skin. He wished he had more time after Asher's injuries to get his head together before he spoke to Jenna. He didn't think the outcome of his conversation with her would have been any different, but maybe he would have made more sense.

And now, she was everywhere in this house. The bed, the kitchen, the shower, the couch.

He'd finally found a place where nobody was around, yet he was going to have to move again to be alone. Because this house was far from empty.

He'd been in a shit mood. A throwback to his early twenties, when the pain of losing Jenna was still fresh. Asher seemed half scared of him. What did it matter anyway? He'd be going home to his mom soon. Brent had called him on his mood, but then Brent told him he was a grumpy asshole every day, so Cal didn't think that counted.

The front door opened, and Jack walked in, a cap pulled low on his forehead, gray eyes dilated from the harsh sun outside. He didn't say a word to anyone, instead walking directly to Asher and hauling him upright with a grip on the kid's biceps. The chatter in the room dimmed as Jack's eyes roamed Asher, taking in the stitches and the arm cast and a couple bruises and road rash.

Asher's eyes were huge, staring up at Jack. The big man's jaw clenched, and he patted Asher roughly on the back of his neck. He let him go, and as Asher sank slowly back onto the couch next to Julian, Jack's head whipped to Gabe. "You!" he shouted and advanced on him like a predator.

"Oh, shit," Gabe said under his breath and squeezed himself into the wall like he could melt into the plaster.

Cal heaved a sigh and went after his dad, because blood was a bitch to clean up.

"Dad," Cal began as he reached his dad's side, but the guy had his finger in Gabe's face. And Gabe was pale and quivering.

"You little shithead," Jack said. "Please explain why the hell the kid's got a fucking broken arm and had to spend the night in the hospital."

Gabe licked his lips. "Well, uh, he fell off the back of the my bike, and—"

"I know that, ya moron. I want to know how it happened. You can't drive the thing?"

"No, I…I, um, had a problem with it, and I took it to a shop in Brookridge, but they, uh, fucked up, I guess. The thing backfired, and—"

"Why didn't you give it to Cal to fix?"

Jack's question made Cal pause. Since when did his dad take any interest in Cal's ability to fix motorcycles?

Gabe's eyes shifted to Cal, like he wanted help with this conversation. Cal just stared back at him. He'd been under his dad's evil eye enough. Someone else's turn. And no way was he helping Gabe after what he did. Gabe heaved a sigh. "Cal was busy, and I heard this guy did good work but clearly not."

Cal stood motionless as Jack turned his head, piercing him with his eyes that were so like his own.

Jack shook his head, exhaling slowly, and then walked away. Gabe looked like he'd dodged a bullet. And Cal wasn't sure what to think.

He followed his dad, who'd gone out to the garage to get a beer out of the ice chest. The door was open, the sun lighting the inside of the garage. The chrome of Cal's bike gleamed in the middle, like a huge metal elephant. His dad took a drag of his beer and then lit up a cigarette. Cal stared at it longingly. He could smoke again now, right? No reason to quit; no one to quit for.

Cal scratched the patch on his arm. "What was that look for in there?"

Jack took another pull of beer, wiping his mouth with the back of his hand before sticking his lit cigarette between his lips. "I'm not so good at this."

Cal waited.

Jack hollowed his cheeks and blew the smoke out, staring out of the garage doors. "Takes me time to get used to new things. Thought Max would be working with us, but he ain't. He's off working as a big-shot teacher, and that's great. But it threw me for a loop that he didn't want to work at the garage with us."

That had been a point of contention when Max was a senior in college. Cal thought he'd get a business degree and then come work at the garage, but Max had other plans. It'd taken his being laid up in the hospital to get the guts to tell Dad what he really wanted to do. And it'd taken his son getting injured for Dad to accept it.

Again, Cal waited.

"So I wasn't prepared for things to change again." Jack's jaw was tight as hell, grinding his molars. Cal could imagine this admission was a little painful. "I like your tools with me and your body in the bay beside mine. I know I can rely on you."

Cal's body went hot. "Thanks, Dad."

"So I'm stubborn. I know that. And every time you asked about changing things, about working on bikes, I dug my heels in more."

Cal held his breath, waiting to hear what came next, because this seemed really important.

"So if you wanna hang out your shingle at the shop, then we'll make it work."

Cal's jaw dropped. "Are you serious?"

"I didn't see a need for it until today. But I'm not having the people of this town go to some hack. You know what you're doing."

Cal blinked. "You really changed your mind?"

Jack squinted at him. "I did. I'm old and set in my ways. Cut me some fucking slack."

Cal stared at the stained concrete under his boots. He knew a thing or two about being stubborn. Change sucked; he got that. Hell, that's what he'd hid behind to drive away Jenna.

The realization flushed through his body like a bucket of ice. He was just like his fucking dad, wasn't he? A gruff mechanic who wasn't willing to take on anything new because of the fear of the unknown. And hell, a couple of weeks ago, Cal was well on his way to smoking a pack a day like his dad. He'd spent all his life, determined not to become his father, and that's what he'd become.

Alone. Stubborn.

An asshole.

Oblivious to Cal's crisis, Jack took another pull of his beer. "You're all assholes for riding bikes, but at least you'll all be safe assholes if you fix shit."

Call tried to focus back on the conversation. "Appreciate the confidence. Dad, I'm still going to be in the shop. I'll still work on cars with you."

Jack picked at the label on his bottle. "Guess you're right."

"Yeah, I *am* right."

"Need a new hire."

"Brent said we can afford it, and I've actually been gathering résumés." Jack shot him a sharp look. Cal decided not to mention the place he'd been about to rent. "Just in case."

Jack was willing to risk this, take on a whole new business after forty years in the business. Cal had thrown in the towel and declared bachelorhood at thirty. What the hell was his problem?

Gravel crunched under tires, and Cal looked up to see a car pulling into his driveway. He squinted but didn't recognize the car, so he walked out of the garage, his dad on his heels.

A silver sedan parked and a sandaled foot stepped out of the driver's side. When the woman stood up, she brushed her brown hair over her shoulder and looked right at Jack.

"Hey, Jill," his dad said. And Cal almost swallowed his tongue.

He'd been a kid the last time he'd seen his mom. And she'd been that young woman in his mind this whole time. Jill now was…well, she was older, with fine lines in her brow and crinkles at the corners of her eyes. Her hair was streaked with gray. She walked slowly toward them, and Cal was surprised at how short she was. Must be why Cal wasn't anywhere near as tall as his dad.

"Hey, Jack," she said, her voice wobbly. "How are you?"

"Can't complain."

Jill's eyes were on Cal now, taking him in, those warm brown eyes—so like Max's and Asher's—coasting from head to toe. "Calvin," she said, a little in awe.

He could only nod. He'd thought he'd feel…sadness. Or anger. Or something when he saw her again. But really, he felt only a mild curiosity.

Cal looked at Jack out of the corner of his eye. He did look sad. And Cal wondered if he still loved Jill, despite what she'd done to his family.

A door opened behind Cal, and then a deep voice said, "Well, holy shit."

Cal braced himself, because the brother with no filter had just appeared.

Jill's smile was shaky. "Hi, Brent."

"An appearance! By God, let's make a float and parade down Main Street."

"Shut up," Jack growled.

Cal elbowed Brent in the stomach, who made a small oomph sound but then kept his mouth shut.

Jill's eyes flicked to Cal, her nerves clear in her rigid posture. "Is Asher here?"

"You interested in seeing him now?" Cal asked.

Jill wrung her hands. "I just…I figured he was in good hands, but then a friend said…well, she said I should go see him."

It was amazing how this woman could have zero maternal instinct. Jenna had more sense when it came to Asher than his own fucking mother. She'd would make a fine mother.

"I-I'm trying," Jill muttered, almost to herself.

Cal didn't know what to say to that. He was past the point that trying would make a fuck of a difference in his life, but Asher still craved attention from his mom. So Cal turned to walk back into the house. "He's inside. Come on in."

Even though it was awkward as hell to have her there, Cal knew it was worth it when Asher's face lit up when he spotted Jill. "Mom!" he cried, standing up. "You came!"

Jill's smile wasn't forced anymore. "Yeah, I'm, uh, here." Her eyes darted around, to Max, whose jaw was hanging on the floor. Her smile fell a little. But Asher was walking briskly toward her, his arms already rising from his sides to embrace her.

Cal looked around—at his family, his employees—and his heart ached, because he knew Jenna should be here. Asher had asked about her, but Cal had been honest, telling him they'd broken up, and the kid looked as upset as Cal.

When Asher sat down on the couch with his mom, Cal heard her say, "Honey, I need to talk to you about your father."

Cal didn't want to hear the rest. He made his way to his back door to retreat to his deck and tried to tune out their murmured words, not wanting to hear that Asher was going to pack up and go home.

And then the kid's voice, shaky but firm, said, "No, I want to stay here."

Cal stopped beside the couch and stared.

Jill's eyes were wide as she shifted her gaze from her youngest son, to her oldest, and then back again. "But, sweetie—"

"I want to stay with Cal," Asher said, his voice no longer shaking. "I like it here. I've made friends. I want to go to high school here."

"Your home is—"

"Here. I've never felt more at home than I do here. I love you, Mom. But nothing's tying you to Virginia if you've left Dad. How about you move here?"

There was a coughing sound behind them, and Jack pounded his chest and then strode off into the kitchen, his boots heavy on Cal's hardwood floor.

Jill watched her ex-husband's retreating back. "Ash—"

"Can I stay here, Cal?" Asher turned those deep brown eyes up at him.

And Cal couldn't move. Those were Max's eyes, the same ones he'd looked into when the kid was a baby. Those were Asher's eyes, the same ones that had looked at him as a surrogate father for the last month or so.

Cal could tell him no, that he'd be better off with his mom, that it was less complicated for everyone. That Cal didn't want him or this responsibility or fucking any of it.

But that would be a lie.

As worry seeped into Asher's gaze while Cal stayed silent, Cal realized how fucking stupid he was. "You want to?"

Asher stood up. "Of course."

"But I did a shitty job, Asher. You got hurt on my watch."

Asher smiled a little. "I got hurt because I did something dumb. If you'll let me, I want to stay because I love this town and this family. You've been the best dad-slash-older brother I think I could ever have. I don't want to give that up." He picked at his cast. "Unless you don't want me here. Then I'll leave."

He thought about life if Asher left. No more brownies. No more bath mats ruined from hair dye. No more John Hughes movie marathons.

Just…nothing. Nothing but him and his beer and his recliner and his job. He'd be able to work on motorcycles, but that goal didn't seem so amazing anymore when he didn't have anyone to share it with.

Fuck, he'd been an idiot.

He wasn't tapped out. The reserve was there, always there, and it was constantly replenished by his own family. By Asher.

By Jenna.

Cal took a step forward and hugged the kid. "Of course I want you. If it's okay with your mom, then you can stay."

When they broke apart and looked down at Jill, there were tears in her eyes. "Of course I want you to be happy, Asher. And if that's here, then that's where you'll stay."

Asher fist-pumped his cast in the air. Cal had to walk away. He needed some alone time, so he continued out the back door and shut it firmly behind him. He stood on his deck and stared at the tree line, his fingers itching for a smoke. But he knew he wouldn't pick one up again.

The door behind him opened and closed. Brent braced his hands on the railing, eyes on the skyline.

"You made the right decision about the kid," Brent said after a long moment of silence.

Cal picked at a loose nail on the railing. "Do you think I'm like Dad?" he blurted.

Brent turned to him, eyebrows raised. "What?"

"You know, stubborn. Set in my ways. That kind of thing."

Brent blinked. "Yes."

"Yes? No hesitation or explanation, just yes?"

Brent turned and leaned his hip on the railing, turning his body to face Cal. "I'm not gonna lie. The only time in the last ten years you haven't acted like Dad is when you were with Jenna. Then you fucked that up somehow, like the moron you are, and now you're Jack 2.0 all over again."

"Shit."

"I don't get it. Honestly. You didn't punch Dylan. You told me she didn't believe you did. So how the hell she isn't here, or in your bed, or living in your house like she'd practically been for the last month is a mystery."

"I told her I didn't have anything else to give. I was tapped out, drained dry. I got you and Max and Dad and Asher, and that takes up all my energy. I like my iron circle. I can handle what happens in it, so I don't have to deal with things out of my control."

"Out of your control?"

"With Jenna and her brother. And then Asher in the hospital. I hate how this all makes me feel. It hurts, Brent. It hurts like hell."

Brent's eyebrows were dipped, his lips pressed in a thin line. He stood close to Cal, so close that Cal had to crane his neck to look up at him. Brent ran his tongue over his teeth before he spoke. "It's okay that it hurts. Fuck, man, so you feel shit? That's what makes you human. If you don't feel pain, then you don't feel the opposite either."

The opposite of pain.

Jenna's laughter in his ear. Her head on his bare chest, hair tickling his skin. Kissing her while she squirmed in his lap. Holding her hand in his truck.

Brent's hand rested on his shoulder. "This last month, it kinda felt like I got my brother back, the one I used to have."

Laughing at Brent's singing at the garage. Playing video games while Brent narrated in different voices. Drinking beer on his deck.

But this pain right now…it fucking hurt. Was it all worth it? Cal squeezed his eyes shut as Brent's palm warmed his skin.

"I know it's hard to care, Cal. I fucking know. But where would Max and I be if you didn't? Where would Asher be? And where would you be?"

Cal's world was tilting. As soon as he thought he had it down on lock, someone took a finger and spun the globe, and everything was a blur all over again.

Brent sighed. "You have more to give. You always will, Cal. That's who you are. You thought you were done before Asher showed up, and you dug deep and gave that kid everything you had. So maybe Jenna took that bullshit that you're done, but I don't. You're not. You'll never be."

The blur was slowing down. Cal was able to focus again, and when he did, it was on his brother's face, so like his own. "What do you think I should do?"

"If you want to keep living like you've been, then I guess you do nothing. And you keep to yourself, until you look in the mirror one day and see Jack."

Cal's stomach rolled.

"Or," Brent said, "you get outside that iron circle you've made for yourself, and you apologize to Jenna for being a dick."

Cal hugged him, just reached up and wrapped his brother in his arms. He couldn't remember the last time he'd done that. "Thanks, man. Appreciate the advice."

Brent squeezed the back of Cal's neck. "Learned from the best."

Chapter Twenty-Seven

JENNA OPENED UP all the windows in her house and let the August breeze blow through. That's exactly what she needed. Some airing out. She wished she could do the same thing for her heart.

She shook her head as she stuck the vacuum back in the closet. Nope, not going there. She wiped her hands and looked around. It was a Saturday, and she probably could have spent all day working, but she needed a break.

Instead of letting her quit MacMillan Industries, her father had fired Dylan and begged her to stay. He'd finally admitted the damage his son was doing to the company, and his actions at the country club had been the last straw.

It had been a tough decision, because leaving this town might have been what was best for her, but she'd enjoyed reconnecting with Delilah. She'd come to know the employees of MacMillan Industries and cared about them. So she'd said yes.

And she vowed to remain single for a long time to come.

She wore a loose tank top and a pair of shorts and pulled her hair back into a ponytail. She planned to barricade herself in her home all weekend. If she needed food, she'd call out.

She walked into the kitchen to begin assembling dinner when there was a knock at her door.

She frowned and kept still. Maybe whoever it was would go away if she waited it out. She had patience.

But the knock came again. And again.

And then the doorbell started ringing.

With a groan of frustration, Jenna padded to the front door in her bare feet and threw it open.

Asher and Brent stood on the front porch. The teenager held a bouquet of flowers in his casted arm. She hadn't seen him since the day he got home from the hospital. And that'd been a week ago. "Asher."

He smiled and held out the flowers. "Hi, Jenna."

"How are you feeling?"

"I'm good."

Her gaze shifted to Brent and then back to Asher. "And what are you guys doing here?"

Brent nodded to the flowers. "You're supposed to take those, and then you're supposed to get into my truck."

Jenna glanced at the huge black monster in her driveway. "Excuse me?"

Brent grinned, but it seemed a little forced. "Will you please come with us?"

Jenna blinked, because she knew who was behind this, and she wanted no part of that. "I'm sorry, but I think it's best if I stay here. Away from all Paytons."

Asher took a step forward. "Please? It's really important, Jenna."

Shit. He'd sent the kid. If that wasn't the most effective weapon to get her to do his bidding, then she didn't know what was. He must have trained the kid too, because she'd never seen Asher go to quite this length with those puppy-dog eyes.

Brent was biting his lip, for once not making a joke. Asher's body was vibrating.

And so that's why she sighed, grabbed her purse and a thin sweatshirt, slipped on her Converse sneakers, and walked out to the truck.

The boys climbed inside, Asher in the middle. And no one talked. Not a word. Jenna didn't know what to say. The whole cab of the truck was loaded with words, and if she vocalized one, it might have suffocated them all.

She figured out where they were going about halfway there, but she didn't let herself believe it until Brent pulled into the parking lot and shifted the truck into park. "He said to take Carson Trail."

That was the one they'd always used in high school. She stared at her hands fisted on her lap. "I don't know if I can do this."

Silence. Only the humming and vibration of the truck. Until Asher said, "I think you can."

So she hopped out of the truck, waved at Brent and Asher, and made her way down the easiest trail, not the one she'd traveled with Cal weeks ago. That had been the safe trail that day, the one with no memories, so they could create their own. Being on Carson Trail felt like rewriting history a little bit. How it ended was still to be determined.

Back in high school, the paths were overgrown, the paint on the trees marking the trail faded. Now, the brush had been cleaned up and swept back, the dirt leveled. The splashes of paint leading the way was fresh and bright on the tree trunks. Even if it hadn't been, she still knew where to go.

There was still that old fallen log off the side as she rounded the first bend. It was more decayed now, but the gnarled roots still stretched out, grasping at nothing.

Even the smell was the same, dirt and moisture and everything that made River's Edge her and Cal's sanctuary.

She ran her fingers over the bushes lining the trails. She jogged over a small bridge that was raised over a mostly dried-out creek bed.

When she reached the area of the trail where she had to go off path to reach their spot, there was a clump of wildflowers tied to the tree. She pulled them out with shaky fingers, burying her nose in the petals.

And then, with careful steps, she went off path and wove her way among the trees and rocks by memory in the direction that would lead her to Cal. The sound of rushing water drew closer, and with one more hop over a fallen log, she pushed aside a branch.

Cal sat on a blanket with his back to her, his wrists propped on his bent knees.

Her mind blipped back ten years. To when Cal had shorter hair. To when his shoulders weren't quite as broad, his skin not as weathered. She took another step forward, a fallen branch cracking under her sneaker, and Cal looked over his shoulder. He stood slowly, hands in his pockets, as she approached.

It was then she saw the difference in his eyes, in his expression. Since she'd been back to town, Cal had done nothing but brace himself, constantly preparing for what would knock him down next.

But this Cal, he faced her head on, his expression open and no longer guarded.

She stopped five feet away from him and waited.

"Thanks for coming," he said.

"You sent the kid. You knew what you were doing to get me here."

A ghost of a smile crossed his lips, and then he looked away, his tongue slipping out to wet his lip. "So I've been doing a lot of thinking."

She pursed her lips to keep from talking.

"I thought that eighteen-year-old kid who wanted the wife and family and you was an idiot. I thought he was full of dreams that in reality, I couldn't fulfill. I spent ten years telling myself I wanted nothing to do with him and everything he wanted." He shook his head and looked down at his boots. "And now, I'm finally starting to realize he was the one who had it right all along."

Her breath stuttered. The sound of the river now mixed with the pounding of her heart in her ears.

He lifted his head. "I know I messed up, Jenna. You were patient with me while I figured this out, and then I messed up, kinda like I knew I would. When we talked the day Asher got home from the hospital…well, I thought he was going back to his mom. She left her dumb-ass husband, and all I could do was feel sorry for myself. I wanted it all gone, everything that reminded me of how great this summer has been." He took a step forward. "And then Asher asked to stay. He said I gave him a family." Cal thumped his fist on his chest, and a bright smile came over his face. God, he was beautiful like this, pouring his heart out to her in a way he never did, in a way the eighteen-year-old Cal hadn't known how. "I was so focused on whether I was doing everything right and that one setback threw me. But when I looked in the mirror and realized that if I kept going the way I'd been before you and Asher…well, I was turning into my father." Another step forward, and Jenna held her ground. "I'll always be a stubborn bastard, Sunshine. But I want to be that with you. And I'm standing here now, telling you that I'm done trying. No more trying. I'm just doing. I'll be your man if you'll be my woman again."

She wasn't sure Cal had ever said that many words at one time in his life. But he had now, and he'd said them to her. She'd seen Cal without his clothes on, yet he'd never been this naked in front of her. He still wore that bright open smile, and his eyes were bluer than she'd ever seen them, reflecting the sunlight filtering through the trees.

This was what she'd wanted to hear for weeks, this conversation where they laid it all out on the table. But she had one question, which had been niggling in the back of her head ever since that night at the country club. "Before you got that call, those words you said to me...did you mean them?"

His brows furrowed. "When we were dancing?"

She nodded, breathless.

He smiled slowly, a slight flush staining his cheeks. "I meant them then, Jenna. And I mean them again now. I love you."

She didn't want to be stubborn. She didn't want to punish him for the week of hell he'd put her through, because that wasn't who she was. She trusted Cal, deep in her heart, and trusted that he was telling the truth now. He was decisive, and she had to allow him a couple of speed bumps to get over the decision he'd made recklessly ten years ago. She was just glad he finally came around.

Jenna took a step forward, until their chests brushed, and she looked up into his eyes. "I don't think I ever stopped being your woman, not for ten years."

"I love you, Sunshine," he growled, and then his big hands gripped her face, and his body slammed into hers, and his mouth attacked her, demanding, hot, needy, pressing her lips open so he could taste her.

She moaned into his mouth, circling his wrists with her fingers, digging in her nails. They sealed this moment with a kiss.

Then they were stumbling back to the blanket, and Cal's fingers were undoing her jean shorts. Her mind raised a tiny red flag, because they were in public, but that flag wilted because in this moment, she didn't care.

In fact, it turned her on a little. Their first time had been here, right at River's Edge. So this was only fitting.

Cal lowered her to the blanket, shoving her shorts down over her hips. His lips were fused to hers, and she was fine with that, unwilling to part. Her hands had slipped under his T-shirt to touch as much of his hot skin as she could.

She heard the lowering of his zipper and the crinkle of a condom wrapper. She bucked her hips when she felt his erection between her legs.

"This okay?" he panted against her mouth.

"More than okay."

"I love you," he said, struggling to roll the condom onto his hardness. It was like he couldn't say it enough.

She laughed against his lips. "I love you too, you stubborn bastard."

And then he was inside of her, his hands gripping her hips, his face shoved into her neck. She wrapped her arms around his shoulders and then kicked off her shorts and underwear so she could wrap her legs around him.

"I missed you," he said against her skin. "I'm sorry." And he muttered other words that didn't matter anymore; they truly didn't. Because she was staring at the sky, with Cal's hard body on top of hers. The sun beat down on her face, on Cal's back, and she was full, so full to bursting with Cal, with love, for the future she'd only dreamed about as a teenager.

He was bringing her to the edge with his words and his fingers between her legs, and she let it happen, let the orgasm begin at her center and spread throughout her limbs until the tips of her fingers and toes tingled. She gasped into Cal's ear, his hair catching on her lips. And then Cal was coming too, pulsing inside of her, his hips stuttering between her thighs.

And then...there was his hot breath misting on her skin, his weight on top of her. And the world kept turning. The water kept flowing. The trees kept growing. And she loved Cal Payton with everything that she was.

CAL HAD BROUGHT sandwiches, with the hope that Jenna would stay. By the time they'd gone another round again and dug into the food, the sun was beginning to set.

They were dressed now, although if they hadn't seen anyone yet, they probably wouldn't. It'd always been a stellar make-out spot.

Jenna sat across from him, dropping blueberries in her mouth. Her lips were red and swollen from his kisses; her cheeks were flushed. He knew her inner thighs probably felt the remnants of his beard.

His cock gave a half-hearted jerk, but he knew he was done for now. He wasn't eighteen anymore.

"So Asher is here to stay?" Jenna asked.

"Yeah, he said he wants to go to school here. He asked Jill, and she said okay. She went back to Virginia for now, but she's making noises about moving up here again." Jenna widened her eyes, and Cal chuckled. "Yeah, I know." He leaned back on his hands. "Good news too. Dad agreed I can work on bikes."

Jenna's mouth dropped open, and she crawled across the blanket to kiss him. "That's amazing! How did that happen?"

"It took Asher's getting hurt for him to realize how badly this town needs a certified mechanic, which sucked that's what it had to take, but there ya go."

Her eyes shone. "I'm happy for you."

"Me too."

"Well, news on my side is that Dylan got fired."

Cal nearly swallowed his tongue. "What?"

"My dad saw what was going on. He got Dylan a job with a friend out in Denver. So Dylan's gone. Out of our lives."

Cal looked to the water. "Huh."

"I'm sorry that happened, Cal. I hope you know that."

"I'm sorry too. But it's done."

Once they finished eating, Jenna lay with her head on Cal's lap. He stroked her hair, knowing they needed to go before it got dark but neither wanting to leave.

"We'll come back here, right?" Jenna asked quietly.

" 'Course," he answered. "This is our spot."

She opened her eyes and looked up at him. "Now that I know you're so good at communicating, I'll hold you to a higher standard."

"Shit," he muttered.

She laughed. "It's okay. Change is good."

He smiled and bent over to give her a kiss. "I'll deal with any change, as long as you're there."

Chapter Twenty-Eight

Two months later

CAL STARED AT the young woman sitting across from him in the back room of the garage. He'd interviewed ten mechanics. Nine men. One woman. And the woman Delilah knew had the best references and the best résumé.

But change was good. He could do this, welcome a woman into the inner workings of the testosterone-fueled Payton and Sons.

In fact, if anything, maybe she'd keep Brent in line.

Alex Dawn was short. Cal wondered if she even hit five feet. She was pretty, if not a little severe-looking, with a sharp nose and chin. Her eyes were strikingly blue, and she lined them heavily with black eyeliner, which made them stand out even more, like glittering sapphires in her pale face.

For this interview, she'd dressed casual, as he'd told her to on the phone. He didn't need to interview someone all dressed up. This was a fucking garage.

So she wore a pair of oversized jeans, black boots, and a faded AC/DC shirt. She looked at him with her chin tilted. The chip on her shoulder probably weighed more than she did.

Cal liked her. A lot.

He reached across the table. "Congratulations, Alex, you're the newest employee of Payton and Sons."

A grin he hadn't seen before cracked her face, splitting her red-painted lips. "Cool" was all she said in response. And then she cracked her gum.

"Come on out, and I'll introduce you to everyone," he said.

It was a Friday afternoon, so everyone was a little punchy and ready for the weekend.

He took one look at Brent and Jenna standing at the front of a bay and knew Brent was being a pain in the ass.

"Come on," Brent was saying, "just, like, writhe around on the hood a little."

Jenna stood with her arms crossed over her chest, tapping her sandaled foot. Cal marveled that she hadn't kicked his brother in the junk yet. "I'm not recreating a Whitesnake music video for you."

Brent pressed his lips together. "I think you're being a little uptight about this. All I'm asking is for a couple hip thrusts, a split or two, and maybe one hair flip."

She glared at him.

Brent appeared unfazed. "I'm sure Cal would be with me on this."

Cal guided the new hire forward and narrowed his eyes at his brother. "Will you shut up and behave yourself?"

Brent's eyes immediately found the other vagina in the room, as expected, and his eyes widened as he took in Alex at Cal's side. "Hey, honey. You're a little short and, uh, not blonde for Tawny Kitaen, but I'm still not opposed to watching you dance on a car."

Alex said nothing; she just stared at Brent like he was an insect. It was glorious, and Cal could barely contain himself. He glanced at Jenna and could tell right away by the grin on her face that she shared his glee.

Cal gestured to Alex. "This is our newest employee, Alex Dawn, so keep your mouth shut, Brent, or she'll sue you for sexual harassment."

Brent's jaw dropped. And Cal nearly cheered. But Brent recovered quickly and maintained some level of maturity when he stuck out his hand. "Welcome."

Alex eyed his hand, shook it, and then shoved her hands back in her pockets. Brent rubbed his palm, mouthing *ouch*. Cal was happy to see Alex was already showing Brent she could handle him.

He introduced Alex to everyone else, including Asher and Julian, who'd just gotten there from school, as well as Gabe and of course, Jenna. Alex thawed a little with Jenna and talked a little about herself, so Cal learned Alex had moved to Tory recently with her sister.

As Alex left, she eyed Brent one last time before walking out to her truck. "See you Monday, boss!" Alex called over her shoulder.

When Cal looked at his brother, Brent was watching her go, shaking his head.

Cal stared at Jenna; she stared back, and then they both burst into laughter.

"So that's going to be amazing," Jenna said when she caught her breath.

"God, that woman probably weighs a hundred pounds soaking wet," Cal said, "but she's a force, huh? I wonder what her sister's like."

"If either has a sharper tongue than Brent," Jenna responded, "then I would pay money to see them go toe-to-toe."

Cal chuckled and grabbed her around the waist, tugging her to him.

"Hey, you're going to get me dirty!" she protested but only with words, because she plastered herself to Cal and wrapped her arms around his neck.

"Clean is overrated," he said against her lips.

She kissed him back. "I always did love you dirty."

Keep reading for a sneak peek at the next sizzling
book in Megan Erickson's Mechanics of Love series,

DIRTY TALK

*Brent Payton has a reputation for wanting to have fun all
the time. It's well earned, after years of ribbing his brothers
and flirting with every girl he meets, but he's more than
just a good time, even though nobody takes the time to see
it. When a new girl walks into his family's garage with big
thoughtful eyes and a body to die for, this mechanic wants
something serious for the first time.*

*Ivy Dawn is done with men, all of them. She and her sister
uprooted their lives for men too many times, and she's not
willing to do it again. Avoiding the opposite sex at all costs
seems easy enough, until the sexy mechanic with the dirty
mind bursts into her life.*

*Brent can't resist the one woman who sees past his devil-
may-care façade, and Ivy finds it harder and harder to
deny how happy he makes her. But Ivy has secrets she
hasn't shared, and when the truth comes out, she must
decide if she's willing to take one more chance on love or
let him go forever.*

Available Fall 2015

An Excerpt from

DIRTY TALK

A THROAT CLEARED. And Brent looked over to see a woman standing beside them, one hand on her hip, the other dangling at her side, holding a paper bag. Her dark eyebrows were raised, her full red lips pursed.

And Brent blinked, hoping this wasn't a mirage.

Tory, Maryland, wasn't big, and he'd made it his mission to know every available female within the town limits and about a ten-mile radius outside of that.

This woman? He'd never seen her. He'd remember if he had.

Gorgeous. Long hair so dark brown, it was almost black. Perfect face. It was September and still warm, so she wore a tight striped sundress that ended mid-thigh. She was tiny, probably over a foot smaller than him. Fuck, the things that little body made him dream about.

He wondered if she did yoga. Tiny and limber was his kryptonite.

Narrow waist, round hips, big tits.

No ring.

Bingo.

He smiled. Sure, she was probably a customer, but this wouldn't be the first time he'd managed to use the garage to his advantage. Usually, he just had to toss around a tire or two, rev an engine, whatever, and they were more than eager to hand over a phone number and address. No one thought he was a consummate professional anyway, so why bother trying to be one.

He turned to her and leaned his ass against the counter, crossing his arms over his chest. "Can I help you?"

She blinked, long lashes fluttering over her big blue eyes. "Can you help me?"

"Yeah, we're full service here." He resisted winking. That was kinda sleazy.

Her eyes widened for a fraction before they shifted to Alex at his side and then back to him. Her eyes darkened for a minute, her tongue peeked out between those red lips, and then she straightened. "No, you can't help me."

He leaned forward. "Really? You sure?"

"Positive."

"Like, how positive?

"I'm 100 percent positive that I do not need help from you, Brent Payton."

That made him pause. She knew his name. He knew he'd never met her, so that could only mean that she heard about him somehow, and by the look on her face, it was nothing good.

Well, shit.

He opened his mouth, not sure what to say but hoping it would come to him, when Alex began cracking up next to him, slapping her thighs and snorting.

Brent glared at her. "And what's your problem?"

Alex stepped forward, threw her arm around the shoulder of the prickly but hot-as-hell woman in front of them, and smiled ear to ear. "Brent, meet my sister, Ivy. Ivy, thanks for making me proud."

They were both smiling now, that same full-lipped, white-teethed smile. He surveyed Alex's face, then Ivy's, and holy fuck, how had he not noticed this right away? They almost looked like twins.

And the sisters were looking at him now, wearing matching smug grins, and wasn't that a total cock-block. He pointed at Alex. "What did you tell your sister about me?"

"That the day I interviewed, you asked me to recreate a Whitesnake music video on the hood of a car."

He threw up his hands. "Can you let that go? You weren't even my first choice. I wanted Cal's girlfriend to do it."

"Because that's more appropriate," Alex said drily.

"Excuse me for trying to liven it up around here."

Ivy turned to her sister, skirt swirling around those thighs he might sell his soul to touch. She held up the paper bag. "I brought lunch. Hope that's okay."

"Of course it is," Alex said. "Thanks a lot, since someone stole my breakfast." She narrowed her eyes at Brent. Ivy turned to him slowly in disbelief, like she couldn't believe he was that evil.

Brent had had a lot of bad first impressions in his life. A dad of one of his high school girlfriend's had seen Brent's bare ass—while Brent was lying on top of his daughter—before the dad ever saw Brent's face. That had not gone over well. And yet *this* first impression might be even worse.

Because he didn't care about what that girl's dad thought of him. Not really.

And he didn't *want* to care about what Ivy thought of him, but dammit, he did. It bothered the hell out of him that she'd written him off before even meeting him. Did Alex tell her any of his good qualities? Like…Brent racked his brain for good qualities.

By the time he thought of one, the girls had already disappeared to the back room for lunch.

About the Author

MEGAN ERICKSON grew up in a family that averages five foot five on a good day and started writing to create characters who could reach the top kitchen shelf.

She's got a couple of tattoos, has a thing for gladiators, and has been called a crazy cat-lady. After working as a journalist for years, she decided she liked creating her own endings better and switched back to fiction.

She lives in Pennsylvania with her husband, two kids, and two cats. And no, she still can't reach the stupid top shelf.

Discover great authors, exclusive offers, and more at hc.com.

Give in to your Impulses . . .
Continue reading for excerpts from
our newest Avon Impulse books.
Available now wherever e-books are sold.

HEART'S DESIRE
By T.J. Kline

DESIRE ME NOW
By Tiffany Clare

THE WEDDING GIFT
A Save the Date Novella
By Cara Connelly

WHEN LOVE HAPPENS
Ribbon Ridge Book Three
By Darcy Burke

An Excerpt from

HEART'S DESIRE

by T.J. Kline

Jessie Hart has a soft spot for healing the broken, especially horses and children, but her business is failing. The one man who can save Heart Fire Ranch is the last man she wants to see, the man who broke her heart eight years ago . . .

Jessie heard the crunch of tires on the gravel driveway and stepped onto the porch of the enormous log home. Her parents had raised their family here, in the house her father had built just before her brother was born. The scent of pine surrounded her, warming her insides. Even after her brother and sister had built houses of their own on either end of the property, she'd remained here with her parents, helping them operate the dude ranch and training their horses. She inhaled deeply, wishing again that circumstances hadn't been so cruel as to leave her to figure out how to make the transition from dude ranch to horse rescue alone.

Leaning against the porch railing, she sipped her coffee and enjoyed the quiet of the morning. When a teen girl walked toward the barn to feed the horses, she lifted her hand in a wave. The poor girl was spending more time at the ranch than away from it these days, since her mother had violated parole again, but Jessie loved having her here. Aleta's foster mother, June, had been close friends with Jessie's own mother, and she understood the healing power horses had on kids who needed someone, or something, just to listen. Now that Aleta was living with June again, she was spending a lot of time at the ranch.

Jessie looked down the driveway as Bailey drove her truck closer to the house. She could just make out Nathan through the glare on the windshield. The resentment in her belly grew with each ticking second at the sight of him. Clenching her jaw and squaring her shoulders for the battle ahead, Jessie walked down the stairs to meet Justin's former best friend and the man who'd broken her heart.

The truck pulled to a stop in front of her, and Bailey jumped from the driver's seat wearing a shit-eating grin. Jessie narrowed her eyes, knowing exactly what that meant—she was in for a week of hell from this pain-in-the-ass, penny-pinching bean counter.

She didn't understand why he'd insisted on returning to the ranch. If Justin hadn't begged her to give Nathan a chance to help, she would have been perfectly content never to speak to his lying ass again.

She watched him turn his broad shoulders to her as he removed his luggage from the back seat. When he faced her, Jessie was barely able to contain her gasp of surprise. After he left, she'd avoided any mention of Nathan Kerrington like the plague, going as far as changing the channel when his name was mentioned on the news. She'd been praying that the past eight years had been cruel, that he'd gained a potbelly, or that he'd developed a receding hairline. She pictured him turning into a stereotypical computer geek.

This guy was perfection. Well, if she was into muscular men who looked like Hollywood actors and wore suits that cost several thousand dollars. Every strand of his dark brown hair was combed into place, even at six in the morning, after a flight from New York. There wasn't a wrinkle in his stiffly starched shirt.

His green eyes slid over her dirty jeans and T-shirt before climbing back up to focus on her face. Memories of stolen kisses and lingering caresses filled her mind before she could cast them aside. His slow perusal sent heat curling in her belly, spreading through her veins, making her feel uncomfortable. Was he just trying to be an ass? If so, it was working. She felt on edge immediately, but she wasn't about to let him know it. She crossed her arms over her chest and kicked her hip to the side.

"Nathan Kerrington. You've got some brass ones showing up here."

An Excerpt from

DESIRE ME NOW
by *Tiffany Clare*

Amelia Grant has just escaped her lecherous
employer with nothing but the clothes on
her back. In the pre-dawn hours of London,
a horse and carriage comes barreling
down on her, and a stranger rushes to
her aid, sweeping her off her feet . . .

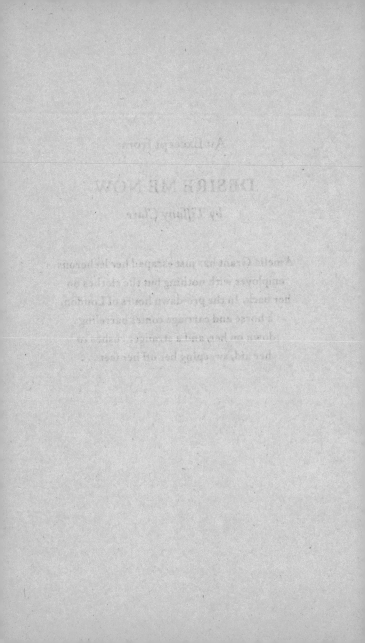

"**W**hy did you kiss me?" She wasn't sure she wanted to hear the answer, but a part of her needed to know. And talking was safer right now.

"I have wanted to do that since you first stumbled into my path. Do you feel something growing between us?"

She'd been ignoring that feeling, thinking and hoping it would pass with time. She'd assumed she'd developed hero worship after Mr. Riley had rescued her and then taken care of her when she'd been at an ultimate low.

She couldn't deny the truth now. She did feel something for him; something not easily defined as mere lust but a deep desire to learn more about him and why he made her feel so out of sorts with what she thought was right.

Not that she would ever admit to that.

Who was she to garner the attention of this man? Women probably threw themselves at his feet and begged him to ruin them on a regular basis. That thought left her feeling cold. She eyed the door, longing for escape.

"Do not leave, Amelia." He stepped closer to her, near enough that she could kiss him again if she so desired. She ignored that desire. "Work for me as we planned. Just stay."

There was a kind of desolation in his voice at the thought

of her abandoning him. But that was impossible. And she was reading too much into his request. Logically, she knew she couldn't feel this sort of attachment to someone she had just met. Someone she didn't really know.

"I am afraid of what I will do," she admitted, more for herself than for him.

"Then do not think about it. Go with what your instincts tell you. If there is one thing I have always done, it is to follow my first inclination. I would not be in the position I am today, had I ignored those natural reflexes."

He caressed her cheek again. She nearly nestled into his palm before realizing what she was doing. With a heavy sigh, she pulled away from him before she made any more mistakes. This was not a good way to start her first official day as his secretary.

She couldn't help but ask. "And what do your instincts say about me?"

"I do not need my instincts to tell me where this is going. It is more base than that. I desire you. And there is nothing that can stop me from fulfilling and exploring what I want. You will be mine in the end, Amelia."

Her heart picked up speed at his admission. Her breathing grew more rapid as she assessed him. She desired him too. She, Amelia Marie Somerset, who wanted nothing more than to escape one vile man's sick craving to marry her and claim her, was willing to let the man in front of her ruin her, only because she felt different with him than she had with anyone else.

What would she lose of herself in the process of courting dangerous games with this man? Focusing on the hard angles of his face and the steady expression he wore, one thing was certain.

This man would ruin her.

And more startling was the realization that she would do nothing to stop him.

An Excerpt from

THE WEDDING GIFT
A Save the Date Novella
by Cara Connelly

In the next Save the Date novella, mousey
Jan Marone finally allows herself to live,
laugh, and love . . . with a sexy fireman
during a weekend wedding in Key West!

"**I**'m sorry, ma'am, there's nothing I can do."

Jan Marone wrung her hands. "But I have a reservation."

"I know, I'm looking at it right here." The pretty blonde at the desk tapped her screen sympathetically. "I'll refund your deposit immediately."

"I don't want my deposit. I want a room. My cousin's getting married tomorrow, and I'm in the wedding."

The girl spread her hands. "The problem is, when one of the upstairs tubs overflowed this morning, the ceiling collapsed on your room. It's out of service for the weekend, and we're booked solid."

"I understand," Jan said, struggling to remain polite. Hearing the same excuse three times didn't make it easier to swallow. "How about a sister hotel?"

"We're independently owned. Paradise Inn is the oldest hotel on the island—"

Jan held up a hand. She knew the spiel. The large, rambling guesthouse was unique, and very Old Key West. Which was exactly why she'd booked it.

"Can you at least help me find a room somewhere else?"

"It's spring break. I'll make some calls, but . . ." A discouraging shrug and a gesture toward the coffeepot.

The girl didn't seem very concerned, but Jan smiled at her anyway. "Thanks, I appreciate you trying."

Parking her suitcase beside the coffee table, she surveyed the lobby wistfully. The windows and doors stood open, the wicker furniture and abundant potted plants blurring the line between indoors and out. The warm, humid breeze drifted through the airy space. Her parched Boston skin soaked it up like a sponge.

To a woman who'd never left New England before, it spelled tropical vacation. And it was slipping through her fingers like sand.

Growing ever gloomier, she wandered out through a side door and into a lush tropical garden—palm trees, hibiscus, a babbling waterfall.

Paradise.

And at its heart, a glittering pool, where six gorgeous feet of lean muscle and tanned skin drifted lazily on a float.

Ignoring everything else, Jan studied the man. Thick black hair, chiseled jaw, half smile curving full lips. And arms, perfect arms, draped over the sides, fingers trailing in the water.

He seemed utterly relaxed, the image of sensual decadence. Put him in an ad for Paradise Inn, and women would flock. Gay men would swarm.

As if sensing her attention, the hunk lifted his head and broke into a smile. "Hey Jan, getcha ass in the water!"

Mick McKenna. Her best and oldest friend.

He rolled off the float and jacked himself out of the pool. Water streamed from gray board shorts as he crossed the flagstones.

Stopping in front of her, he shook his hair like a Labrador.

"Geez! Don't you ever get tired of that?" She brushed droplets off her white cotton blouse.

He laughed his big, happy laugh. "Never have, never will. Get your suit on. The water's a perfect eighty-six degrees."

"I can't. They don't have a room for me."

The grin fell off his face. "What the hell?"

"Water damage." She shrugged like it wasn't tragic. Like she hadn't been anticipating this weekend for months.

"They must have another room." Mick started to go around her, no doubt to raise hell at the desk, McKenna-style.

She stopped him with a hand on his arm. "I tried everything. They're digging up a room for me somewhere else on the island."

He tunneled long fingers through his hair. "Take my room," he said.

An Excerpt from

WHEN LOVE HAPPENS
Ribbon Ridge Book Three
by Darcy Burke

In the third Ribbon Ridge novel from
USA Today bestseller Darcy Burke,
Tori Archer is about to discover that even the
best kept secrets don't stay buried for long . . .

Tori Archer sipped her Nocktoberfest, Dad's signature beer for the annual Ribbon Ridge Oktoberfest, which was currently in full swing. She clung to the corner of the huge tent, defensively watching for her "date" or one of her annoying siblings that had forced her to go on this "date."

It wasn't really a date. He was a professional colleague, and the Archers had invited him to their signature event. For nine years, the family had sponsored the town's Oktoberfest. It featured Archer beer and this year, for the first time, a German feast overseen by her brother Kyle, who was an even more amazing chef than they'd all realized. Today was day three of the festival and she still wasn't tired of the fondue. But really, could one ever tire of cheese?

"Boo!"

Tori jumped, splashing a few drops of beer from her plastic mug onto her fingers. She turned her head and glared at Kyle. "Did you sneak through the flap in the corner behind me?"

"Guilty." He wore an apron tied around his waist and a custom Archer shirt, which read CHEF below the bow and arrow A-shaped logo. "How else was I supposed to talk to you? You've been avoiding everyone for the past hour and a half. Where's Cade?" He scanned the crowd looking for her not-date, the engineer they'd hired to work on The Alex, the hotel and restaurant venue they'd been renovating since last spring. With a special events space already completed, they'd turned their focus to the restaurant and would tackle the hotel next.

Tori took a drink of the dark amber Nocktoberfest and relished the hoppy flavor. "Don't know."

Kyle gave her a sidelong glance. "Didn't you come together?"

"No. Though it wasn't for your lack of trying. I met him here. We chatted. He saw someone he knew. I excused myself to get a beer." *An hour ago.*

Kyle turned toward her and frowned. "I don't get it. Lurking in corners isn't your style. You're typically the life of the party. You work a room better than anyone I know, except maybe Liam."

Tori narrowed her eyes. "I'm better at it than he is." Their brother Liam, a successful real estate magnate in Denver, possessed many of the same qualities she did: ambition, drive, and an absolute hatred of failure. Then again, who *wanted* to fail? But it was more than that for them. Failure was never an option.

Which didn't mean that it didn't occasionally come up and take a piece out of you when you were already down for the count.

Kyle snorted. "Yeah, whatever. You two can duke it out at Christmas or whenever Liam decides to deign us with his presence."

Tori touched his arm. "Hey, don't take his absence personally. He keeps his visits pretty few and far between, even before you moved back home. Which is more than I can say for you when you were in Florida."

Kyle's eyes clouded briefly with regret and he looked away. "Yeah, I know. And hopefully someday you'll stop giving me shit about it."

She laughed. "Too soon? I'm not mad at you for leaving anymore. I get why you had to go, but I'm your sister. I will always flip you shit about stuff like that. It's my job."

He returned his attention to her, his blue-green eyes— nearly identical to her own—narrowing. "Then it's my duty to harass you about Cade. He's totally into you. Why are you dogging him?"

It seemed that since Kyle and their sister Sara had both found their soul mates this year, they expected everyone else to do the same. Granted, their adopted brother Derek had also found his true love, and they'd gotten married in August. What none of them knew, however, was that Tori was already spoken for—at least on paper.